The Book of
Knights

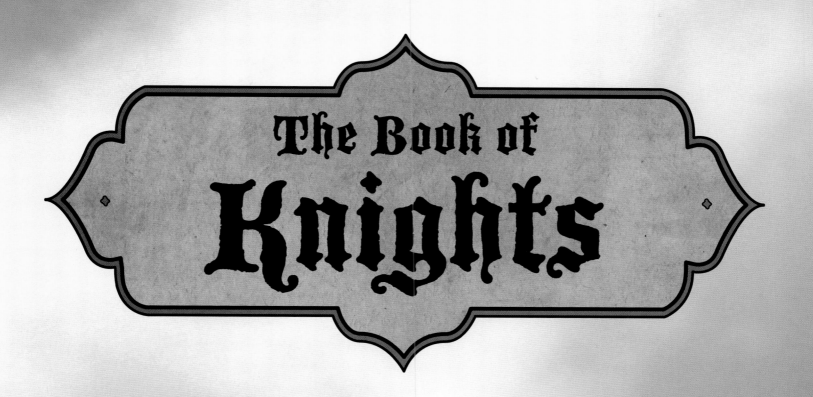

The Book of Knights

L.A. Williams,
with Donato Giancola, Mark Poole,
and Ruth Thompson

STERLING

New York / London
www.sterlingpublishing.com

STERLING and the distinctive Sterling logo are registered trademarks
of Sterling Publishing Co., Inc.

Library of Congress Cataloging-in-Publication Data

Williams, L. A. (Lawrence Allen), 1965–
The book of knights / L.A. Williams ; with Donato Giancola, Mark Poole, and Ruth Thompson.
p. cm.
Includes bibliographical references and index.
ISBN 978-1-4027-4556-0 (trade cloth : alk. paper) 1. Knights and knighthood—History. 2. Knights and
knighthood—History—Pictorial works. 3. Knights and knighthood in art. 4. Knights and knighthood in
literature. 5. Knights and knighthood—Folklore. 6. Arthurian romances. I. Giancola, Donato. II. Poole,
Mark, 1963– III. Thompson, Ruth, 1966– IV. Title.
CR4509.W48 2010
940.1—dc22
2010018220

2   4   6   8   10   9   7   5   3   1

Published by Sterling Publishing Co., Inc.
387 Park Avenue South, New York, NY 10016
© 2011 by L.A. Williams
Distributed in Canada by Sterling Publishing
c/o Canadian Manda Group, 165 Dufferin Street
Toronto, Ontario, Canada M6K 3H6
Distributed in the United Kingdom by GMC Distribution Services
Castle Place, 166 High Street, Lewes, East Sussex, England BN7 1XU
Distributed in Australia by Capricorn Link (Australia) Pty. Ltd.
P.O. Box 704, Windsor, NSW 2756, Australia

Design and layout by Gavin Motnyk

Sterling ISBN 978-1-4027-4556-0

For information about custom editions, special sales, premium and
corporate purchases, please contact Sterling Special Sales
Department at 800-805-5489 or specialsales@sterlingpublishing.com.

Contents

·1·

In the Days of the Knights

Introduction

noble figure in polished armor, armed with a brilliant gleaming sword and standing against the forces of darkness, the wandering hero chancing upon someone in dire need of help and lending his hand, or the young adventurous youth eager to set out on a quest in order to prove his worth and merit—the knight has stood forth, both in history and in legend, as an inspirational ideal. Children and adults alike have long sought the examples of courage, strength, and chivalry found in both the metaphor and the reality of the knight. In days past, stories of their bravery, determination, and pursuance of noble principles were passed down as both guidance and entertainment. The knight of reality and the knight of legend were, of course, very different. Real knights were embroiled in the details and struggles of daily living, much as we are today. But in the midst of their struggles— perhaps because knights aspired to a nobility of purpose—they were responsible for the stories and legends that grew from them. The real knights were the inspiration for the legendary knights, who in turn proceeded to inspire the next generation and, as history unfolded, to perpetuate their ideals and values.

Real knights were disciplined warriors: they stood in battle, ready to die for their cause. They were also rowdy brawlers who would fight at a moment's notice, just for the fun of it. Most of them lived lives of relative luxury compared to the average person, but it was not uncommon to find entire orders of knights that took vows of poverty. For example, the symbol for the Knights Templar is the image of two knights on one horse—possibly an indication of their initial poverty at a time when each knight was expected to own at least three: a battle horse only to be used in fighting, a second horse for riding, and a third used for pack and luggage. Just as King Arthur and his knights embarked on many quests, real medieval knights were required to pursue the quests of their sovereign. In England during the Anglo-Norman period, each landowner was required either to serve forty days a year as a knight or to outfit and supply a knight to serve in his stead.

In this *Book of Knights* you will find a brief introduction to the life and history of the real knight and then a leap into the stories of the knights of legend. As you will see in the forthcoming pages, where there are knights, there are incredible feats of bravery, tales of giants and other adversaries of horrible countenance—and, of course, there are dragons.

Becoming a Knight

Knighthood was more than a profession: it was a noble calling whose virtues pervaded every aspect of the knight's life. Being a knight meant that every facet of one's life reflected the heroism, valor, humility, dignity, and self-sacrifice synonymous with the title.

Many men possessed the skills and breeding necessary to be a knight. Nevertheless, knighthood was a rare privilege reserved for an elite few. Good fortune—and, sometimes, extraordinary luck—might place a young man on one of three paths that led to this valiant destiny.

The most traditional path to knighthood extended from noble heritage. If a boy was born into a noble family—if his father was a lord or king, or his mother a lady or queen—then in about his seventh year he might be sent to a neighboring castle and begin instruction as a page. Although it was assumed that good breeding in a noble family was an essential foundation for the education and discipline that becoming a knight entailed, there was a more practical aspect to the association between knighthood and nobility. Being a knight meant being able to keep a horse and being able to buy and maintain costly weapons and a suit of armor. Only the landed gentry had sufficient wealth for their offspring to afford the expense of knighthood.

As a page, the young boy would learn the basic tenets of courtly etiquette and begin to learn the fundamentals of chivalry, the code of knightly conduct that encompassed the virtues of courage, honor, and service. The chivalrous knight was expected to respect God and Church, always be benevolent and generous, be courteous toward women, redeem the captive, aid the oppressed, speak the truth, avoid deceit and dishonor, defend the integrity of fellow knights, never refuse a challenge from an equal, never turn his back on a foe, and never seek material reward for his knightly service.

A page also would be taught a wide variety of skills and knowledge—not just horseback riding and rudimentary combat training but also reading, writing, religion, music, falconry, and other disciplines essential to court life. In addition to receiving education and instruction, a page performed many menial tasks: he helped to dress his lord in the morning, he served at meals, and he ran errands for the lords and ladies of the castle. The humility that these duties instilled in him was considered fundamental to his developing good manners.

After about seven years of study, training, and servitude, during which he proved his competence and willingness, a page could advance to the position of squire. There, he would be given greater responsibilities, the most important of which was assisting a particular knight in all aspects of life. He would serve the knight meals, clean his armor and weapons, and assist him in tournaments. A squire was also responsible for the grooming and stabling of his patron knight's horse. His greatest honor was to accompany his patron to the battlefield.

A squire engaged in more realistic combat training as well. He began to use heavier swords, lances, and armor to condition his body, and he fought in jousts and other forms of simulated battle. He learned skills of both mounted combat and ground combat, as well as how to coordinate his fighting with the efforts of fellow knights. An essential part of training for every aspiring knight was to know when he had to rely on himself and when he could depend on his compatriots for teamwork and support.

The Knighting Ceremony

Around the age of twenty, a worthy squire was knighted in a grand ceremony, which evolved and took many different forms during the medieval period. This ceremony was often more than just a secular, military rite of passage; in fact, many such observances were important social gatherings that incorporated religious rites. An example of a more elaborate medieval knighthood ceremony is presented thus:

The day before, he would begin fasting, and the knight-aspirant's sword would be blessed by a chaplain and left on the altar of a nearby chapel or church. That evening, he would don ceremonial garb of white and red—the white symbolizing purity, the red the blood he was willing to shed for his king. He would also wear black hose and shoes symbolic of death and acceptance of his mortality, and a white cingulum, or belt, as an emblem of chastity. The squire then spent the night in prayer and meditative contemplation.

Before sunrise on the morning of the ceremony, he would bathe in a ritual that symbolized the washing away of impurities. As the dawn broke, he would confess his sins to a priest and receive absolution. The ceremony usually would begin outside, shortly after he took a light breakfast. He would appear dressed in white linen and kneel before his lord, who would ask him his reasons for wanting to be a knight. If the knight-aspirant answered satisfactorily, the lord would signal his approval and the ceremony would continue to its end. In front of family, friends, nobles, and fellow knights, the squire would don blessed pieces of his armor and be girded with a blessed sword befitting his new station. He would remove the sword from its sheath and brandish it three times before re-sheathing it. Kneeling before his patron knight, lord, or some other noble of high standing, he would be "dubbed" on each shoulder three times. Then, invoking the name of God or a patron saint, the patron knight or noble would declare him a true knight. Before a final blessing, he would be instructed in the knightly virtues of never trafficking with traitors, always honoring ladies, observing fasts and abstinences, and ever respecting his maker. A great celebration followed, with food, dancing, and music.

There were other possible pathways to knighthood for those not fortunate enough to be nobly born. If a soldier showed great courage and skill in battle, he could be knighted by his lord and forgo the lengthy apprenticeship served by pages and squires. Less frequently, a lord or king who needed soldiers for a skirmish might knight men—even commoners and the lowly born—en masse just before the battle.

Regardless of his heritage or social station, once a man was knighted, he was expected to adhere to the highest moral code in his service to king and country. It was his duty to be loyal, courageous, faithful, humble, generous, and courteous to those less fortunate than himself. He was expected to lead an exemplary life.

Being a Knight

A newly knighted individual, though his station was much improved, was still required to maintain a training regimen and continue his military study, along with the many expectations placed upon him, not the least of which was to serve his king or queen on the battlefield. Furthermore, it was incumbent upon him to train the next generation of pages and squires.

In times of peace he would test himself in the jousting arena, meeting his peers with lance, sword, and fist. In times of war he would strive to be the first to rise to the call of service to his lord or land. It was his duty to ensure that his soldiers were well versed in hand-to-hand combat and were competent horsemen, because he would be expected to lead them—whether on foot, over mountain passes, or over great plains on horseback—into battle.

On the ground or mounted, the knight's trappings were sometimes the only thing that stood in the way of his injury or death. Be it leather, chain mail, or plated, a knight's armor was one of his most valued possessions. Even though its design and aesthetic properties changed greatly over time, its function has always remained the same: protect the knight in combat so that he might live to fight again.

Orders of Knights

Knighthood was not a solitary profession. When a knight swore personal allegiance to a feudal lord, noble, or king, he became a member of a fraternity of fellow knights. They lived, trained, and fought together and were united in their observance of the code of chivalry.

The earliest knights often served no formal master, but rather were bound in honor to one another by the vows of their specific orders. Orders of knights first came to prominence in the twelfth century, when many organized as armies to fight in the Crusades. Orders such as the Teutonic Knights and the Hospitallers of St. John of Jerusalem were known for their code of Christian conduct and devotional acts as much as for their military might. In the fourteenth and fifteenth centuries, when knights more commonly served royalty, the Most Noble Order of the Garter, the Order of the Golden Fleece, and other knightly orders were defined by the rituals and affiliations that bound them as soldiers to a monarch or noble patron.

The Knights Templar are possibly the most famous of all knightly orders. First organized in the early twelfth century to serve as protectors of Europeans making pilgrimages to the Holy Land, they were named for the site of their headquarters, which was built on the supposed ruins of the Temple of Solomon in Jerusalem. The Knights Templar were originally a monastic order who were endorsed by the Catholic Church and exempt from all authority save that of the Pope. Knights of the order wore signature white mantles emblazoned with red crosses and played key roles in some of the most famous battles of the Crusades. Over two centuries, the Knights Templar grew so wealthy and powerful that they were perceived as a threat by many royals who had benefited from their services. In 1312, Pope Clement V formally disbanded them.

Female Orders

Knights were the elite soldiers of the medieval era, and, as befit the traditions of the times, their ranks were exclusively male. However, different countries made various provisions for women to hold the title of knight. Orders of knights often included non-military personnel, including priests and brothers. Several monastic orders, such as the Hospitallers of St. John of Jerusalem, were also affiliated with convents and thus included their sisters and female residents. In medieval France, the wife of a knight assumed the title of chevalière, which made her a knight by marriage if not by deed. A woman who was awarded a fief with a knight's fee (the amount of money necessary to support a knight and pay for his service) attached to it was honored with the title of chevaleresse.

In very rare instances, women were knighted for their heroism in battle. In twelfth-century Spain, for instance, a count of Barcelona created the Order of the Hatchet to honor the women of Tortosa for their valorous defense of the city. When the Earl of Barcelona denied Tortosa military assistance to fend off a Moorish siege, the beleaguered town had considered surrendering until some of the town's women donned men's clothing, took up weapons, and assisted in the routing of the enemy. As their reward, the women of Tortosa and their descendants were given their own order, with its own special heraldry. They were also exempted from having to pay taxes, and were allowed to keep jewels and valuables left by their deceased husbands.

Joan of Arc

Although she was never formally knighted, Joan of Arc has for centuries provided historians and mythmakers with the classic image of the female knight. In the final decades of the Hundred Years' War, Philip III, Duke of Burgundy, had entered into an alliance with Henry V of England, who sought the French crown. In 1429, with northern France under both British and Burgundian domination, Joan was an uneducated seventeen-year-old farm girl in the northeastern territory of Lorraine. Claiming that she had received divine instruction to drive invading forces out of her country, Joan petitioned the French court for permission to travel to Orléans, then under siege by the British army. Dressed in a man's suit of armor and, as legend has it, leading the French army, Joan aggressively reversed the defensive battle strategy that had drawn out the siege for five months. In little more than a week, she led her countrymen to victory.

The battle proved a turning point for the French military. Within two and a half months, the French army liberated Reims from Burgundian occupation, paving the way for the coronation of the French king at Reims Cathedral. Under her leadership, the nation's morale was rejuvenated, and for most of the following year the French army routed invading forces from the country's northern provinces. In May 1430, Burgundian forces captured Joan during a skirmish in Compiègne when she insisted that she and her rearguard be the last to retreat from the battlefield. She was exchanged by the Burgundians to the British for a large sum, tried for heresy, and, after a lengthy trial, burned at the stake the following year.

Joan's exemplary leadership inspired many and contributed to France's eventual victory in 1453. Numerous artistic renderings have since depicted her mounted on a white horse, wearing a full suit of armor and bearing a standard with the image of Jesus flanked by the angels Gabriel and Michael, each presenting to him a fleur-de-lis—an enduring symbol of France.

Heraldry

Across the battlefield, two opposing forces would face each other. Political, social, or economic, the reasons for their skirmish could be anything from an incidental slight between lords to an attempt by one lord to take land—and therefore power—from another. The knights all looked the same. They wore the same armor. Their swords were likely made at the same forge. Yet on one side stood a billowing flag with, say, the image of a raging, rampant lion, and on the other a banner perhaps depicting a great bird of prey, wings outstretched with a radiant sun behind.

The art of devising, describing, and regulating hereditary symbols used to differentiate individuals, manors, institutions, churches, and other entities began as a method to ensure that knights were recognized by their followers in a battle. On the battlefield, the ability to quickly tell friend from foe could mean the difference between victory and defeat. Early heraldic designs were simple and easily recognizable. Later, as heraldry became formalized and branched away from military use, the elements became increasingly complex.

While there were strict guidelines for the design of a coat of arms, in application there were a great number of variations from the guidelines. The escutcheon, or shield, was composed of the "field" and "charges." The field displayed colors, metals, and furs, which were the essential background design elements. The charges placed upon the field were divided into two categories: ordinaries, and "other charges." Ordinaries included simple geometric figures, such as the chevron (an inverted V), while other charges varied widely, from animals to religious symbols. Often a coat of arms included a helmet, which by its style and orientation indicated the rank or station of the bearer. A mantle, sometimes used to frame the design, was secured to a wreath above the helmet. While it often resembled the leaves of a plant, the mantle was said to represent the tattered lambrequin, a cloth that protected the knight's head and neck from the elements and decreased the effect of sword-blows, often becoming shredded in the course of battle.

Though, artistically, the individual elements of the design were open to interpretation, the language used to communicate the coat of arms was very specific. The written depiction of a coat of arms is called the blazon and consists of a brief description of the shield—including the field and charges—and sometimes the crest. There are, of course, many unofficial and nonstandard coats of arms ranging in complexity from a shield of a single color to complicated illustrations that rival intricately woven tapestries.

Armor and Ground Combat

A knight's armor and weapons set him apart from all others in his kingdom. They were the tools of his trade as a combat professional and the visible emblems of his elite class.

In the thirteenth century, a knight's armor consisted primarily of a coat of chain mail made from small interlocking links of iron or steel, "woven" like cloth into loosely fitting garments that allowed great mobility. Mail was often fashioned into a hauberk, a garment extending down to the knees that often featured a coif or hood exposing only the face. A cloth surcoat decorated with the knight's heraldic insignia was frequently worn over the mail.

Gradually, knights came to appreciate the protection afforded by heavy metal plates sewn to the surcoat, which by the fifteenth century led to the development of full-plate armor worn over an arming doublet, or cloth coat fitted with arming points where the plates attached. The central component of plate armor was the cuirass, a carapace of molded steel that extends from the shoulders to mid-torso and consists of the breastplate and backplate. The protection provided by the cuirass was extended several inches by a skirtlike culet behind and a fauld in front. Some knights also wore mail under their armor to cover areas exposed between armor pieces.

A knight protected his shoulders with dome-shaped cups of metal called pauldrons and his elbows with similarly contoured couters. The upper arms would be fitted with rerebraces and the forearms with vambraces, gutterlike metal protectors strapped on with leather ties. Gauntlets—metal gloves with extended cuffs and fingers—covered the hands.

Knights on foot were especially vulnerable to swords wielded by mounted riders. A knight would protect his legs with chausses—lengths of mail that covered the lower extremities and sometimes permitted the attachments of cuisses to cover the thighs, poleyns to cover the knees, and greaves that protected the front and back of the lower legs. Sabatons covering the top of the feet completed his outfit.

The most distinguished part of a knight's armor was his helmet. Initially, the helmet consisted of little more than a metal skullcap that was effective for deflecting blows from above, but this still left a good deal of the face exposed, even with the addition of a nose protector and chin flaps. The introduction of the great helm in the early thirteenth century addressed this problem by sheathing the knight's head and face in a bucket-like cylinder of steel punctuated with slits for the eyes and mouth. However, the great helm severely limited its wearer's vision. It was superseded eventually by the bascinet, a helmet often fitted with a beaklike visor that could be raised and lowered. Later variations on the helmet included the visorless barbute, notable for the Y- or T-shaped pattern cut into its front plate as an aid to vision and breathing, and the armet, a four-piece helmet consisting of a skullcap, two hinged cheekpieces that locked at the front, and a visor.

A knight also had a vast arsenal of weapons at his disposal. Mounted knights played an essential role in breaking through infantry lines, and they often carried lances measuring twelve feet or longer. Knights on the ground might carry halberds, spear-tipped pikes equipped with an ax blade and a hook useful for grappling with mounted combatants. Most knights fought with arming swords, which could be carried in one hand so that a shield could be carried in the other. A longsword gave a knight greater reach but was more unwieldy—its blade was three feet long, and it weighed about three pounds. The two-handed great sword featured a blade four to six feet long and weighed up to six pounds. In addition, knights fought with longbows and crossbows.

Knight vs Squire

Pauldron

Rerebrace

Chain mail

Vambrace

Great sword

Backplate

Breastplate

Culet

Gauntlet

Hauberk

Cuisse

Poleyn

Helmet

Arming doublet

Fauld

Couter

Agincourt

A knight outfitted with weapons and a full suit of plate armor was carrying as much as sixty additional pounds. While this added weight usually translated to formidable protection, it was often unwieldy and made maneuvering on the battlefield difficult—even perilous—as was proved at the Battle of Agincourt, a historical turning point in the way knights waged war.

On the morning of Friday, October 25, 1415, British forces outside the French town of Agincourt assembled approximately 900 men-at-arms across a field approximately 750 yards wide, and flanked them on either side with approximately 5,000 longbowmen. They were greatly outnumbered by French forces that approximately consisted of 8,000 armored men-at-arms, 1,400 mounted soldiers, 4,000 archers, and 1,500 crossbowmen. Initially, the French forces repelled the British invaders; but several days earlier, rain had turned the field into a muddy quagmire, and the vanguard of fully armored French knights found it difficult to clamber over the mounting casualties before them. Chaos ensued as they were met from behind by successive waves of their advancing countrymen. Hemmed in by woods on either side of the field, the French knights found it nearly impossible to maneuver without stumbling into one another or sinking knee-deep into the mud. Their ranks disordered and their battle plans in disarray, the armor-burdened knights became easy targets for the more lightly armored British forces and longbowmen, who were able to pick them off from a safe distance. Casualties at the end of the battle day were staggering for the French: an estimated 7,000 men lost, compared to little more than 400 for the British. In retrospect, Agincourt marked the beginning of the end of the knight-in-shining-armor heyday.

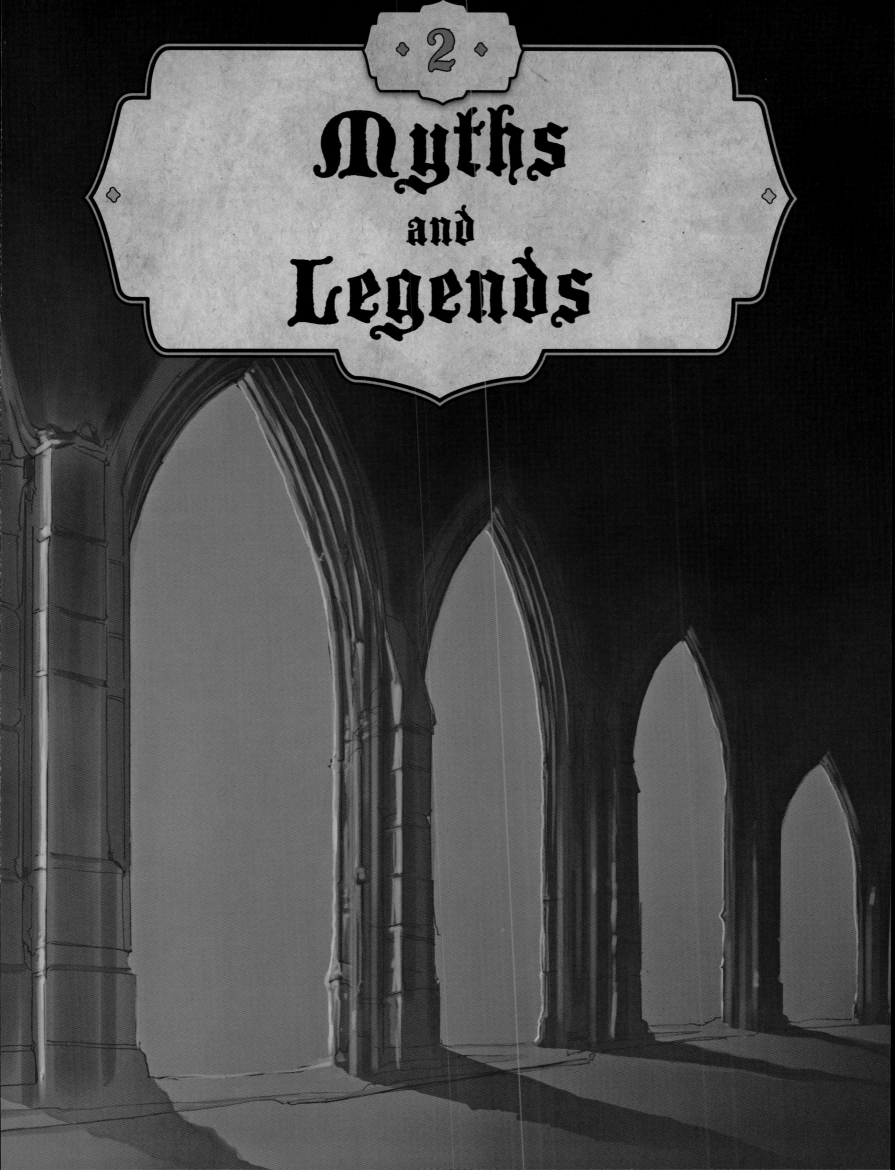

2
Myths
and
Legends

The Tale of Beowulf

Beowulf was a mighty warrior who sailed with his comrades from Geatland (now part of Sweden) to aid the Danish king Hrothgar in his battle against the monster Grendel. Hrothgar had built a magnificent mead (feasting) hall called Heorot to serve as his throne room, but Grendel, a malignant monster who lived at the bottom of a nearby murky lake, pillaged it shortly after its completion, slaughtering thirty of Hrothgar's best men. Grendel's nightly attacks then continued for twelve years, forcing the Danes to abandon the hall.

When Beowulf arrived in Hrothgar's kingdom, boasting of his prowess at fighting monsters, the Danes feted him at Heorot, inadvertently alerting Grendel to their presence. That evening, when Grendel stole upon the sleeping warriors in the hall, Beowulf grappled violently with the monster. The warriors awoke and came to Beowulf's aid, but unearthly forces protected Grendel's flesh from their swords. Luckily, however, Beowulf possessed an almost Herculean grip and wrenched one of the monster's arms from its socket. The mortal wound drove Grendel from the hall and back to his underwater den to die. Beowulf was celebrated as a hero, and Grendel's arm was immediately mounted on the outside of Heorot as an emblem of victory.

The Danes' jubilation, though, was short-lived. The next day, Grendel's mother, a formidable sorceress, came to Heorot to avenge her son. Retrieving Grendel's arm, she made off with one of Hrothgar's warriors and fled to her lair. With Hrothgar leading the way, the Danes followed in pursuit. Arriving at the edge of a foul lake, the warriors came upon the head of the ill-fated retainer and sighted a spot of blood on the water. As Beowulf donned his helmet and chain mail, the great Danish hero Unferth offered the Geat his ancient, poisonous sword, Hrunting.

Beowulf then plunged into the lake and swam for the better part of a day. When he confronted Grendel's mother, he found that Unferth's poisonous sword was useless against her. Fortuitously, in the midst of an armory of weapons pried from the hands of fallen warriors, Beowulf caught sight of a sword that had once belonged to a race of ancient giants. He seized it and cut off the sorceress's head. Discovering Grendel's corpse in the den, Beowulf beheaded it as well. He then returned to land bearing Grendel's head and the hilt of the giant's sword, which he later presented to Hrothgar.

Beowulf returned home a legend and was eventually made king of Geatland, where he ruled for half a century. In his final act of valor, he died slaying a dragon that had menaced his kingdom. Beowulf's body was burned on a funeral pyre, and the cairn covering his ashes was filled with jewels and riches from the dragon's hoard.

With its grand scope and dramatic heroism, the tale of Beowulf has stirred the world's imagination for well over a thousand years. The epic poem was first written down between the eighth and eleventh centuries, but it was likely told much earlier and passed down through oral tradition. To some extent, Beowulf's fearsome battles with a variety of supernatural nemeses recall the adventures of Odysseus and other heroes of classical epics. Yet other aspects of the legend—Beowulf's weapons and regalia, his selfless service to the king, and the innate nobility that is inseparable from his valor and awesome might—anticipate Arthurian legends and the lore of the medieval knights.

Siegfried and Brünnhilde

Told in many versions, with characters whose names vary with different tellings, the story of Siegfried and Brünnhilde is both a heroic epic and a tragic love story.

In Richard Wagner's *Ring of the Nibelung* cycle, Siegfried began life as the adopted child of Mime, an ill-tempered dwarf who kept the young man's true parentage a secret. Mime raised the young hero in the hopes that he would, one day, defeat Fafner, guardian of the coveted magical Ring. As a youth, Siegfried was utterly fearless and amazingly strong—traits he had inherited, unknowingly, from his real father, Siegmund, a slain warrior and son of Wotan, the leader of the Norse gods. Mime, an accomplished swordsmith, had never been able to forge a blade that Siegfried could not break effortlessly, and though Mime possessed the fragments of Siegmund's sword, Nothung, he lacked the skill to reforge them. In the midst of Mime's despairing, a disguised Wotan visited the dwarf and revealed that only a man who was without fear could restore the blade. That man turned out to be Siegfried, who fashioned a sword so strong that he was able to split Mime's anvil in two with a single blow.

Mime grew increasingly concerned at Siegfried's power, so he promptly dispatched the young warrior to slay Fafner, a dragon feared for his immense jaws, cadaverous breath, acidic spittle, and barbed, stinging tail. Siegfried surprised the dragon in his lair and, after a violent battle, struck Fafner fatally in the heart with Nothung. When some of Fafner's blood seared Siegfried's hand, he licked his injury to soothe it, and soon discovered that the blood had endowed him with the power to understand the songs of birds. A small woodbird that watched the battle then proceeded to tell Siegfried of treasures secreted in Fafner's cave. Only two items out of the hoard interested Siegfried: the Tarnhelm, a magical helmet that allowed the wearer to cloak his identity, and the all-powerful Ring.

The woodbird also warned Siegfried of Mime's intent to murder him, so he killed his former caretaker when Mime approached him with a poison drink. Then, the woodbird sang of a beautiful woman asleep in a ring of fire on a mountain peak. Eager to continue his pursuit of the meaning of fear, Siegfried followed the bird up the stony face of the mountain.

The woman was Brünnhilde, daughter of Wotan. As a Valkyrie, one of the armored emissaries of the gods, Brünnhilde's job was to bring slain warriors to Wotan's great hall, Valhalla, which served as a home for those who died gloriously in battle. When she disobeyed her father by aiding Siegfried's father, Siegmund, who had been chosen for death, Wotan condemned her to mortality and stranded her on a remote mountaintop. After placing her in a deep sleep, he commanded Loki, a trickster god capable of assuming many guises, to take the form of flame that encircles her. Undaunted by the flames, Siegfried stepped boldly through the fire. Only after he removed her armor did Siegfried realize that a woman lay before him, and, confronting fear for the first time, he kissed her.

Brünnhilde opened her eyes and beheld her rescuer and, though she felt despair for her loss of immortality, she found her passions awakened for the heroic Siegfried. The next day, before Siegfried left to continue his adventures, he and Brünnhilde exchanged tokens of their love: Brünnhilde gave Siegfried her warhorse, Grane, and Siegfried gave Brünnhilde the Ring he had claimed from Fafner's treasure hoard. He did not know that whoever wore the Ring could use its power to rule the world, nor did he know that the Ring also bore a curse that doomed the wearer.

Siegfried's travels eventually brought him to the Hall of the Gibichungs, a people ruled over by King Gunther. Gunther recognized Siegfried as a hero and, in a scheme to snare him and enhance his kingdom's reputation, he and his half-brother, Hagen, tricked Siegfried into wedding Gunther's sister, Gutrune. After Gutrune offered Siegfried a potion that made him forget his past, including his intense love for Brünnhilde, he fell in love with Gutrune and vowed to marry her. Gunther then decided to take Brünnhilde for his own wife and employed Siegfried to press his suit. Using the Tarnhelm, Siegfried assumed the countenance of King Gunther and returned to Brünnhilde's mountain, where he overpowered her and took back the Ring.

When Brünnhilde discovered that it was actually her lover who had betrayed her, she became enraged and revealed to Hagen the secret for slaying Siegfried: the otherwise invincible warrior had one spot on his back that was not magically protected. Hagen had already recognized the Ring taken back from Brünnhilde as a powerful talisman. Determined to take it for himself, he speared Siegfried in the back during a hunt, killing him. By the time the hunting party returned with Siegfried's body, Brünnhilde had learned the truth about the potion of forgetfulness and the Ring. Bereft at the understanding that her lover would never have willingly betrayed her, she took the Ring and commanded a funeral pyre to be built for Siegfried. When it was lit, she mounted Grane and rode into the flames. With her death, the curse of the Ring ended.

The Black Knight

The Black Knight is a persona of both legend and of historical reality. Whether appearing as an innocuous freelance knight in black armor or as a mysterious warrior of the most fearsome sort, bearing enchanted weapons and fantastic powers, the Black Knight is the "unknown foe."

In history, a knight in black armor was either unaffiliated to lord or land, or traveling in disguise so as not to be recognized. The armor that he wore was either forged to be bluish black or, as it became tarnished (a freelance knight typically couldn't afford a squire to polish his armor), painted black to avoid rust or obscure his standard.

In Arthurian legend, the Black Knight is a recurring character. Usually treacherous and opportunistic, he stands against king and court and disregards the rules of conduct and battle, sometimes using dark forces to tip the scales in his favor.

• The Black Knight •

By Henry Wadsworth Longfellow (1893)

'Twas Pentecost, the Feast of Gladness,
When woods and fields put off all sadness,
Thus began the King and spake:
So from the halls
Of ancient Hofburgh's walls,
A luxuriant Spring shall break.

Drums and trumpets echo loudly,
Wave the crimson banners proudly,
From balcony the King looked on;
In the play of spears,
Fell all the cavaliers,
Before the monarch's stalwart son.

To the barrier of the fight
Rode at last a sable Knight.
Sir Knight! your name and scutcheon say!
Should I speak it here,
Ye would stand aghast with fear;
I am a Prince of mighty sway!

When he rode into the lists,
The arch of heaven grew black with mists,

And the castle 'gan to rock.
At the first blow,
Fell the youth from saddle-bow,
Hardly rises from the shock.

Pipe and viol call the dances,
Torch-light through the high hall glances;
Waves a mighty shadow in;
With manner bland
Doth ask the maiden's hand,
Doth with her the dance begin;

Danced in sable iron sark,
Danced a measure weird and dark,
Coldly clasped her limbs around.
From breast and hair
Down fall from her the fair
Flowerets, faded, to the ground.

To the sumptuous banquet came
Every Knight and every Dame.
'Twixt son and daughter all distraught,
With mournful mind

The ancient King reclined,
Gazed at them in silent thought.

Pale the children both did look,
But the guest a beaker took;
Golden wine will make you whole!
The children drank,
Gave many a courteous thank;
Oh, that draught was very cool!

Each the father's breast embraces,
Son and daughter; and their faces
Colourless grow utterly.
Whichever way
Looks the fear-struck father grey,
He beholds his children die.

Woe! the blessed children both
Takest thou in the joy of youth;
Take me, too, the joyless father!
Spake the grim Guest,
From his hollow, cavernous breast,
Roses in the spring I gather!

Excerpted from

Childe Roland to the Dark Tower Came

By Robert Browning (1885)

My first thought was, he lied in every word,
That hoary cripple, with malicious eye
Askance to watch the working of his lie
On mine, and mouth scarce able to afford
Suppression of the glee that pursed and scored
Its edge, at one more victim gained thereby.

What else should he be set for, with his staff?
What, save to waylay with his lies, ensnare
All travellers who might find him posted there,
And ask the road? I guessed what skull-like laugh
Would break, what crutch 'gin write my epitaph
For pastime in the dusty thoroughfare,

If at his counsel I should turn aside
Into that ominous tract which, all agree,
Hides the Dark Tower. Yet acquiescingly
I did turn as he pointed: neither pride
Nor hope rekindling at the end descried,
So much as gladness that some end might be.

So, quiet as despair, I turned from him,
That hateful cripple, out of his highway
Into the path he pointed. All the day
Had been a dreary one at best, and dim
Was settling to its close, yet shot one grim
Red leer to see the plain catch its estray.

For mark! no sooner was I fairly found
Pledged to the plain, after a pace or two,
Than, pausing to throw backward a last view
O'er the safe road, 'twas gone; grey plain all round:
Nothing but plain to the horizon's bound.
I might go on; nought else remained to do.

So, on I went. I think I never saw
Such starved ignoble nature; nothing throve:
For flowers—as well expect a cedar grove!
But cockle, spurge, according to their law
Might propagate their kind, with none to awe,
You'd think; a burr had been a treasure trove.

No! penury, inertness and grimace,
In some strange sort, were the land's portion. "See
Or shut your eyes," said Nature peevishly,
"It nothing skills: I cannot help my case:
'Tis the Last Judgment's fire must cure this place,
Calcine its clods and set my prisoners free."

A sudden little river crossed my path
As unexpected as a serpent comes.
No sluggish tide congenial to the glooms;
This, as it frothed by, might have been a bath
For the fiend's glowing hoof—to see the wrath
Of its black eddy bespate with flakes and spumes.

So petty yet so spiteful! All along
Low scrubby alders kneeled down over it;
Drenched willows flung them headlong in a fit

Of mute despair, a suicidal throng:
The river which had done them all the wrong,
Whate'er that was, rolled by, deterred no whit.

Which, while I forded,—good saints, how I feared
To set my foot upon a dead man's cheek,
Each step, or feel the spear I thrust to seek
For hollows, tangled in his hair or beard!
—It may have been a water-rat I speared,
But, ugh! it sounded like a baby's shriek.

Glad was I when I reached the other bank.
Now for a better country. Vain presage!
Who were the strugglers, what war did they wage,
Whose savage trample thus could pad the dank
Soil to a plash? Toads in a poisoned tank,
Or wild cats in a red-hot iron cage—

The fight must so have seemed in that fell cirque.
What penned them there, with all
the plain to choose?
No foot-print leading to that horrid mews,
None out of it. Mad brewage set to work
Their brains, no doubt, like galley-slaves the Turk
Pits for his pastime, Christians against Jews.

And more than that—a furlong on—why, there!
What bad use was that engine for, that wheel,
Or brake, not wheel—that harrow fit to reel
Men's bodies out like silk? with all the air
Of Tophet's tool, on earth left unaware,
Or brought to sharpen its rusty teeth of steel.

· · · · ·

And just as far as ever from the end!
Nought in the distance but the evening, nought
To point my footstep further! At the thought,

A great black bird, Apollyon's bosom-friend,
Sailed past, nor beat his wide wing dragon-penned
That brushed my cap—perchance the guide I sought.

For, looking up, aware I somehow grew,
'Spite of the dusk, the plain had given place
All round to mountains—with such name to grace
Mere ugly heights and heaps now stolen in view.
How thus they had surprised me,—solve it, you!
How to get from them was no clearer case.

Yet half I seemed to recognise some trick
Of mischief happened to me, God knows when—
In a bad dream perhaps. Here ended, then,
Progress this way. When, in the very nick
Of giving up, one time more, came a click
As when a trap shuts—you're inside the den!

Burningly it came on me all at once,
This was the place! those two hills on the right,
Crouched like two bulls locked horn in horn in fight;
While to the left, a tall scalped mountain . . . Dunce,
Dotard, a-dozing at the very nonce,
After a life spent training for the sight!

What in the midst lay but the Tower itself?

The round squat turret, blind as the fool's heart
Built of brown stone, without a counterpart
In the whole world. The tempest's mocking elf
Points to the shipman thus the unseen shelf
He strikes on, only when the timbers start.

Not see? because of night perhaps?—why, day
Came back again for that! before it left,
The dying sunset kindled through a cleft:
The hills, like giants at a hunting, lay
Chin upon hand, to see the game at bay,—
"Now stab and end the creature—to the heft!"

Not hear? when noise was everywhere! it tolled
Increasing like a bell. Names in my ears
Of all the lost adventurers my peers,—
How such a one was strong, and such was bold,
And such was fortunate, yet each of old
Lost, lost! one moment knelled the woe of years.

There they stood, ranged along the hillsides, met
To view the last of me, a living frame
For one more picture! in a sheet of flame
I saw them and I knew them all. And yet
Dauntless the slug-horn to my lips I set,
And blew. "Childe Roland to the Dark Tower came."

Rinaldo and the Magic Shield

The story of Rinaldo's magic shield, which first appeared in a sixteenth-century poem by the Italian poet Torquato Tasso, takes place in Jerusalem during the First Crusade. Most of the operas adapted from this tale describe an attempted assassination of Rinaldo, a Christian knight, by the powerful sorceress Armida. As she prepared to stab Rinaldo in his sleep, she fell madly in love with him and whisked him away to her enchanted isle. Rinaldo fell under her charms, neglecting his duties to the Christian army as he grew idle in the luxury of her garden, so two of his best knights came to his rescue bearing a wondrous shield made of diamond. They confronted Rinaldo and forced him to see his pallid reflection in its mirrored surface, wakening his warrior spirit and shattering Armida's spell.

Handel's opera *Rinaldo* presents a slightly different version of events: in an attempt to weaken his military advances, Armida lures Rinaldo to her island by kidnapping Almirena, his fiancée. In pursuit, Rinaldo and two companions make their way to Armida's shore, where a siren entices him into a boat. When he arrives at Armida's palace on the peak of a frightful mountain, the sorceress offers him her love, but Rinaldo spurns her advances. She responds by transforming herself into the likeness of Almirena, drawing Rinaldo temporarily under her spell. Meanwhile, Rinaldo's abandoned comrades enter a magician's cave at the foot of the mountain. The magician wishes to see Almirena released, so he grants the warriors magic wands to fight the horrible creatures at Armida's command. At the thrilling climax of the story, Rinaldo attacks Armida and rescues Almirena as his faithful knights transform the garden and palace into a site just outside Jerusalem with their wands.

Hereward the Wake

Hereward the Wake was an eleventh-century Anglo-Saxon hero who led resistance movements in the aftermath of the Norman invasion of England. Not only has his life inspired legends, but these legends, in turn, have been incorporated into the tales of the renowned fictional outlaw Robin Hood.

One such legend tells of young Hereward, who, on a visit to Cornwall, discovered that King Alef had betrothed his beautiful daughter to a giant in order to keep her from marrying Prince Sigtryg, the son of a Danish king. In a display of chivalry, Hereward challenged the giant and killed him, after which King Alef threw him into a prison cell. The princess then arranged for Hereward's release and sent him to fetch her prince. Hereward, ever brave, set out to fulfill her request, enduring many trials along the way. Eventually Hereward reached Prince Sigtryg but then discovered that, during his absence, King Alef had betrothed his daughter to yet another man: the wild Cornish hero Haco. At once, Prince Sigtryg sent a band of forty warriors to rescue the princess, whose wedding feast was scheduled for that very day. A disguised Hereward gained admission to the event and found out that the warriors had been captured and that Haco planned to release them, incapacitated by blinding, after the wedding. After informing Prince Sigtryg of Haco's plot, Hereward and company waited silently in the ravine where the forty Danes were to be blinded, springing out as Haco and his Cornishmen passed them. A great fight ensued, from which Hereward and the Danes emerged victorious, slaying Haco and freeing the captives. Prince Sigtryg and the fair princess were subsequently wed, while Hereward was recognized as a great hero and friend to their kingdom.

The Hound of Ulster

Deep in Irish legend there lived a warrior like no other. Born to a mortal mother, his father was believed to be Lugh of the Long Hand, an Irish deity also known as the God of Light. At the age of seven, the young warrior—then named Sétanta—killed a ferocious guard dog while visiting the smith Culann in the village of Cúailnge. In recompense for slaying Culann's prized watchdog, the young boy assumed the name Cúchulainn ("Culann's hound") and replaced the dog at its post until another watchdog was reared.

Cúchulainn was a fierce and terrible warrior to behold. In the midst of combat, he transformed into a hulking berserker filled with rage, his battle lust contorting his body and causing gouts of blood to erupt from his head. His favored weapon was the Gáe Bulga, a barbed spear said to thirst for blood and cause thirty wounds within the body of its victim.

The adventures of Cúchulainn were many and varied. In a competition with Conall Cernach and Lóegaire, great warriors in their own right, Cúchulainn was placed in a room with three demonic cats. He alone stood his ground and defeated the beasts while the others fled.

In another tale, the Hound of Ulster—as Cúchulainn came to be known—was confronted by a horrifying one-eyed giant named Goll mac Carbada, who demanded a tribute. Undaunted, Cúchulainn leaped upon the giant and slew him in single combat.

Perhaps his greatest triumph took place when Medb, an ancient queen, had dispatched her army against Ulster. A curse laid down upon the men of Ulster sent them into a deep sleep, so Cúchulainn alone kept the entire opposing army at bay—some men dying of fright at the mere sight of him—until the enchanted army of Ulster could recover and come to arms.

· Saint George and the Dragon ·

Saint George, the patron saint of England, is believed to have been a Roman from the Near East who lived in the third or fourth century C.E. According to legend, during one of his many travels he came upon a land decimated by blight. A hideous dragon had taken residence in the local swamp, and whenever the beast came near the town, its poisonous breath threatened the inhabitants. To keep the dragon at bay, the townspeople fed it their sheep, but as the livestock began to deplete, townspeople were taken in their stead. Thus, in order to keep the dragon

placated, a human victim was selected daily for sacrifice by drawing lots.

Fortuitously, on the very day that their princess, who had been chosen as the monster's next victim, was led to the swamp, Saint George arrived on the scene. A knight renowned for his courage and righteousness, he vowed to save her.

The princess pleaded with George, urging him to flee and save himself, as the great beast raised its head out of the water and advanced toward them. Making the sign of the cross, George charged the dragon at full speed and drove his lance into the creature. As the dragon lay grievously injured, George asked the princess for her girdle (belt), which he tied around the dragon's neck. The weak, shackled dragon had no choice but to follow the princess and Saint George into town, where the brave knight delivered the final, killing blow, ending the dragon's pestilent reign once and for all.

Don Quixote

Don Quixote de la Mancha is a fictional character who lived his imaginary life in the world of knights, dragons, and adventure. In Miguel de Cervantes's well-known tale, the aging dreamer is obsessed with the codes of chivalry and knighthood and the eternal quest to vanquish insurmountable odds. Where we see only windmills, Don Quixote saw fantastic giants to be reckoned with. Everyday people were transformed into rival knights, lords, and princesses, and inns became medieval castles in his eyes. In the end, however, these castles crumbled as the delusional knight slowly regained his sanity. The profound melancholy that settled on Don Quixote as he finally renounced the ideals of chivalry speaks to the ever-enduring power of mythmaking and storytelling. Knights, dragons, giants, heroic exploits, and the stories from whence they come thrive in the corners of our imaginations—and, real or otherwise, these stories enlighten, enliven, entertain, encourage . . . and inspire.

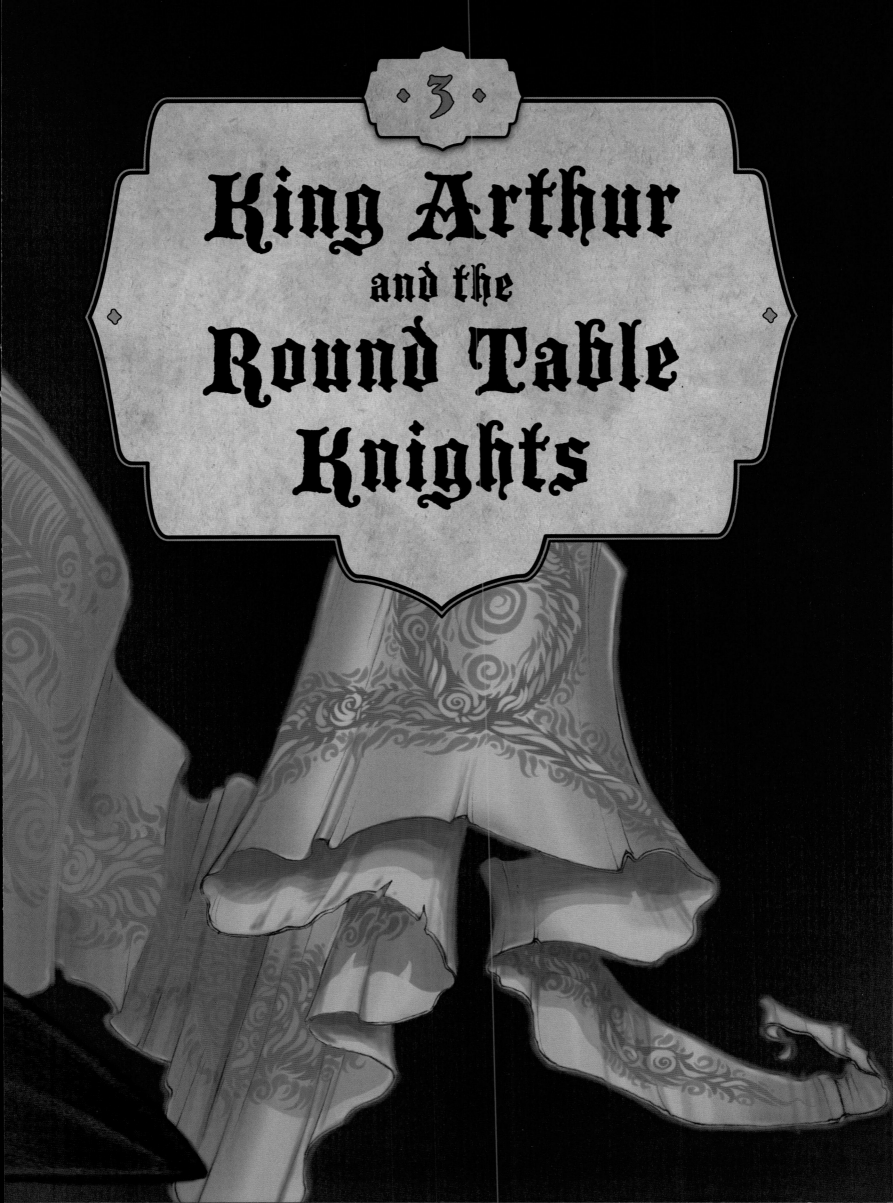

·3·

King Arthur
and the
Round Table
Knights

Merlin

Through many acts of heroism and courage, King Arthur built a legendary kingdom, but it was the enigmatic presence of the wizard Merlin that infused these tales with a deep sense of magic and mystery that is still felt today.

Merlin Ambrosius, Merlinus Caledonensis, Myrddin Emrys—the Arthurian sorcerer is known by many monikers. Likewise, his tales are numerous and varied. As legend has it, his mother was a princess and his father an incubus. At his birth, the infant Merlin was baptized in order to negate the evil influence of his demonic sire. While christened and thus transformed into a force for good, Merlin retained the shadowy gifts of prophecy and sorcery, which he used to

shape King Arthur's destiny. It was the wizard's talents that first placed the magic sword into the stone and that, later, guided the sword into Arthur's hand, making the young squire a king. When Arthur broke that sword against the might of King Pellinore, it was Merlin who led him to Nimue, the Lady of the Lake, and Excalibur. The sorcerer aided and advised Arthur through many of the challenges that he faced.

Merlin remained the king's most valuable adviser, giving prophetic knowledge and guidance to many of his knights, until Nimue, herself a powerful and ambitious sorceress, lured the wizard into an enchanted prison that stilled his counsel and bound his magic forever.

Uther and Pendragon

At the time of Merlin's birth, King Vortigern, an evil usurper, reigned in Britain. He lived in constant fear that the rightful heirs of the kingdom would return to reclaim the throne, so he began to build a strong fortress tower. Three times during its construction, however, the tower collapsed without any apparent cause. After consulting his astrologers, the king learned that the tower was cursed and that, in order to lift the curse, he would have to bathe the cornerstone of the tower's foundation with the blood of a child born without a mortal father.

Vortigern sent his messengers all over the kingdom in search of such a child, and they discovered Merlin in the forest. The boy was taken to the king, but young Merlin was able to avoid his own sacrifice by revealing the true cause of the tower's instability. In fact, the king was attempting to build a fortress over the den of two immense dragons, whose frequent battles shook the earth above them. Vortigern ordered his workmen to dig beneath the tower, where they discovered precisely what Merlin had described to them: two enormous serpents, one white as milk, the other red as fire. As the crowd looked on in amazement, the serpents slowly rose from their dens and expanded their enormous wings. Only Merlin was brave enough to witness the combat, which resulted in the red dragon being slain and the white one disappearing through a cleft in the rock.

As Merlin later explained, these dragons represented the invasion of Uther and Pendragon, the rightful heirs to the throne. Before long, they landed with a great army and burned Vortigern alive in the very tower he had taken such pains to construct. When Pendragon ascended the throne, Merlin became his chief adviser, often assisting the king with his magical arts. Among other endowments, he had the power to transform himself into any shape he pleased, appearing on one occasion as a dwarf and at others as a damsel, a page, or even a stag.

King Arthur

Arthur would never have known, as he stood before the sword in the stone, of all the legends that would spring from this momentous occasion. Drawing the sword would make him king of the renowned kingdom of Camelot, the backdrop against which many of the adventures of Arthur and his Knights of the Round Table would unfold.

The stories of King Arthur and Camelot are the legends by which all other medieval myths and fantasies are measured. Featuring prominently the values of chivalry, courage, love, and nobility, the tales also present examples of treachery, betrayal, and deceit. They depict Arthur and his loyal followers as men and women of the highest caliber who are still human and, therefore, flawed. Arthur constructs the realm of Camelot and dispatches his noble knights on their many quests. The knights often must battle their own weaknesses and fears in addition to the dragons, beasts, and seemingly insurmountable foes that they face. In reading these tales, we observe men and women striving to do right and to be true to the chivalric code to which they are bound. Sometimes they fall—and the stories are the better for it, as we see these brave warriors overcome their mistakes and reach once again for the ideals that Arthur and Camelot represent.

The characters that revolve around Arthur are many and varied. There is Merlin, a half-demon sorcerer and Arthur's counselor, and King Pellinore, a warrior knight so strong that he nearly kills Arthur in combat. There is Queen Guinevere and her ill-fated romance with Lancelot, the strongest and most courageous of the Knights of the Round Table. These are but a few of the players who populate Arthur's realm.

Yet it is Arthur who remains at the center of all the action. Arthur was the humble squire who pulled the sword from the stone. He was the king who broke that sword in combat, only to be led to the fabled Excalibur by his counselor, Merlin. It was Arthur's voice that issued the command to build Camelot and the Round Table and then sent his knights in search of the Holy Grail. Finally, it was King Arthur that fought the evil Mordred to the death on the plains of Camlann. Of course, there are many accounts of gallant knights throughout the ages; but, after all are told, it is Arthur who presides as the rightful king of knightly legend.

The Sword in the Stone

Arthur, the legendary king of the Britons, is forever associated with the sword Excalibur. But before his hand grasped that mighty sword, he distinguished himself by wielding another: the mythical Sword in the Stone.

As a squire, young Arthur accompanied his knighted foster brother, Sir Kay, to a jousting tournament. In the midst of battle, however, Kay broke his sword and sent Arthur home in search of a replacement. Unable to locate a sword, Arthur spied an unattended blade of great quality near the church. Effortlessly, he drew the sword from its resting place, unaware that prior to this simple act, a host of valiant knights had struggled, without success, to wrest the sword from the stone.

When Arthur returned and handed the sword to Kay, the knight immediately recognized it as the Sword in the Stone, which heralded Arthur's rightful ascendancy to the British throne. Though Kay desperately wanted to claim the sword and the kingship it represented as his own, truth ultimately prevailed, and young Arthur became king.

The Sword in the Stone remained with Arthur until it was destroyed in an epic duel with King Pellinore. In fact, if not for the magical intervention of Merlin, Arthur might have been slain by the fierce and powerful warrior. After casting Pellinore into a deep sleep, the sorcerer rescued Arthur by stealing him away into the safety of the forest.

Camelot

The kingdom of Camelot may not have existed in the world of real men, but its prominence in our minds as the center of King Arthur's realm—where his court and Round Table reside and the ideals of romantic knighthood prevail—is as real as any stone-and-mortar castle in existence.

The knights of Camelot swore oaths to serve their king and kingdom. Camelot, with its shining towers, gleaming walls, and idyllic courtyards, was a worthy symbol for which many brave warriors sacrificed their lives. And this metaphoric icon of peace, prosperity, and strength survives even today. Though Camelot may never have been built, as long as it reminds us of what can be accomplished with perseverance, honor, discipline, sacrifice, and—most of all—passion, it will never be destroyed.

Excerpted from

• Camelot •

By Benjamin Gilbert Brooks (1917)

Dank fogs and foul mists from the poisoned deep
Thickened above strange pools, aglimmer
With shapeless white moons elf-dismembered, dimmer
Than snakes that through the sombre brushwood creep.
Where grey breaths mingled in slow dance
Men's faces flashed in one fierce glance.
The cold bleak fury of the sudden lance
Tore them like paper masks: so white
They vanished in the night.
A mad wind hurried from the east
Whirling afar the cloudgates fleeced.
The chill grey dawn spread out behind.
From clarion wild and throbbing tremulous drum
Went up a cry of Arthur come.
Proud, with proud princely lips, he rode
Where the dim-wreathèd vapours flowed.
Between the banners green and gold
Were calm bluff face and silent eyes
And thick lank hair driven red along the wind.
A thousand knights and spearmen bold
About their monarch tramped and wheeled.
The tangled lance, like bristles in black field,
Pierced the grey torment of the storm-swept skies.

O'er Camelot Town by trumpet sound
A white sun burnt like burnished brass,
And bronze-cheeked horsemen turban-crowned
O'er-swarmed the plain, and swept around
Speared thick as bladed grass.
A Queen they brought to Arthur's hand
To spare the wasting of their land.
Lo! stately amid white foaming ostrich plumes
Went ponderous elephants vermilion-dyed,
Pricked on by shrill calls from their oiled black grooms.
Then, in a golden tower's mauve-curtained pride,
Moved forth dark Guenivere to meet the King.

• • • • •

Whereupon right low
The King, ruthless no more, bent him in greeting,
While sombre horns and wailing kettledrums beating
Noised o'er the ground bass shouts of Arthur's men
A strange barbaric hum. Among the crowd
Great Launcelot (long, horse-cheeked, and swarthy-browed,
His black hair ringed with red gold) paused, drew rein,
Tamed the proud hoofs and turning in the way,
Towards Camelot's ivory gates, led back the wide array.

Knights of the Round Table

The Round Table was a symbol of equality among men and the highest order of chivalry in Camelot. The requirements to receive and retain a seat—or siege, as it was called—at the table were very strict indeed. Being noble born was not a guarantee of knighthood in Camelot. In fact, a knight of the Round Table was required to display unshakeable courage and fighting skill in battle. Additionally, every knight in Arthur's court pledged the following: to never murder or commit vile acts, to never be a party to treason, to never align himself in wrongful battles for money or love, to be always merciful, and to remain loyal to the king, the land, and each other without fail.

There are many legends about the Knights of the Round Table, whose numbers range from 13 to 1600, depending on which story you consult. It would be nearly impossible to list all of the names associated with the legends, but a partial roster includes Sir Aglovale, son of King Pellinore of Listinoise; Sir Agravaine, son of King Lot of Orkney; Sir Anselm, son of Lord Valette; King Bagdemagus of Gore; Sir Bedivere (Bedwyr), who threw Excalibur back into the lake when Arthur died; King Bors of Gannes; Sir Brunor le Noir, also known as "La Cote Male Tailée," who arrived at Arthur's court wearing the ill-fitting coat of his late father; Sir Cador of Cornwall; Sir Caradoc Briefbras, also known as "Caradoc of the Shrunken Arm"; Sir Colgrevance; Sir Constantine, son of

Cador, who became king after Arthur's death; Sir Dagonet, the court jester; Sir Dinadan, son of Sir Brunor Senior and brother of Sirs Brunor le Noir and Daniel; Sir Ector, Arthur's foster father and Sir Kay's father; Sir Ector de Maris, the son of King Ban of Benwick; Sir Elyan the White, the son of Sir Bors; Sir Erec, the son of King Lac; Sir Gaheris, the son of King Lot and brother of Sirs Gawain, Agravaine, and Gareth; saintly Sir

Galahad, the son of Lancelot, whose seat was the Siege Perilous; Sir Galehaut, Lord of the Distant Isles and a friend of Lancelot; Sir Galeshin, son of Elaine of Tintagil and King Nentres of Garlot; Sir Gareth, also called Beaumains ("Goodhands"); Sir Gawain; Sir Geraint, son of King Erbin of Dumnonia; Sir Gingalain, Gawain's son, also known as Le Bel Inconnu ("The Fair Unknown"); Sir Griflet, one of Arthur's chief advisers; King

82

Hoel; Sir Kay (Cai, Caius); Sir Lamorak, the son of King Pellinore and lover of Morgause (Arthur's half-sister and King Lot's widow); Sir Lancelot (Launcelot du Lac); King Leodegrance, the father of Guinevere and keeper of the Round Table; Sir Lionel, the son of King Bors; Sir Lucan, King Arthur's butler; Sir Maleagant, King Bagdemagus's son and Guinevere's abductor; Sir Meliant de Lis; Sir Mordred, Arthur's illegitimate son by Morgause and destroyer of the kingdom; Sir Morholt; Sir Palamedes the Saracen ("Unchristened"); Sir Pelleas, husband of Nimue, the Lady of the Lake; King Pellinore; Sir Percival, son of Pellinore; Sir Sagramore le Desirous; Sir Safir, the brother of Sirs Palamedes and Segwarides; Sir Tor; Sir Tristan; King Urien; Sir Yvain (Owain), the son of King Urien and his wife, Morgan le Fay; and King Arthur himself, presiding.

Sir Lancelot

Rescued from a burning castle and raised by Nimue, the Lady of the Lake, Launcelot du Lac ("Lancelot of the Lake") quickly became known as one of the most handsome, powerful, and courageous warriors in all of Camelot when, as a young man, he entered the court of King Arthur.

Sir Lancelot embarked on many thrilling adventures, yet the same character who could slay lions and defeat any knight who stood in his path could not conquer the most powerful of human emotions. After persuading Arthur's enemy, Sir Galehaut, to peacefully surrender and receiving a seat at the Round Table as a reward for his diplomacy, Lancelot commenced an affair with Arthur's wife, Guinevere. Ultimately, this act of treachery barred him from attaining the Holy Grail, but the awful ramifications did not end there. Sir Agravaine discovered the sin of Lancelot and Guinevere and forced it into the open, not only causing strife for the king and queen of Camelot, but destroying the unity of the Round Table knights.

Excerpted from

The Lady of Shalott

By Alfred, Lord Tennyson (1833)

On either side the river lie
Long fields of barley and of rye,
That clothe the wold and meet the sky;
And through the field the road runs by
To many-towered Camelot;
And up and down the people go,
Gazing where the lilies blow
Round an island there below,
The island of Shalott.

Willows whiten, aspens quiver,
Little breezes dusk and shiver
Through the wave that runs for ever
By the island in the river
Flowing down to Camelot.
Four grey walls, and four grey towers,
Overlook a space of flowers,
And the silent isle imbowers
The Lady of Shalott.

There she weaves by night and day
A magic web with colours gay.
She has heard a whisper say,
A curse is on her if she stay
To look down to Camelot.
She knows not what the curse may be,
And so she weaveth steadily,
And little other care hath she,
The Lady of Shalott.

And moving through a mirror clear
That hangs before her all the year,
Shadows of the world appear.
There she sees the highway near
Winding down to Camelot:
There the river eddy whirls,
And there the surly village-churls,
And the red cloaks of market girls,
Pass onward from Shalott.

Sometimes a troop of damsels glad,
An abbot on an ambling pad,
Sometimes a curly shepherd-lad,
Or long-haired page in crimson clad,
Goes by to towered Camelot;
And sometimes through the mirror blue
The knights come riding two and two:
She hath no loyal knight and true,
The Lady of Shalott.

But in her web she still delights
To weave the mirror's magic sights,
For often through the silent nights
A funeral, with plumes and lights
And music, went to Camelot:
Or when the moon was overhead,
Came two young lovers lately wed;
"I am half sick of shadows," said
The Lady of Shalott.

A bow-shot from her bower-eaves,
He rode between the barley-sheaves,
The sun came dazzling through the leaves,

And flamed upon the brazen greaves
Of bold Sir Lancelot.
A red-cross knight for ever kneeled
To a lady in his shield,
That sparkled on the yellow field,
Beside remote Shalott.

. . . .

His broad clear brow in sunlight glowed;
On burnished hooves his war-horse trode;
From underneath his helmet flowed
His coal-black curls as on he rode,
As he rode down to Camelot.
From the bank and from the river
He flashed into the crystal mirror,
"Tirra lirra," by the river
Sang Sir Lancelot.

She left the web, she left the loom,
She made three paces through the room,
She saw the water-lily bloom,
She saw the helmet and the plume,
She looked down to Camelot.
Out flew the web and floated wide;
The mirror cracked from side to side;
"The curse is come upon me," cried
The Lady of Shalott.

In the stormy east-wind straining,
The pale yellow woods were waning,
The broad stream in his banks complaining,
Heavily the low sky raining
Over towered Camelot;
Down she came and found a boat
Beneath a willow left afloat,
And round about the prow she wrote
The Lady of Shalott.

And down the river's dim expanse,
Like some bold seer in a trance
Seeing all his own mischance,
With a glassy countenance
Did she look to Camelot.

And at the closing of the day
She loosed the chain, and down she lay;
The broad stream bore her far away,
The Lady of Shalott.

Lying, robed in snowy white
That loosely flew to left and right—
The leaves upon her falling light—
Through the noises of the night
She floated down to Camelot:
And as the boat-head wound along
The willowy hills and fields among,
They heard her singing her last song,
The Lady of Shalott.

Heard a carol, mournful, holy,
Chanted loudly, chanted lowly,
Till her blood was frozen slowly,
And her eyes were darkened wholly,
Turned to towered Camelot.
For ere she reached upon the tide
The first house by the water-side,
Singing in her song she died,
The Lady of Shalott.

Under tower and balcony,
By garden-wall and gallery,
A gleaming shape she floated by,
Dead-pale between the houses high,
Silent into Camelot.
Out upon the wharfs they came,
Knight and burgher, lord and dame,
And round the prow they read her name,
The Lady of Shalott.

Who is this? and what is here?
And in the lighted palace near
Died the sound of royal cheer;
And they crossed themselves for fear,
All the knights at Camelot:
But Lancelot mused a little space;
He said, "She has a lovely face;
God in his mercy lend her grace,
The Lady of Shalott."

The Grail Quest

One day while he was holding court at the Round Table, a clap of thunder followed by a flash of brilliant light surprised King Arthur and his knights. Then a chalice covered by a white cloth appeared in the hall, before quickly fading from view. This magnificent vision corresponded with the arrival of young Sir Galahad, son of Lancelot, who safely took the Siege Perilous—a seat deadly to all except he who was prophesied to locate the legendary cup of Christ. Arthur realized immediately that this was a sign to begin the quest for the Holy Grail, the lost cup from which Christ had drunk at the Last Supper before bequeathing the precious relic to Joseph of Arimathea, who carried it to the West.

Of all the strong and brave Knights of the Round Table who set out that day, only Sir Percival, Sir Bors, and Sir Galahad ever came close to locating the Grail. After a series of adventures, the trio found themselves together in a ship, sailing past wondrous and dangerous sights. They came upon another ship, and, encouraged by Sir Percival's sister, they boarded it. There, upon a table of silver, they finally glimpsed the most beautiful and sacred Grail.

In time, the wind steered their ship to a kingdom stricken with grief with the death of its king. Seeing the nobility and courage of the three knights, and without a successor for their king, they chose the youngest knight, Sir Galahad, to rule their land.

Once he became king, Sir Galahad ordered a chest constructed of gold and precious stones in which to keep the Holy Grail. One morning, a year after Sir Galahad received his crown, the king and his two companions went to pray and saw a man kneeling before the Grail, surrounded by a host of heavenly angels. The stranger announced himself as Joseph of Arimathea. After kissing the cheeks of his fellow knights, Sir Galahad knelt in prayer, and—to the dismay of his companions—his soul departed from his body, followed by a multitude of angels. The two remaining knights then witnessed a hand reach down to the Holy Grail, which then took it up to Heaven, never to be seen on Earth again.

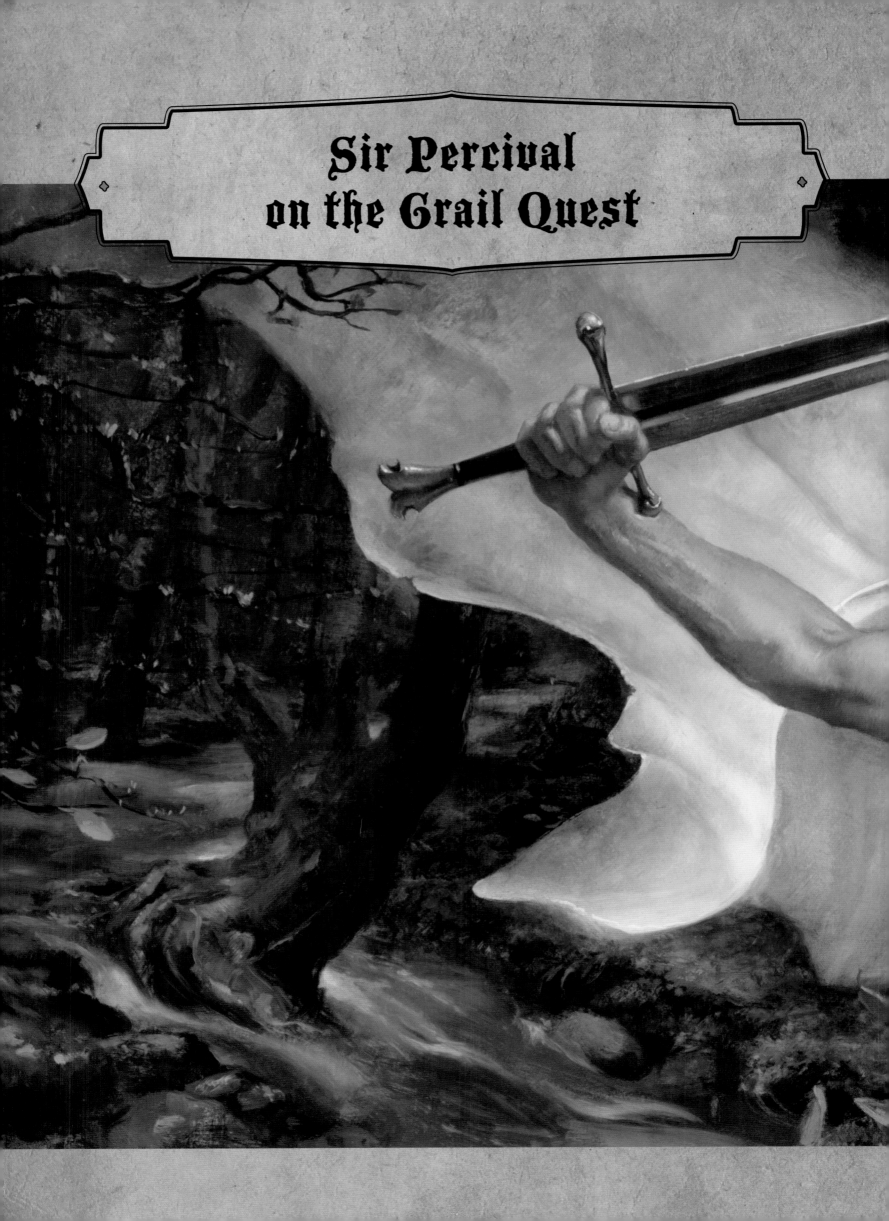

Sir Percival
on the Grail Quest

As King Arthur and his court sat down for the annual Pentecost feast, a young, unknown peasant entered the room. The men were stunned by the youth's handsome face and powerful physique. The stranger strode up to the dais at which King Arthur and the Knights of the Round Table were seated, and he began to speak. He praised the king and his valiant knights and then asked that Arthur listen to his three requests. The first request he made immediately, but the other two were to be granted to him in a year's time. His first request was simply to be fed sufficiently for the next year. King Arthur willingly accepted the young man's proposal, and the stranger was sent to the kitchen to eat and drink his fill. In exchange for food and lodging, he promised to work in the castle's kitchen as a servant. No one suspected him of being noble born, and his humble nature did not permit him to brag of it.

For a year, the young man—dubbed "Beaumains" (fair hands)—toiled under the suspicious Sir Kay, the steward of the kitchen, in the service of the knights and nobles of Camelot. Sir Kay's poor treatment of him did not damage his disposition, so willing and guileless was he, but Beaumains would have his redemption soon enough. On the very day that Beaumains had completed his year of service at Camelot and was to petition King Arthur to grant his remaining requests, a damsel by the name of Lynette came to Arthur's hall and pleaded for a knight to retrieve her sister, Lyonesse, who had been kidnapped by a grievous character called the Red Knight, one of the most dangerous warriors in the world. Beaumains came forth and, as his second request, asked Arthur for the opportunity to rescue Lady Lynette's sister from the Red Knight. His final request was that the valiant Sir Lancelot, whom he greatly respected, make him a knight. Arthur willingly granted Beaumains what he desired, although he would not be made a knight until he had displayed his valor.

Lady Lynette, insulted by the king's offer of a simple kitchen servant to help her, stormed out of the castle, but the youth would not be denied his opportunity. He rode after the lady as she left Camelot, and though she scorned him with each passing moment, he bore it with a knightly decorum.

Shortly after Beaumains's departure, Sir Kay overtook the young man and demanded that he return to the kitchen to serve his superiors. Tired of being belittled by Sir Kay, Beaumains refused, which angered the older knight so much that he drew his spear to attack the youth. With lightning-quick reflexes, Beaumains deflected Sir Kay's spear with his sword and delivered a hard blow, knocking Sir Kay from his horse and rendering him unconscious.

Sir Lancelot, who witnessed the fight, then challenged the young man to a joust. They charged one another so fiercely that both men were thrown from their horses and badly bruised. Unsatisfied, they began to fight one another in hand-to-hand combat, which lasted for over an hour. Lancelot was so impressed and, indeed, intimidated by Beaumains's strength and stamina that he called off the fight, saying they had no real quarrel. Beaumains asked Lancelot if he had proved himself worthy to be a knight, and Lancelot agreed that he had shown great valor and strength; but he refused to knight Beaumains until he knew the young man's real identity. So Beaumains finally revealed who he was: Gareth, brother of Sir Gawain, a renowned Knight of the Round Table. Lancelot then bestowed

upon Gareth, formerly Beaumains, the order of knighthood before returning to Camelot.

Despite Sir Gareth's triumphs, Lady Lynette continued to berate and mock the young man as they continued on their journey to rescue her sister. She still did not know his true identity and saw him as nothing more than a lowly kitchen knave. Nevertheless, he ignored her ridicule, pledging to keep his promise to King Arthur and to complete his task of rescuing Dame Lyonesse.

Eventually they came to a strange, bleak country. In the distance, next to an enormous black boulder, sat a fearsome-looking knight outfitted entirely in black armor. The Black Knight called out to Lady Lynette, asking about her escort, to which she responded that she was forced to ride with a poor kitchen servant. The Black Knight then attempted to force Sir Gareth to relinquish his horse and harness to him. However, the young knight said that the Black Knight would have to fight him for his horse and harness and insisted that he, Gareth, would pass through this bleak land whether the Black Knight liked it or not.

At this challenge, the Black Knight stood, gathered his large black shield and his spear, and mounted his ebony steed. Moments later, the formidable knight was bearing down on Sir Gareth. They fought for over an hour, clashing with numerous weapons, but the young knight finally won when, in a swoon, the Black Knight fell from his horse and died.

Gareth's victory was short lived, however, for very soon a knight covered in gleaming green armor appeared. The lady, still scornful of Sir Gareth, told the Green Knight that the kitchen servant with whom she was forced to travel had killed his brother, the Black Knight. Angered, the Green Knight drew his sword against the young man. Gareth was undaunted and fought courageously, eventually defeating the Green Knight, who, rather than perish, begged his conqueror for mercy. When Lady Lynette asked that he not slay the knight, Sir Gareth yielded to her request and freed him. In return for his act of mercy, the Green Knight swore allegiance to Sir Gareth and promised to help guide the two travelers through the forest.

At dinner that night, the Green Knight spoke of his admiration for Sir Gareth's remarkable fighting skills and went on to say that the young knight must be of noble blood. However, Lady Lynette still did not believe that Sir Gareth was anything more than a lowly kitchen knave and continued to berate him. Sir Gareth and Lady Lynette traveled on for a while, encountering various foes along the way. Witnessing the young knight defeat enemy after enemy who wished them harm, Lady Lynette finally began to feel ashamed of how she had mistreated such a noble and courageous gentleman and, finally, apologized to Sir Gareth.

Eventually they came upon the castle of the Red Knight of the Red Lands. Amid the trees, Sir Gareth beheld a horrible sight: from many large, twisted trees hung the lifeless bodies of forty knights. When Sir Gareth and Lady Lynette neared the menacing castle walls, they discovered a giant horn hanging from a sycamore tree, and Sir Gareth, angered at the sight of so many good men slain, blew the horn to issue a challenge to the man responsible for these dreadful deeds.

The Red Knight promptly emerged from his castle, attended by his barons and servants. He was a giant man, covered all over in blood-red armor that glowed as if it had just been forged in a smith's furnace. He mounted his warhorse and sat, glaring down at the young knight. Looking beyond the terrible warrior, who was rumored to possess the strength of seven men, Sir Gareth could see the beautiful Dame Lyonesse watching from a tower window. The Red Knight warned Sir Gareth that he would meet the same fate as the others should he refuse to be on his way, but the brave knight announced that he would rescue the damsel or die trying.

So Sir Gareth and the Red Knight joined in ferocious combat. So mighty and skilled were the two warriors that they fought for a full day. It seemed that the Red Knight would emerge victorious, but, at the last moment, the young knight, inspired by the beauty and kindness in Dame Lyonesse's countenance, rallied and defeated the Red Knight. The vanquished warrior begged for mercy, and Sir Gareth told him that, if he restored Dame Lyonesse's lands and earned her forgiveness, he might live. The Red Knight assured Sir Gareth that he would do as commanded; so, after the defeated warrior had released Dame Lyonesse, Sir Gareth sent him to Camelot to relate the entire gruesome story to King Arthur and to place himself at the mercy of Sir Lancelot and Sir Gawain.

But Sir Gareth, having fallen in love with Dame Lyonesse, was heavy-hearted when she refused to welcome him into her castle. Though she loved the courageous young knight, she would not wed him until he had spent another year as a knight in King Arthur's service. Downcast but determined to prove his worth, Sir Gareth rode off to achieve more great deeds and to establish himself as a rightful knight of Camelot.

Gawain and the Green Knight

The story of Sir Gawain and the Green Knight is one of the most popular of the Arthurian tales. His trials began during the New Year's celebration in the kingdom of Camelot. During the festivities, an unexpected visitor arrived at King Arthur's court. This was not just any visitor: this gigantic, powerful knight was green from head to foot. As the king and his court stared speechless at the fearsome Green Knight, he stepped forward and issued a challenge: he who is brave enough to trade blows must come forth, take the gleaming ax from his mighty grasp, and strike him as he sits motionless.

No one in Arthur's court was eager to accept the challenge, so the Green Knight began to mock their honor and courage, provoking Arthur to seize the ax and wield it threateningly. Then—quite suddenly—the king's young nephew, Gawain, intervened. After receiving Arthur's blessing, the young man swore the following oath to the Green Knight: he would attempt to strike the giant with a deadly blow. Should the Green Knight survive, Gawain would seek him out in one year and one day's time, and volunteer to receive an equal blow. Having accepted Gawain's pledge, the Green Knight knelt before him and bared his thick neck. Then Gawain took the giant's enormous axe and cleaved the Green Knight's head from his body. Horrified, the court watched as the body stood, collected its severed head, and abruptly departed.

When late autumn arrived, Gawain left to fulfill his oath. Worn and weary from his grueling quest to find the Green Knight and his abode at the Green Chapel, he came upon the castle of Lord Bertilak and took refuge. Each day that Gawain rested, Lord Bertilak hunted. At Bertilak's suggestion, the two decided that, at the end of each day, they would trade whatever they had obtained.

The first morning, as Bertilak departed, the lady of the castle surprised Gawain with a kiss. She returned to seduce him for two days, but Gawain only accepted chaste, courtly kisses from her, which he then traded to Bertilak in the evening. On the third and last day, Lady Bertilak succeeded in persuading Gawain to accept a magical girdle (belt) that protected its wearer from all harm. Thinking of the ordeal he was about to face with the terrible Green Knight, Gawain withheld her gift from the lord of the castle, merely offering him three kisses in exchange for a fox skin. That night during their evening discussion, Bertilak revealed the route to the Green Chapel.

The next day, Gawain left the castle to fulfill his obligation to the Green Knight. He had traveled for less than a full day when he came upon a bubbling, boiling stream next to a dark crevice in a hill. This was the Green Chapel.

Hearing the sounds of weapons being sharpened, Gawain called out to the Green Knight. His adversary emerged and, just as the Green Knight had done a year prior, Gawain knelt and bared his neck. When the Green Knight swung the mighty ax, however, Gawain's courage failed him, and he flinched, despite the magical girdle he was wearing. After chastising the young knight, the giant swung the axe again—not with the intent to kill him, but to see if Gawain would falter. This time, Gawain's bravery stuck—he did not move, and the Green Knight halted the axe before it fell upon the young knight. Gawain

dared his fearsome adversary to swing again with all his might, but the Green Knight only allowed the blade of the axe to fall lightly upon Gawain's neck. Rather than being killed, the brave knight was left with a scar that he would carry forever.

When the trial was over, the Green Knight revealed that he was none other than Lord Bertilak. Gawain, feeling ashamed of his deception concerning the girdle, admitted his wrongdoing, but the lord only laughed and promptly forgave him. Bertilak went on to admit that King Arthur's half sister, Morgan le Fay, had used her sorcery to transform Bertilak into the Green Knight and orchestrate the whole series of events in order to shame Arthur and the Knights of the Round Table.

Upon his return to Camelot, Gawain was embarrassed as he related the tale to the Round Table knights. King Arthur, however, saw only bravery and humility in the young knight. In his honor, the king instructed all his knights to wear a green sash as a reminder that courage is meant to be tested and will ultimately prevail.

The Knight of the Lion

Sir Yvain (Sir Owain) was one of the many knights of King Arthur's court. One day, he set out on horseback to carry out a personal quest. He rode deep into the forest and, hearing a loud, terrible cry reverberate from within the woods, came to a clearing. There, a ferocious giant serpent held a struggling lion by the tail, burning the beast with its fiery, venomous breath. The two were joined in bitter combat, and neither would yield, so Yvain decided to intervene. Deeming the lion less wicked than the serpent, the young knight mustered all his strength and delivered a powerful blow to the monstrous reptile, cutting it in half. He continued to strike the serpent until it lay in pieces.

Having killed one fearsome creature, the young knight readied himself for an attack from the other deadly foe. Freed from the serpent's grasp, the lion leaped toward Yvain. However, instead of attacking him, the lion bowed its head at Yvain's feet in gratitude. From that day forward, the wild creature barely strayed from his side and fought beside him in many battles against horrible foes.

One noteworthy adventure helped to spread word of this unlikely pair far and wide. While on his way to defend the honor of Lady Lunete, who had been accused of treason and sentenced to death, Yvain happened upon a village in peril. The lord of the region pleaded with the knight to stand up against a giant who had beset them. Yvain agreed, and the very next morning

he met the giant, called Harpina of the Mountain, in combat. As the two battled fiercely, the lion crept onto a battlement and leaped upon the monster, tearing nerves and flesh from its massive body. Yvain dealt a final blow, and the giant crashed to the ground with a boom that sounded as if an enormous oak tree had been felled.

Thus Sir Yvain, the Knight of the Lion, became exalted throughout the lands, and many stories were told about his adventures with his faithful companion.

The Fair Unknown

In the midst of his adventures, Sir Gawain met a beautiful female fairy named Blanchemal in a deep wood. Gawain and the fairy fell into a romance with each other and had a child, whom Blanchemal raised in isolation, never revealing to him his knightly lineage or even his name. One day, while wandering in the woods, the young boy came upon the remains of a fallen knight. Seeing this awakened his desire to become a knight himself, so he traveled to King Arthur's court and asked to be knighted—a strange request, indeed, from an untried youth with no name. Nevertheless, Arthur agreed and named the boy Le Bel Inconnu ("The Fair Unknown"). Arthur, bound by his agreement to make the boy a knight, sent him to rescue Queen Esmerée, who had been captured and transformed into a dragon by the cruel wizard Mabon. After a lengthy journey, the Fair Unknown found himself amid the ruins of a once-magnificent city, where a huge ethereal knight on an imposing fire-breathing steed confronted him. The youth leaped into combat with the horrible apparition and slew him with a fatal stroke from his sword. No sooner was the horrible knight revealed to be Mabon than a hideous serpent rose up in front of the Fair Unknown. Realizing that this must be the dragon form of the kidnapped queen, he overcame his fear and stilled his sword as the creature lowered its fearsome head and granted him a kiss. At once, he heard a mysterious voice in his ear that spoke the name "Guinglain." With the revelation of his true name, the city around him sprung back into life and Mabon's curse was lifted. Before him stood the beautiful queen, now restored to her former glory. Eventually, he married her and ruled the city at her side.

Tristan and Isolde

he tale of Tristan and Isolde was one of the most heroic and tragic in the kingdom of Camelot. Although a courageous and fearless knight, Tristan was ultimately defeated—not in battle, but by his ill-fated love of Isolde.

Tristan was born to King Meliadus of Leonois and Queen Isabella, sister to King Mark of Cornwall. When Tristan was still an infant, his father was lured away by a fairy while on a hunt, and his mother died on her journey to locate him. Eventually the queen's squire restored Tristan to his father's care, where he developed special aptitudes for hunting, chess, and music. After King Meliadus died, his widow sent the talented youth to his uncle's residence at Cornwall.

Some time later, Sir Morholt, brother to the queen of Ireland, arrived at the court to collect tribute from King Mark, but the king had decided that he would pay the Irish throne no more. Unfortunately, the knights of Cornwall were known for their cowardice, and no one volunteered to fight against the great Irish champion. Tristan desired to enter the order of the knights, so he stepped forward and agreed to fight Sir Morholt in exchange for the grant of knighthood. King Mark, though afraid he would lose his nephew in the battle, consented.

Tristan and Sir Morholt fought for over half a day. Despite severe wounds, Tristan eventually managed to strike Morholt through his helmet, leaving a fragment of his sword embedded in the Irishman's skull. Mortally wounded, Morholt fled to his ship and back to Ireland, where he died.

At the conclusion of the battle, Sir Tristan was himself gravely wounded. His attendants tried all manners of healing cures, but none worked against the poison that had laced

Morholt's sword, so Tristan decided to seek aid in the kingdom of Loegria (England). After setting out to sea, however, a great storm drove the ship to the coast of Ireland. Relieved that he had escaped the dangerous seas alive, Tristan took out his harp and began to play. King Anguish of Ireland and his fair daughter, Isolde, heard the beautiful music and sent for the unknown harpist. When Tristan arrived at their court, he realized he was in Ireland, so when the king asked him his name, he introduced himself as Tantrist.

During his time in Ireland, Tristan began to instruct Isolde in the arts of minstrelsy and poetry. As the days passed, they grew increasingly fond of one another, but fate intervened when, one day, a young damsel of the court entered the closet that held Tristan's sword and noticed that a notch missing from his blade was similar in shape to the piece of metal found in the skull of Sir Morholt. She told the queen of her findings, and Tristan was promptly called before the court and reproached for his dishonesty. As punishment, Tristan was ordered to leave Ireland without delay and to never return, or else face death.

Upon his return to Cornwall, Tristan so eloquently described the beauty of Isolde that King Mark decided to marry her himself, so he demanded a boon of Tristan: that Tristan return to Ireland as Mark's messenger and ask King Anguish for Isolde's hand in marriage.

During his journey back into enemy territory, a tempest came and blew Tristan to the coast of England, near King Arthur's court at Camelot. Once again, Tristan kept his identity hidden as he participated in many tournaments and games, gaining prestige. One day, Tristan witnessed the arrival of the king of Ireland at Camelot, who

was there to free himself from a charge of treason against King Arthur. King Anguish needed a youthful knight to fight against Blaanor, his accuser. Tristan made his true identity known to Anguish and consented to his request, on the condition that, if Tristan were successful, he would be granted any favor he might ask.

The young knight fought Blaanor and defeated him, so the judges of the field declared the king of Ireland free from the charge against him. Immensely grateful, King Anguish asked Tristan to return with him to his kingdom. Isolde was overjoyed to see Tristan and, knowing that her father had promised to grant the knight anything he asked, she hoped that her beloved would ask her hand in marriage. Tristan, on the other hand, was very heavy-hearted, for he had sworn an oath to bring Isolde back to Cornwall to wed his uncle. This was the favor Tristan asked of King Anguish, who readily accepted King Mark's proposal to wed his daughter.

While they were readying for their departure, the queen took one of her devoted attendants aside. She had seen the love shared between Tristan and Isolde, so she gave her attendant a love potion to administer to Isolde and King Mark on the evening of their marriage ceremony. The voyage to Cornwall was favorable, but Isolde soon complained of thirst. In response, Tristan brought her a bottle—the love potion that the queen's attendant had been so imprudent as to leave in plain sight—and both drank its contents.

King Mark was extremely pleased with his young bride and heaped honors upon Tristan, making him chamberlain of the palace, which gave the young knight access to Queen Isolde at all times. Soon after the wedding, Tristan and Isolde began an extended love affair. One day, Isolde and Tristan were in her quarters, sitting at a chess table (although not attending to the game), when the cowardly knight Andret spied them through the keyhole and alerted King Mark to the debauchery taking place in his palace. The

king saw enough to confirm his suspicions and rushed into the room with his sword drawn. He would have killed Tristan, but the young knight managed to draw his sword and chase the king through the palace. No one in the court dared intervene.

This outrageous event resulted in Tristan's banishment from Cornwall and Isolde's imprisonment in a tower on the bank of a river. Tristan traveled through various countries, embarking on all kinds of adventures and becoming a knight of great renown. Meanwhile, Isolde was beset with grief, spending her days singing sweet melodies to her beloved Tristan. Meanwhile, Tristan remained steadfast in his allegiance to Isolde, relishing every correspondence they shared.

Eventually, Tristan arrived in Brittany, where he earned the favor of King Hoel by aiding him in a war against rebel armies. In gratitude, King Hoel proposed that Tristan marry his beautiful daughter. Resigned to the fact that he and Isolde would never be united, Tristan accepted the proposal.

Later, as the rebels attempted another uprising, Tristan suffered a terrible wound. Although he had grown fond of his wife, his thoughts returned to his true love. Hoping that Isolde might be able to heal him, he sent for her, telling his messenger that the ship would wear white sails if she was on it and black sails if she was not. Black sails meant his impending death. As Tristan lay close to death, the ship approached wearing white sails, but his wife, jealous of the serious love he still felt for Isolde, told him the sails were black. In despair, Tristan died moments before the queen of Cornwall arrived at his side. Holding the lifeless body of her one true love, Isolde died from grief.

Upon hearing their tale, King Mark felt great compassion and had them buried next to each other in his own chapel. Legend has it that a vine sprang from Tristan's grave and, covering the walls of the chapel, descended into the grave of Isolde. To this day, that wondrous plant shades the tombs of the star-crossed lovers.

Knight of the Swan

Long ago, in the kingdom of Brabant, a dying duke entrusted his daughter, Elsa, to a powerful vassal by the name of Frederic von Telramonde. This esteemed warrior sought Elsa's hand in marriage, but she would not have him, so he called upon Henry the Fowler, King of Germany, to settle the dispute. The king decided that Elsa should select as her husband the knight who managed to defeat Frederic in battle, but her father's fearful knights refused to take up arms against the mighty villain.

In answer to her prayers, a young knight arrived in a beautiful boat drawn by an enormous white swan. He defeated Frederic in combat and took the young duchess as his wife. In exchange, he asked only that she refrain from asking his name or from whence he came. Elsa agreed to his request.

After many years, curiosity got the better of Elsa. Unable to live in mystery any longer, she asked her husband the forbidden question: *Who are you, and from where did you come?* Heartbroken, the knight answered that he was Lohengrin, son of Percival, a Knight of the Round Table and a protector of the Holy Grail. After kissing his two children, the swan-drawn boat appeared to take Lohengrin away. Turning his back on Elsa, he stepped into the boat and drifted down the river, never to be seen again.

Lohengrin's tale is a poignant example of the idealized knight and how, in order to adhere to the knightly code of honor and the rules that bound his order, he was expected to sacrifice the pursuit of worldly happiness.

The Questing Beast

Among the tales surrounding King Arthur and the Knights of the Round Table, the story of King Pellinore and the Questing Beast is one of the strangest. A seemingly impossible-to-capture monster with the head and neck of a serpent, the body of a leopard, the hindquarters of a lion, the hooves of a deer, and the wretched bark of a pack of thirty hounds, the Questing Beast is a powerful metaphor for the incestuous relationship between King Arthur and his half-sister, Morgause, which begat Sir Mordred and the eventual destruction of Arthur's kingdom. Furthermore, the beast could be seen to represent the occasionally pointless, fruitless quests that knights were required by honor, loyalty, or circumstance to undertake.

In Sir Thomas Malory's version of this tale, King Arthur encountered the beast while hunting in the forest. Shortly thereafter he came across the beast's pursuer, King Pellinore, whose bloodline was bound to the hunt and capture of the hideous creature. Unfortunately Pellinore himself was never able to accomplish the task, and after his death Sir Palamedes the Saracen resumed the futile chase.

A thirteenth-century text of unknown authorship, however, provides a conclusion to this "endless" quest. According to the Post-Vulgate Cycle, Pellinore's son, Sir Percival, watched the beast vanish into a deep lake after Sir Palamedes pierced it with his lance.

Excalibur

Distraught by the loss of the illustrious Sword in the Stone, which broke in battle against the shield of Sir Pellinore, King Arthur traveled with the wizard Merlin through the woods. Merlin assured him that they would soon find a suitable replacement as they came to a beautiful, tranquil lake. Lo and behold, held aloft by an arm clad in white silk in the center of the water was the sword of which Merlin spoke.

Just then, Merlin and Arthur saw a woman walking upon the water toward them. Arthur asked Merlin who this amazing damsel was, and the wizard replied that she was Nimue, the Lady of the Lake, and that Arthur must kindly ask to be granted the magnificent weapon. The Lady of the Lake agreed to let him take the sword and its protective scabbard if he promised to grant her a favor at a time of her choosing. The young king agreed; so, accompanied by Merlin, he climbed into a nearby barge, rowed to the center of the lake, and took the sword. Immediately, the arm holding the sword

withdrew into the water, and Arthur admired his new weapon, Excalibur. Forged on the magical isle of Avalon, it was adorned with jewels and precious metals. However, Merlin warned him that he should hold the scabbard in even higher regard than the sword itself, for as long as Arthur kept the scabbard with him, he would lose no blood, nor would he be sorely wounded.

It was said that Excalibur's blade shined so brightly at times that none could look directly at it. In the tales of Camelot, it was a bright icon of honor, purpose, and strength. Though King Arthur possessed many magic weapons, none captivated the imagination as much as Excalibur.

Morgan le Fay

A very powerful sorceress, a healer, a manipulator, an adviser, and the greatest adversary to the reign of King Arthur, Morgan le Fay was, perhaps, the single most influential character in the contemporary legends of King Arthur and the Knights of the Round Table.

This mighty enchantress was ruler of the magical isle of Avalon. She was said to have gathered her powers in a Christian nunnery, according to Sir Thomas Malory's *Le Morte d'Arthur*. Some early tales suggest that she expanded her powers under Merlin, and still others claim that she had once been a fairy or goddess herself.

Human or not, if there were fearsome beasts or formidable enchanted warriors to be dealt with in the lands of Camelot, one would be wise to look for the hand of Morgan le Fay orchestrating in the background.

Morgan le Fay was a complicated character. Reviled by her half-brother, King Arthur, and the Knights of the Round Table, she repeatedly attempted to plot their downfall. However, despite stealing the enchanted sheath of Excalibur that made the king impervious to injury, she was also recounted as a healer who brought the broken body of King Arthur to Avalon after he suffered mortal wounds in the battle of Camlann.

Mordred

Mordred, illegitimate son and nephew of King Arthur, was the quintessential villain of Arthurian legend. His twisted, opportunistic nature impelled him to seek the crown of Britain and take Guinevere as his queen when Arthur and most of his knights were off to war. After faking news of Arthur's demise, he declared himself king of Camelot and chased Guinevere to the Tower of London, where she took refuge. Upon reports of Arthur's imminent return from battle, Mordred then gathered an army at the port of Dover, where his uncle was expected to arrive. A fierce, deadly battle ensued.

Eventually the battle made its way to Camlann, and when nearly all of the knights lay dead on the field, Mordred and Arthur met in hand-to-hand combat. Arthur ran at Mordred with his spear and pierced the treacherous knight through his body, just as Mordred's sword struck Arthur's helmet and caused a fatal wound. In his final act, Arthur had defeated a true enemy—one that threatened not only his kingdom but his legacy of knightly honor.

Avalon

Said to be a paradise on Earth, Avalon was a mythical kingdom of abundance and magic. A place of bountiful food, eternal springs, and powerful healing properties, some legends suggest that the only way to arrive at the wondrous land was through the very lake where Arthur had received Excalibur from Nimue, the Lady of the Lake.

By some accounts, Morgan le Fay was the fairy queen of Avalon who accompanied King Arthur's body on a funeral boat to its final resting place. Legend also says that Arthur sleeps there still, but will return with his Knights of the Round Table when the need arises.

◇ Bibliography ◇

Britannica Online Encyclopedia. http://www.britannica.com.

Ellis, F.S., ed. *The Golden Legend or Lives of the Saints*. London: J. M. Dent & Sons, 1931. http://www.fordham. edu/halsall/basis/goldenlegend/GL-vol3-george.html.

Ford, David Nash. "Sir Galahad, Arthurian Literary Character." David Nash Ford's Early British Kingdoms. http:// www.earlybritishkingdoms.com/bios/galahad.html.

Graeme, Roland. "Review of *Armida* by Joseph Haydn." *The Opera Quarterly* 18.1 (Winter 2002). http://muse.jhu.edu/ journals/opera_quarterly/v018/18.1graeme01.html.

Malory, Thomas. *Le Morte Darthur: Sir Thomas Malory's Book of King Arthur and of his Noble Knights of the Round Table, Volume 1.* Electronic Text Center, University of Virginia Library. http://etext.virginia.edu.

Martin, Richard. *Bulfinch's Mythology.* New York: Harper-Collins, 1991.

Owen, D.D.R., trans. *Chretien DeTroyes: Arthurian Romances.* London: Everyman Library, 1987. http://omacl. org/Yvain/.

Savage, Anne, "Beowulf – Introduction," McMaster University Department of English, http://www.humanities. mcmaster.ca/~beowulf/main.html.

The Academy of Ancient Music Web site. http://www.aam. co.uk/index.htm.

Thorpe, Benjamin, ed. *Northern mythology: comprising the principal popular traditions and superstitions of Scandinavia, north Germany, and the Netherlands, Volume 3.* London: Edward Lumley, 1852.

Weston, Jessie L. *The Legend of Sir Gawain: Studies upon Its Original Scope and Significance.* London: David Nutt, 1897. http://www.lib.rochester.edu/CAMELOT/sggk.htm.

Index

The End

They reckon death a blessing,
Yet make of life an anxious joy,
A villa thin with gilded laughter,
All these condemned.

DECIMUS JUNIUS JUVENALIS
Satire Number Twelve

Chapter One

(NOEL HESS—AFTERWARD)

WHEN AT LAST they found her and took her out of the water
I knew I had to go down and look at her. It was more than
that sweaty curiosity that surrounds the sudden death of a
stranger on a city sidewalk. But there was some of that, too.
In all honesty I had to admit that there was some of that,
too.

I had left Randy, my husband, asleep in the bedroom she
had assigned to us, that smallest of the guest bedrooms. I
supposed she had selected it coldly for us, with an objective
consideration of our status, half guest, half employee.

Randy had remained awake for a time, dithering about the
future, growing increasingly more haunted, until at last emotional exhaustion had taken him, aided a bit by the sleeping
pills I began to use long ago, when he first took her on as a
client, even before her affairs became his exclusive concern,
before she began to devour him with the dainty and absent-
minded finesse of a mantis.

I had left him there and gone to the big living room,
overlooking the lake. There was one small light in the room,
in a far corner. A mammoth trooper stood at parade rest,
hands locked behind him, leather creaking as he breathed
with big slow lungs, looking out the window at the pattern
of the lights and the boats. I wondered where the others were.

5

I felt very tiny and feminine beside the trooper. He smelled of wool and leather and, oddly, the woods.

"It must be getting chilly out there," I said. "I could have Rosalita make some coffee."

He looked down on me. "That's been taken care of, ma'am."

His tone made me feel ineffectual. "Do you think there's much chance of finding ... the body?" I asked him.

"Lake bottom is bad on this side, ma'am. Lots of big rocks. They keep hanging up the grapples on the rocks. But they'll get her. They always do."

"There seem to be an awful lot of boats out there."

"People around here pitch in when there's a drowning. I don't know as I remember your name. I'm Trooper Maleski."

"I'm Mrs. Randolph Hess."

"I got you placed now, Mrs. Hess. Your husband is another one worked for her. Hard to keep people straight here. Some of them in pretty bad shape when we got here. I guess there was a lot of drinking."

"Not everyone," I said, and I wondered why I should be so defensive.

"She put on a lot of parties here, they tell me. Pretty fancy layout. Lot of privacy. You get a lot of drunk people around the water and sooner or later you're going to have an accident." His voice was full of ponderous morality. We had kept our voices low. It seemed instinctive in the wake of death.

"I guess this Mrs. Ferris was a pretty well-to-do woman."

"A wealthy woman, Mr. Maleski."

"They'll be reporters here in the morning, I'd say. They'll get the word and drive up here. Or maybe rent a float plane, the smart ones. What kind of job has that fellow Winsan got?"

"He's a public-relations man."

"I get it now. He's out in one of the boats trying to help out. He's sure eager to find her before any newspaper people get up here. I guess he doesn't want them to find out she was swimming naked. But I'd think that would come out in the coroner's report anyway."

"Steve would try to prevent any scandal he could, Mr. Maleski."

"He's got himself a job this time. They'd already started dragging for her when that deputy sheriff found her swimming suit shoved in the big pocket of that robe. It makes it harder, dragging for her."

6

His slow words made a mental image that was, for a moment, entirely too vivid. The room went far away from me and there was a noise like the sound of surf in my ears. Reality returned slowly. I stood beside him and we looked out. The gasoline lanterns on the boats made vivid patterns on the water. The lights were so perfectly white they looked blue. In contrast the flashlights and the kerosene lanterns were orange.

The look of lights moving on the water stirred some reluctant memory in me. It took a long time to bring it clear, as though I forced a key to turn in a rusted lock. Then I remembered and was saddened by the memory. When I was small my parents had taken me to the west coast of Florida, to a shabby little fishing village. There had been a secret in the house. I was aware of the existence of a secret, without knowing what it was. I knew only that it was bad. People were always talking in whispers in the next room. And one night my father fell down and died, and I knew what the secret had been. We had rented a house on a bay there, and during the October nights the commercial fishermen had spread their gill nets in the bay waters, and they had lights on their staunch and clumsy boats, and there had been a great number of them out the night my father had died. It had perhaps been a very good night for fishing.

The trooper had been silent a long time. He said, quite unexpectedly, "You know, Mrs. Hess, I can't get over that Judy Jonah. I guess I've seen her on the TV a hundred times. I used to think she was the funniest woman in the world. She hasn't seemed so funny lately. But anyway, I always thought she was a great big woman. She's not much bigger than you are, is she?"

"They say you look bigger than you are."

"That must be it. I guess she hasn't got much to be funny about tonight, eh?"

"Not very much."

"You could have knocked me over with a pin feather when I walk in and see her. Last person in the world I expected to see up here in the woods."

"Do you know where she is now, Mr. Maleski?"

"She was down on the dock a while back, just looking, wearing a man's jacket. She must have gone around in the back someplace."

I thought of Judy. She wasn't going to do any more

7

weeping than I would. Not over Wilma Ferris. We had other things to weep over.

"Have you been up here before? I guess you would have," the trooper said.

"Many times."

"I guess she put a lot of money in this place. Fanciest place for miles around. Maybe in the whole country. You know, I always thought it was a kind of crazy house, all this glass and a flat roof in snow country, and those terrace things sticking out. I mean it looks funny as hell from the lake when you're out in a boat. But standing in here like this, I guess a fella could get to like this sort of thing."

"That was her stock in trade."

"What do you mean, Mrs. Hess?"

"The way people could get to like this sort of thing." The way Randy got to like it too well, and what it was doing to Mavis Dockerty while Paul had to stand by and watch it happen to her, and the way Gilman Hayes was soaking it all up. Even Steve Winsan and Wallace Dorn and myself—all of us jumping and whirling in marionette blindness while Wilma Ferris toyed with apparent purposelessness with our strings.

"I guess I see what you mean," the trooper said. "She used it for sort of business purposes. Like getting a fella off guard."

"Like that," I said.

"There was the eight guests and Mrs. Ferris and the three Mexican servants. Twelve in all. Is that right?"

I counted them in my mind. "That's right."

"If anybody wants servants up here, they got to bring them up. There isn't anybody up here does much of that kind of work. How about these Mexicans? Where'd she find them?"

"They came up from Mexico. She has a house down there. In Cuernavaca. She has them come up here for the summer."

"Is her house down there like this one?"

"No. It's very, very old. With a high wall around it. A Spanish house near the center of the town. She has ... had that house and this one and the apartment in New York."

"Nice work if you can get it," the trooper said. "I've seen her in the village a lot of times. Well, not a lot. Maybe three or four times. I've only been up here two years. I used to be in the troop up in Malone. She was a good-looking woman. How old would you say she was?"

"She kept that a state secret, Mr. Maleski. When she was divorced the last time, *Time* covered it in their Milestones

8

column and said she was forty-two. Wilma was furious. She wanted to be considered as being about thirty-four or so. I would say she was probably forty-five. She didn't look it."

The trooper grunted. "Damn well told she didn't! Forty-five. That's hard to believe."

"She worked at it, Mr. Maleski."

I suddenly realized that I was looking at the outline of the hills in the east and had been able to see them for some time. I stepped closer to the window. The stars had paled; just a few of them were visible.

"Dawn coming," the trooper said. "Going on for five now, daylight time."

The lights on the boats had lost some of their intensity. The water was no longer jet. It was the color of wet slate. And I heard the call then from one of the boats, a cry that had a different note from those that had gone before. All the other boats seemed to stop, and I sensed a change in the big body of the trooper beside me, a new alertness. The other boats began to move in a new way, began to converge.

"Looks like they got her," the trooper said.

He walked ponderously to the door that opened onto the main terrace. I followed him. He opened the door and then realized I was going along with him. He stopped as though to bar the way. "You better stay in the house here. Might be messy to look at."

"I'm going down there, Mr. Maleski."

Talking there so long in quiet voices, we had achieved a sort of friendliness. I saw it leave his face. I was no longer a woman he had talked to in a friendly way in the semidarkness. I was—one of *them*. One of the moneyed drinkers, the nude swimmers, the mate traders.

"Suit yourself," he said.

I followed him down the long curve of the stone steps to the narrower terrace that sent the twin prongs of the concrete docks out eight feet into the lake. They were each ten feet wide and they were set about fifty feet apart, so that they carried out the basic U pattern of the big house on the rock ledge thirty feet above the surface of the lake.

"Got her?" the trooper yelled toward the lights.

"We got her, Joe," somebody answered. And somebody said something in a low voice and there was a male snort of bawdy laughter, quickly stilled.

9

"Get those floods on, Joe, so we can see where we're coming in."

He asked me where the switches were. I said I would do it. I hurried up the steps and went to the box on the side of the house by the main terrace. I did not know which ones they wanted, so I turned them all on, all the batteries of sealed-beam lights that so brightly flooded the terraces and the twin docks and the house walls and the surrounding woods that the gray promise of dawn was suddenly gone and it was full night again.

I hurried back down to be on the dock again when she was brought in. Judy Jonah was already there. Others were coming. Gilman Hayes, who giggled nervously. Mavis Dockerty, sobbing aloud again. Wallace Dorn, cloaked in solemn dignity. The lights on the boats were going out, one by one. But they did not head for home. They followed the boat in, the boat containing the body of my enemy.

Steve Winsan climbed up onto the dock from another boat. He glanced at me. His good square face was pulled tight with strain. But even in the urgency of that moment he managed to put something into his look that was for me alone. And warmed me. The bier came alongside the dock. There were two old men in it. Twin Charons, with the reptilian wiriness of old men who do physical work. The trooper in the other boat bawled unnecessary instructions. Trooper Maleski and Steve Winsan knelt side by side to lift the body up. I moved close behind them. I could see down over the broad shoulder of the trooper. I saw her foot, very still and very white, projecting from under the edge of a greasy tarp. Wilma Ferris under a greasy tarp. I could imagine her nose wrinkled in distaste.

"Hook catch her in the arm," one of the old men said to all of us. "Slipped when she come up. Nearly lost her, but Jimmy, he grabbed her quick. She was about sixty feet off this end of the dock. I'd judge she were in forty feet of water."

There was a lot of awkward fumbling. The old men tucked the tarp around her and worked the body up to where Maleski and Steve could get hold of it. They had to move back to make room to put her on the dock, and in doing so the big trooper stepped on the trailing edge of the tarp and half stumbled backward, dropping her legs. Steve held onto the tarp and it came loose and she rolled out onto the concrete dock, white, flaccid, heavy. Her dark long hair

10

was pasted to half her face, and the other half had a blue glow in the lights. I saw for the first time the rumored richness of her body and saw how, even in the looseness of death, her breasts were large and firm, her belly taut, her thighs like Greek marble polished by centuries.

There was a silence there in the lights that was like a long exhalation. I saw then that her body was visibly changing color, visibly darkening. The trooper and Steve began fumbling with the tarp and Judy Jonah said in her harsh expressive voice, "Cover her up, for God's sake, you pair of clowns!"

They got the tarp over her. It was a dead thing. When it had been alive it had taken all I had. Using the weapons of money, of dominance, and of the body's richness as they were needed.

There was considerable argument as to whether it should be left on the dock for the coroner's inspection, or if it could legally be taken up to the house. Boats began to pull away, outboard motors catching and then rattling their tin thunder off the dawn mountains, Deputy Sheriff Fish making a point of yelling his thanks at each boat. The coroner, an unexpectedly young man with overlong sideburns, settled the argument by arriving, shooing us all off the dock except the officials, and conducting his examination on the spot.

I felt as if I had soiled myself by going down to look at her in death, and yet I had to be certain she was dead. I had needed an assurance based on more than being told. I looked in on Randy. He slept heavily, his mouth open. What would become of him now? Wilma had forced us to live up to an expected standard. So all we had left from the years of her were debts, a lease on an apartment too big for us, too many expensive clothes, and a large salary that had stopped when her heart had stopped. Somewhere he had to find the nerve, the guts to start again as we had once started together. But it was difficult to think of guts when she had so cleverly eviscerated him over the years, wrapping him in strand after strand before performing the brutal operation. Any single strand could have been broken. But not all of them. She had debased both of us.

I decided not to wake him and tell him. He would know soon enough that they had found it. I went back down the hallway toward the living room. I wondered if Steve were in his room. His door opened so suddenly it startled me.

"Noel," he said, saying it, as he always does, with that

11

special tone that is for me. "I thought that was your step. Nobody else walks quite that way." He took my wrist and pulled me, unprotesting, into his room. He closed the door quietly.

"What a mess!" he said. "God, what a mess! Is Randy carrying on again?"

"He's still sleeping. I gave him pills. He needs to sleep."

He had been washing his hands. His sleeves were rolled up. The crisp brown hair on his strong arms was matted and wet where he had dried hastily and imperfectly. He put his hands on my waist and they felt strong. I am glad I am slim for him. I am glad he likes shoe-button eyes, an upper lip that is a little too long, and my flavor of gravity. He pushed his mouth down hard on my lips, taking away my breath and my will.

"This is still the same," he said against my hair, still holding me.

"No," I said. "It isn't the same. It was simple yesterday, wasn't it? Everything was perfectly dandy." I began to cry. I hadn't wanted to cry. We sat on his bed, his arm around me.

"You better tell me what you mean, Noel."

I had to explain it carefully. "Last night she was there. He had a place to go. Emotionally, I mean. That could be the end of it. With no regrets, because I finally stopped loving him. It took a long time to stop, but I finally stopped. She had become his whole life. And I was just such a little part of it, he would hardly have missed me. But now he needs me, Steve."

"That's a trap," he said. "Females fall into it all the time. Maternal stuff. Poor little man needs you. Don't be ridiculous."

"She turned him from a man into a flunky. He's going to need help if he tries to turn back into a man."

"For richer and for poorer? In sickness and in health?" Steve said bitterly. I did not like the curl of his lip. It was contemptuous of me, of the person I am. And if he loves what I am, what I believe is a part of me ... And he should not show contempt.

"I only know what I have to do."

"Then I'm to consider this the brush-off."

It was not what I wanted him to say, God knows. I did not want such an easy and empty victory. It was his duty to talk me out of it, to give me all the reasons why I should leave Randy as we had talked about it last night. He should

12

have given me all the reasons why he wanted me to leave the sinking ship that was Randolph Hess.

But that was not the dreadful thing, the most dreadful thing. I am sensitive to people. I see little clues in their faces. And I saw, in Steve's face, a concealed relief. As though something were going far easier for him than he had anticipated.

I made myself test him. "Really, Steve, after all, haven't we got just a little bit too serious about all this? I mean it made it more dramatic and all, but ... after all, we *are* a couple of adults, aren't we?"

He looked at me in a startled way and then he laughed softly. "God, Noel, you're a package of surprises. You're right. We are all grown up."

I smiled. "And it didn't mean as much as we said it did."

He ruffled my hair. "I guess not, kitten. But you've been awful good for me. I want you to know that. I mean just knowing somebody like you."

And that was the end of it, of course. I felt more soiled than when I had gone to look at her body. Than when I had sat and looked at the face of my sleeping husband, hating him. More soiled, because at least those emotions had been direct and honest. But this with Steve had been a cheapness. A baseness. Week-end entertainment, married-love variety. I sat and smiled at him and saw how he was. All the pose and the faking. Making his living from poses and fakings and posturings and lies so that there was no longer any Steve Winsan left at all. Maybe there had been such a man once. Now he was an attractive shell stuffed solid with press clippings.

He kissed my ear playfully. It made my ear ring. His hand was on my waist. "Now that we understand each other, kitten, let us do some relaxing. Hell, I think I can steer some people to Randy if he wants to set up an office again. It would be nice to keep you right in New York."

"That's sweet of you," I said.

His square hand left my waist and gently pulled my sweater free of my skirt in back, crept up my spine to the fastening of my bra, and fumbled there a very short time before the fastening was released. It was something he had learned to do very well indeed.

There is something perverse within you. It says that when you have been tricked and humiliated, you must seek further degradation. I sat in numbness, with his hands on me,

13

perfectly willing to respond with completely faked emotions, perfectly willing to accept his meaningless and casual use of me, accepting him as a punishment, as ashes on the head of mourning. There was nothing at all left now, not even a way of escape.

And there was a soft servile tapping at the door and the voice of Amparo, the sturdy and very lovely Mexican maid. "Meester Weensan?"

He ceased his tactile deliberations. "What do you want?"

"The *policía*, they say come right away, sir, to the beeg room, sir. Everywan."

He looked at me and raised his eyebrows and shrugged and called to her that he would be right along. We got off the bed. He rolled his sleeves down and put on his jacket while I fastened my bra and tucked my sweater back in. There was a crudeness in being there like that together, with the homely formulae of fixing our clothing—a crudeness and the death of magic.

He opened the door and looked up and down the hallway and then said, "O.K., Noel." As I started to go by him, out into the hallway, he clapped his square hand against my haunch in what I guessed was supposed to be rude affection and the affirmation of possession.

But I have never liked to be touched except by those I love. I turned sharply and I do not know what my face looked like, but I do know that I made the quick sound of exhalation and warning that a cat will make as I raked at his face. He gasped with pain and jumped back. I went down the hallway alone.

They were in the big living room. The lounge, as Wilma had called it. The big expanse of glass was gray. There was rose color outlining the eastern hills. I realized it was Sunday morning, and there was something shocking in realizing that.

The two troopers, Carran and Maleski, were there, and the bulky officiousness of Deputy Sheriff Fish and the sideburned young coroner, all with the looks of ranks closed against us. José Vega, the butler-bartender-handy man, stood in a corner with the mild docility of the horse he so much resembled. His elder sister, the cook, Rosalita Vega, stood beside him. Amparo Loma, the pretty maid, sat uneasily on a chair as though she had been invited to sit down, had sat down obediently, and suddenly found herself to be the only servant seated and did not know quite how to terminate the embarrassment.

14

My husband came into the room soon after I did. He was fusty with doped sleep, rumpled and vague-looking, yawning and nervous at the same time. He gave me a nod and sat over beside Judy Jonah and asked, too loudly, "What's up, anyway?" Nobody answered him.

Gilman Hayes, Wilma's protégé, sat on the floor near the pale lamp wearing his Basque shirt and ragged shorts, long hard round brown legs crossed. He was looking with contempt at a book of reproductions. Wallace Dorn sat on the couch with the Dockertys. They talked in very low voices. Finally Steve entered the room. He gave me a sharp unpleasant look and sat as far from me as possible. He had two strips of tape on his left cheek. I felt a cold amusement.

"That's everybody," Trooper Maleski said. "You want to take it, George?"

Deputy Sheriff Fish looked both pleased and self-important. He took a step forward and cleared his throat. "We . . . I figured you people better all know the score just as soon as possible. When we got here last night, those of you we talked to give us the pretty clear idea of how it was an accidental drownding. Doc Andros here says she drownded, all right. That was the cause of death, he says. But he didn't like the look of the pupils of her eyes, he says. So he gave her an extra good looking over and he finds out she was stobbed in the back of the head with something sharp. It punched a hole in her head bone and maybe if she wasn't in the water she might of died of it eventually. But being in the water and still breathing, she just naturally drownded. We've been over that dock and those boats there with fine-tooth combs and there's nothing she could have fell on to do that.

"It was a round thing with a sharp point and she got stuck with it right here." He turned around and pointed at his own head to show us. "So that can only mean one thing, and that's a murder. Now Les Riley, the sheriff, is sick abed, but there's going to be other people here that'll want to talk with you folks about this thing. The county attorney—that's J. P. Walther—and a lieutenant from the criminal-investigation part of the state police are both coming, and more than likely they'll both bring along some people with them. In the meantime, by reason of the authority vested in me I'm here and now telling you folks that you all stay right here. Joe, you take up a collection of car keys and label them. I don't want you down on the dock or out on the

15

grounds. You stay right here in this house. That clear to everybody?"

Steve spoke up. "It's clear, sir. I'm sure we'll all cooperate. My name is Winsan. Steve Winsan. As a public-relations counselor, I'm used to dealing with the press. In fact, Mrs. Ferris was a client of mine. Miss Jonah and Mr. Gilman Hayes are also clients. They have reputations to protect, sir. I'm asking you to let me handle the working press on this whole matter. With people like Judy Jonah and Wilma Ferris and Gilman Hayes involved, they're going to swoop down on this place like locusts. It will require careful handling."

"Now, I just don't know about that," the deputy sheriff said dubiously.

Steve interrupted to say, "And by the way, I'd like to write down your name, your full name, so the papers won't get it wrong. And the names of these other gentlemen, of course."

"I guess it's a smart thing to use a man who knows his business," Fish said, looking questioningly at the troopers.

"This whole place will be a three-ring circus before noon," Steve said.

I was perfectly aware that I was going to be violently sick. I did not know how much time I had. As I walked toward the door, Fish said, "Where are you going, lady?"

"To lie down," I told him. I did not look back. No one stopped me. I made our room in time.

I was sick and then I washed and then I stretched out on my unused bed. I tried to think coherently about myself. God knows I had seen enough sharpies in the past few years. I'd seen more than enough slick ones. I'd seen Randy moving ever closer to filth and had kept a certain pride in keeping myself clean. And then I had been taken like a schoolgirl by one of the worst ones. By one of the ones who cultivate a hearty honest manner.

Wilma's death no longer seemed important to me. She had died a long time ago.

I slipped sideways into dreams that moved like acid across my mind, awakening in sweat only to slip back again, helpless against my exhaustion and my regret.

Chapter Two

IT WAS a three-hundred-mile drive to Wilma's place at Lake Vale, and in spite of the work I had piled up, Mavis, my wife, absolutely refused to arrive Saturday instead of Friday. She said that she had accepted the invitation and promised we would arrive Friday in time for cocktails.

And then she gave me that bland look which is such an infuriating copy of Wilma's and said, "But, darling, you work for her, don't you? I should think it would be *important* to you."

Yes, I worked for Wilma Ferris. There was no denying that. But my lovely wife couldn't seem to get it through her thick head that I also had a reputation in the field to uphold. Before I had gone with Ferris, Incorporated, I had been a senior consultant with Ramsey and Shaver, Management Engineers. I had specialized in revamping the sales set up of the client firms. The works. Distribution, outlets, advertising, market surveys.

And it was a black day indeed when I resigned from Ramsey and Shaver and went to work for twice the money for Ferris, Incorporated. I made the change after she spent a whole morning sitting across a desk from me and making good hardheaded sense. The company certainly wasn't sick. It was highly profitable. But not what it could be. She gave me the entire picture. The factory was in Jersey. They had two lines of cosmetics. The Ferris line was the specialty-shop line, high-priced. Symbol of luxury. The Wilma line was the bread and butter. The chain-store stuff, big quantities, low profit margin. But distribution on both lines was a shambles. Sales had started downward. The sales manager had recently done the firm a favor by dropping dead. She wanted the sales trend healthy, the whole sales end revamped. She offered a good salary. I talked it over with Mavis. I accepted it.

17

Because, you see, Wilma Ferris had talked hardheaded sense. At one point her voice got throatier, huskier, and she looked me in the eye and said, "Don't ever try to kid me about the business, Paul. I started it with these two hands in a fourth-floor walkup. I started with Ferris Kreme. I mixed the glop up in a vat. I bought the jars wholesale. I designed the labels and stuck them on. I filled the jars and capped them and peddled them and collected my own accounts. Don't ever try to kid me."

"Why tell me that?"

"Lots of people try. They think they can walk off with a piece of the business just because I spend so damn little time at it. I spend little time at it because I've earned leisure. I've worked for it. I enjoy myself, Paul. I enjoy myself a hell of a lot. I hire people and let them work and leave them alone while I play."

I wish to God she'd left Mavis and me alone.

Because that was the first time and the last time she ever made sense to me. After that I began to learn what she was. But by then our standard of living had gone up to match my new salary.

"Besides," Mavis said, turning from the lengthy business of brushing her hair, speaking as though it were the clincher, "the Hesses will be there, and Judy Jonah and Wallace Dorn, and you'll certainly have a chance to talk business with them, won't you?"

Mavis felt we had to go because it was the first time we had been invited up to that reputedly fabulous place at the lake. But I could guess what sort of mess it would be. We'd been at Wilma's apartment enough times to learn that. And people who knew had told me that if I thought Wilma a bit extroverted during her apartment parties, I should see her at the lake sometime. Or in Cuernavaca.

Mavis took over the packing and by the time we were ready to leave a stranger would have guessed we were about to take a cruise to Norway, stopping at Bermuda on the way back. I shuddered to think of how much of my fat pay was stowed away in those suitcases. I got Herman to help me, and between the two of us we got it all down to the apartment garage and loaded it in the back end of the new car. I know that Mavis looked very nice indeed, but it was spoiled for me because of her hair. She had started to fix her hair like Wilma's. She sees too damn much of Wilma. They're built somewhat alike—both tall women solid in the hip, big-breasted, slim in waist, ankle, wrist. Women that look and act alive and have some warm substance to them. They have none of the anemia of the high-fashion ads. I am a big man but, contrary to legend, my tastes have not run to miniature women.

This fixation of Mavis' needs some explaining. I hear that it happens often. I have just never seen it happen before. I'll have to expain how she *was* in order to explain how she *is*. I met her six years ago. She was twenty-one, to my thirty. She was a file clerk in a client plant in Troy, New York. I worked at the client plant for four months. There was something vague and unformed about her. Un*in*formed, too. Not th∷ I can afford to be any intellectual snob. My college background was too much concerned with work sheets, reserves for depreciation, and time and motion study. But regardless of background, people do seem to acquire some stable theories and philosophies of existence, right or wrong. Mavis believed earnestly in any idea with which she happened to come in contact. And she would jettison it immediately when she ran smack into the next idea.

Her vacillating earnestness so delighted me that I didn't pay much attention to her lack of any vestige of a sense of humor. I can't remember the name of that play by Old Whiskers where he takes a dumb girl and has the guy make her into a lady. There is some of that tendency in every man, I guess. Not that I wanted to make Mavis into a lady. She was ladylike enough. But I thought I could start with this big pretty sort of formless girl and marry her and she would learn what I liked and become what I liked.

It didn't work that way. I married her and she stayed the same old Mavis. Take her to a movie and for the next two days she'd be Betty Grable until she saw the next movie. She kept changing her hair, her accent, her style of dress, even her responses to affection. You couldn't call it shallowness. She just hadn't solidified into any one special individual. And I began to accept the fact that she never would, and accepted her for herself. She amused me. She fed me well. She was warm in bed. And she was decorative. If that is what you get, you can make it do. Even if there is no intellectual stimulation. Almost, I used to think, like having a great big beautiful playful red setter in the house.

That's the way she was. Until we fell into the orbit around Wilma Ferris. Wilma is the strongest woman I know. My God, she's strong. She keeps pressure on you all the time. As

19

they say about certain entertainers, she's always on. There is never any directness or simplicity. Only the impression thereof. And my girl became like a big fluttery moth circling the hot flame. She dived in finally and came out and she wasn't Mavis any more. She was another edition of Wilma. Not deep on the inside, where Wilma is like steel. But all the outward manifestations. Wilma seemed to polarize her. To line up all her molecules or something. So she thinks Wilma is the mostest woman that ever walked the earth, and each day there is less of Mavis and more of Wilma. And the hell of it is, perfecting the facsimile means getting as close to Wilma's standard of living as we can.

That alone I could adjust to. But my Mavis was a good girl. I mean good in the old-fashioned sense. Where things are black and other things are white. Wilma operates in an even shade of gray. And I have sensed that Wilma is superimposing her own moral standards on my Mavis. That frightens me.

I think there was a time when I could have told Mavis a little story about Wilma. And the little story would have severed that umbilical cord through which she feeds Mavis. But I waited too long, and if I told her now she might look at me with that derision I saw that afternoon in Wilma's eyes.

Wilma asked me to come up to her apartment. A chat about our tie-up with the advertising agency, Fern and Howey. But from the moment I walked in, I sensed how it was. She had set her de luxe stage, and all I had to do was reach out. I damn near did. I was very, very close. But I kept remembering Randy Hess, remembering that big ring she had put in his nose, and I didn't want any such ring in my nose. A business relationship was entirely enough. I gingerly untangled myself and made it just obvious enough so that she could hint that I was scared. I said it wasn't that, exactly, and was rewarded with her look of derision. From that afternoon on she started seeing even more of Mavis. It sounds a little crazy to say that because she batted zero with me, she would concentrate on making my wife emotionally dependent on her, but not when you know Wilma. She has to win, somehow. I think it was Steve Winsan who told me about the titled lady in Cuernavaca who consistently and politely declined all invitations to attend parties at Wilma's place. Not long after that the Mexican authorities found

20

an irregularity in the titled lady's residence permit, and the lady had to go back from whence she came.

Wilma had been entertaining the Mexican official who was in charge of those permits.

She has to win, somehow.

I can understand some of it and I don't blame her. She came from nothing. From a complete nothing. The lower East Side, they say, where you learn a hell of a lot about survival. Maybe it was there that she learned she had to win all the time. And maybe if she was still struggling, that desire to win would be channeled in the right direction. But she *has* won, and so it has been diverted to a lot of social and personal stuff, where it becomes just so much malicious mischief, and worse. Like those two husbands she took on. One ended up a hopeless alcoholic, and the first one shot himself. They were sort of unstable guys to start with. I sometimes think she is attracted to instability, that she sort of feeds on it. Randy Hess is a pretty good example of that.

I've made her sound like a mess. Actually she is a hell of a lot of woman. You've got to admire her. But sort of in the way you admire a parade going by. With a lot of drums.

We got in the car and started up the parkway and you could feel what kind of day it was going to be in the city. A bake job. One of those Dutch-oven days followed by a night when all that stone would be radiating heat until dawn.

Mavis said, "Dahling, it would have been a dreadful day to stay in town." Accent, intonation, huskiness—all a lovely imitation of Wilma Ferris. And she was drenched with that damn stuff Wilma uses. Blue Neon, it's called. Twenty bucks an ounce, and our chemists say it's one of the heaviest in the Ferris line. I wished Wilma Ferris would be suddenly taken dead. It wouldn't affect my job. And it might give me my wife back.

Once we got far enough north so that we had a reasonable assurance of keeping moving, I pulled over on the grass and put the top down. I'd needed the new car like a second head, but once Wilma had casually mentioned that she thought closed cars were terribly dull, I knew that sooner or later I would have to trade.

We had the big fight before we got to Albany. I guess I started it. It was some damn thing she said that parroted an opinion of Wilma's. And I asked her if she would please, for God's sake, start being herself and stop being a cheap imita-

21

tion of Wilma. And she told me that Wilma was the finest woman she had ever met, and Wilma was doing so much for her, and I ought to be grateful instead of stinking about it, and it was any wife's job to improve herself and she wanted to be a credit to me, and it helped me for her to be so close to Wilma, her best friend practically, and I wanted to shut her up in a jail or something so she couldn't have any friends, make a nun out of her or something. And then she got as far away from me as she could and she cried in a way that was entirely alien to her. An aloof weeping, full of pain and dignity. I just wished she would cry the way she used to. A lusty, puff-eyed yowling, full of snorts and wet noises.

"It's going to be a dandy week end, isn't it?" I said.

"Divine," she said remotely.

Traffic was heavy, but out of annoyance with her and with myself I drove too fast, so we got to Lake Vale a little before five. I looked at the marked map. Her place was on the opposite side of the lake from the village. Mavis sat forward, obviously excited at seeing the place. She was the one who spotted the sign. A varnished plaque swinging from wrought iron, with the name written on it in brass in flowing script with no capital letter, the same as on the trade-mark: *ferris*. I turned left down the narrow gravel road toward the lake.

Except for the obvious fact of a power line and a phone line going in, the winding rutted road would make you think you were heading for a beat-up cabin. We went through over a thousand feet of woods, a thick stand of birch and pine and maple, all downhill, then we saw the blue gleam of the lake through the trees and saw the house itself. It would take your breath away, that house by the lake. Not just because it was so damn big. I'd heard she brought up some kid architect from Miami on the assumption that at least he'd do something different. He'd done it, all right. Stone and wood and a lot of glass, but none of that business about looking as though it grew out of the rock ledge on which it stood. That place looked as if it had glided in and was ready to take off across the lake as soon as you fired the rockets. Mavis looked at it in a glaze of ecstasy, lips parted, fingers wound in knots.

There was a sizable parking area, with five cars already parked. One beat-up station wagon, Wilma's little steel-blue Austin-Healey, which she drives like a banshee with her hair on fire, a yellow Buick Skylark that I recognized as the Hesses' car, a new-looking black MG that might be Steve

22

Winsan's, and a white Jaguar with a little line-drawing caricature of Judy Jonah on the door, leaving no doubt as to its ownership. I parked our crate at the auto show and a big Mexican with a long sad face came trotting out. I unlocked the rear end so he could get at the luggage. He told us to take the path around the house.

There was a big grass terrace on the right, all set up for English croquet with umbrellaed tables for the gallery. We went around the wing of the house to the big concrete terrace enclosed by the U of the structure. There were two sets of concrete steps that made slow curves down the rocky bank in front of the place to another and shallower terrace and two huge docks that stuck out into the blue lake. Two identical runabouts, fast-looking, well kept, were tied up at the dock. I saw water skis on the dock, or pier I guess would be a better word. They were built like Fort Knox, probably to withstand the ice in winter. Judy Jonah was down on the pier, face down on a red mat, and Gilman Hayes sat near her, his brown back heavily muscled, legs dangling over the edge.

Wilma came hurrying across the big terrace toward us, making little sounds of delight. She spread her arms as though she would hug us both at once. She wore a white dress so painfully simple that you could almost read the price tag. She kissed Mavis and cooed at her, and patted my arm and got between us and led us back to the group. Randy Hess and Steve Winsan untangled themselves from some sort of lounge affairs.

"Of course you know everybody," Wilma said. "That's the point of this whole party. We're all friends. No strangers to adjust to."

Noel Hess smiled at us in her mild way. Steve shook my hand in that outdoor-boy manner he uses as stock in trade. Randy Hess greeted us with that sort of apologetic nervousness of his that reminds me sometimes of a child that suspects he shouldn't be hanging around the grownups so much.

"Your house is absolutely lovely," Mavis told Wilma.

"Thank you, darling. Now come on, dears. I'll show you your room. José should have your luggage in by now."

We went off the terrace through a door in a glass wall and through a perfectly tremendous room, and then down the corridor of what was apparently a bedroom wing, to the first door. José was putting the last suitcase on a rack. We had a big window overlooking the lake. The room was paneled in

23

some silvery wood. Everything was built in. A big dressing room between the bedroom and the bath turned it into a semisuite.

"Gosh!" Mavis said. It was the first honest sound I had heard out of her in a month. She recouped lost ground immediately, saying, "It's perfectly dahling, dahling."

"Suppose I send José in with a drink while you dears are freshening up," Wilma said.

"Please," Mavis said. "A Martini . . ."

"Extra dry, coming up. And you, Paul?"

"Bourbon and water, thanks," I said. Mavis gave me the stone glare. I am supposed to take up Martinis. It makes no difference to her that to me they taste like battery acid and get me howling drunk in twenty minutes. I'm supposed to conform.

Wilma left and we did some unpacking in sepulchral silence. Mavis stalked into the bath first. José brought the drinks, Mavis' in one of those little bottle things the way they're served in the better bars. I laid out a pair of fresh slacks and a gray gabardine shirt. Mavis came out of the bathroom with her dress over her arm and took a fast knock at the Martini.

"Go easy on that nitro, honey," I told her. "Last time you lost your sawdust."

"Did I indeed?" she asked, one eyebrow high, a Wilma look.

"Your samba with that Hayes phony was more utilitarian than graceful."

"Gil Hayes is a talented artist."

"Gil Hayes is a carefully calculated eccentric. The rhythmic integrity of spatial design." I made a rude noise.

"Oh, shut up," she said. It was the second honest sound she'd made within twenty minutes. Maybe there was hope left. From the neck down she looked very pink and pleasant indeed. She detected the examination and turned away quickly, saying, "Don't get messy."

When I came out of the bathroom she was gone, glass and all. I sat on the bed and finished my bourbon and thought dark thoughts about the week end. We couldn't legitimately leave until Sunday before noon. That meant getting through two evenings and one day of fun and games. And it would be a week end like one of those simplified models of the structure of the atom, with Wilma as the nucleus, and all her pet electrons whirling around the edge.

24

I dressed and went out. I found Randy in the big living room. He was biting his lip and fiddling with Wilma's high-fidelity setup. It was built into the west wall. I know a little bit about such things, so I went over and watched him diddle around. There was a Magnecord tape recorder racked the way you see them in radio studios. It had the hubs for one-hour tapes. There was a big Fisher amplifier, a Garrard changer fitted into a drawer, a Craftsman tuner, a big corner speaker enclosure. There was a control panel with switches marked for the various rooms so you could shunt the music around where you wanted it, an electronic mixer panel, and a studio mike. It looked like a good three thousand dollars' worth of equipment. Randy, with shaky hands, was trying to thread the tape around the empty hub and across the heads of the recorder. He gave me a nervous smile. "Little music coming up," he said.

Wilma came in off the terrace. "Really, Randy," she said in a most unpleasant voice. "A simple little thing like that. Just get out of the way. Here. Hold my drink."

He held her glass. Her fingers were deft. She threaded the tape, fastened it to the empty reel, turned on the recorder. The tape began to turn slowly onto the empty reel. "Bring me a fresh one, Randy." He hurried off obediently.

The music started. It was alive in the room. Clear and perfect. It made the back of my neck tingle. She adjusted the volume, frowned at the panel board, then clicked a switch labeled "Terrace."

She said, "You lose something if you try to operate too many speakers at once. This one is the best one here. I'll turn it off so we can get the most out of the terrace enclosure. Don't try to answer any question Judy might ask you about the program."

The abrupt change caught me off balance. I had the stupid idea she meant the program of music. And then I realized she meant the television program we had sponsored until Judy went off for the summer.

"I can't answer any questions because I don't know the answers, Wilma."

She patted my cheek. "That's a dear." She was standing quite close to me. There is an odd quality about her. When you are close to her you are so very conscious of her physically. Her mouth looks redder, her skin softer; her breathing seems deeper. It is an almost overpowering alive-ness, and it has a strong sexual base to it. It is impossible for any normal man to stand close to Wilma and talk to her without having his mind veer inevitably toward bed. It is, perhaps, the same quality that Miss Monroe had. It fogs up your mind when you want it to be clear. And she is perfectly aware of that.

We went back out on the terrace. She frowned. "Randy, it's just a tiny bit too loud out here. Be a dear and run in and turn it down just a shade more."

Randy went buckety-buckety into the living room. Noel looked down into her glass.

Judy appeared on the terrace at the head of the steps. "The sun is gone, people," she said. "Judith turns blue. Feed the girl rum. Hey there, Paul, Mavis. How do you like the gilded wilderness?"

I like Judy. She got her start singing with a band. She didn't have much voice, but what she had she threw around with abandon. When her face is in repose, which is not often, you realize with surprise that she is quite a pretty blonde. And when she stands still, which is equally seldom, you see that her figure is trim and good. But when she is in motion, with that rubbery mercurial face, with all her calculated awkwardness and grotesqueries of stance and movement, you see merely that clown, that Judy Jonah, that crazy gal.

But I feel sad, watching her, because I know television has devoured her, and I know she knows it. The last forty weeks of Judy, the half-hour show that we sponsored until she went off in June for the summer, slipped in the ratings, week by week. There is a limit to the amount of straight comedy the public will take from one person. Situation comedy has a longer life. Judy's was straight. And almost inevitably, she duplicated routines. I knew that Wallace Dorn, the account executive at Fern and Howey who has the Ferris account tucked neatly under his wing, had been scouting around for a new fall show, new talent for Ferris. So I wondered what Judy was doing up here without her agent. I suspected that Wilma had clubbed her into it. It would be so easy to trade on Judy's uncertainty. "Don't bring that horrible man, darling. We won't talk business, believe me."

The music masked the sound of the last car coming in. We didn't know Wallace Dorn had arrived until he walked around the edge of the terrace. He wore his country tweeds and an ascot. He is an ersatz Englishman. There seems to be a constant supply of them in New York. The military mustache, the carefully gobbled enunciation with the ends of sentences falling off into "d'y' know." Much talk of the club, no ice in mine, please, and, on occasion, a silly little stick to carry. Veddy, veddy country, old Wallace Dorn. Bachelor, sportsman, school-tie type.

It was another hour before we were all collected on the terrace, Judy and Gilman Hayes back in clothes, José in a far corner standing behind a little bar on wheels, standing with the remote patience of a horse, and a little Mexican gal, cute as a button, hefty across the hips and shoulders, who appeared among us from time to time to pass little items of melted cheese.

As the alcohol worked on them I could begin to smell more and more of the tension. I didn't know what was up, but Wilma seemed both too gay and too smug, and everyone else too miserable.

I finally had a chance before dinner to cut Steve Winsan out of the herd. I got him aside and said, "What goes, Steve? What the hell is up? Why all the sniping going on in all directions?"

He shook his head sadly. "Lucky boy," he said. "A nice safe clean job. Lucky boy."

"What *is* up? Is it a state secret?"

"I'm just sore enough to tell you, Pappy. I lose one client, I figure on picking up another. Our Wilma lives big. Old Randy, the watchdog, has been nibbling on her very gingerly about personal expenses. There's a tax matter pending. She put too many cookies in this layout. She's living too high. She's a client on a personal basis, you know. Not through the company. Randy thinks I should be cut off at the pockets. And he wants her to drop Muscle Boy as an expensive luxury, which means cutting me off there, because she has been paying the PR shot on Muscle Boy, the shot that made him a big wheel in the gallery world. I handle Judy, too. She's got Judy up here to put the blocks to her. She promised Judy next year's show but didn't put it in writing, and at the same time told Jolly Boy Dorn to dig up something else for fall. He hasn't found anything and Randy whispers to me that she's lifting the account and putting it in another agency. Which Dorn damn well suspects. And don't think he won't put up a battle. Don't think I'm not going to do battle too, my friend. I need a good lever. With same I will pry hell out of Randy and get him to tell Wilma dahling that she better keep me on. My God, if I lose all three, it's better than six hundred a week that Stephan Winsan Associates stop getting. If I wasn't half tight I wouldn't be telling you all this, Pappy. You sure she's not about to cut your throat too?"

"You make me wonder."

"There's one more wheel within a wheel too, Pappy. She tells our Randy that, as her tame and captive business manager, he should not have permitted her current expenses to get into such a state. The poor jerk. He begs and pleads and she ignores him, then she turns around and blames him because she didn't listen to him. She's got him so jumpy if you went up behind him and snapped your fingers he'd jump out of his shoes. This is going to be a gay, gay week end. Keep your guard up."

I tried to follow his advice. Steve's briefing clarified the tension. I could watch the focal points. Judy was overly casual. Wallace Dorn became more British than Churchill. Randy Hess had the severe shakes. Noel acted as though she wished she were somewhere else. Steve was quarrelsome. As my Mavis got drunker, her imitation of Wilma began to border on parody. And you could almost hear Wilma purr. I half expected her to sit on the floor and start cleaning her shoulder with her tongue. We ate abundantly of the highly spiced Mexican food prepared by the doom-faced Rosalita, served by José, her brother, and Amparo, the cutie. It was semibuffet, with each of us filling our plates the first time and with Amparo trotting about with the hot casseroles providing refills. I saw Gilman Hayes sitting on the floor in a shadowy corner and saw the exceedingly primitive caress he conferred on Amparo when she leaned close to serve him. Her only reaction was a bit of excess hip sway when she moved away from him. The stolid *mestiza* face did not change expression. Later I saw José watching Gilman Hayes with an equal lack of expression. I did not think I would care to be looked at in precisely that way.

After dinner there was the softness of the good music in the big lounge, and all the world outside brilliantly flood-lighted. Steve and Wilma played their normal vitriolic game of gin. Judy Jonah, Wallace Dorn, and I played a three-way game of Scrabble at a nickel a point. Noel Hess, pleading a headache, had gone to bed. Randy jittered around, taking care of the music, fussing with the floodlighting, rearranging ash trays, fixing drinks, kibitzing at both games. Randy kept South American music on the turntable at Gilman Hayes's request. The light was bright on the Scrabble board, a spotlight with an opaque shade.

My concentration was bad because I could not help being aware of Mavis dancing with Hayes. I had no cause for complaint, no legitimate cause. But the music was low, slow, and insinuating, and they did entirely too much dancing without moving from one spot. I felt alternately sweaty and cold. I could not turn and look at them. I would see them from the corners of my eyes. Fragments. A slow turn, his hand brown on the softness of her waist. An infrequent image of them in the glass. The music was full of rhythmic tickings and clackings and thumps, with a horn crying. Wilma was saying, in the other corner, "One card at a time, damnit, Winsan," and Wallace Dorn gave a little grunt of satisfaction, then clacked the wooden tiles onto the board.

I suddenly realized that Hayes and my wife were gone. I turned quickly and looked at the empty room. I must have started to rise. But Judy, with a quick shielded movement, pressed my arm. I looked at her. Wallace Dorn was studying his rack, chewing a fragment of his mustache. Judy made a slight motion with her head. I looked in that direction, through the glass, and saw that they were dancing on the big terrace now, in the light of the floods. They had a theatrical look, as though they were on one of those monstrous sets that the Hollywood geniuses create for Astaire. At any moment a silver staircase would unwind from the stars, and down it would come the sharp-shouldered chorus boys and a quarter ton of bare thighs.

I looked at Judy with gratitude, and with respect that she had sensed so quickly what was going on and how I could have made a fool of myself. Her face changed into the public Judy, and she gave me a distorted wink so vast I could almost hear it. Wallace Dorn gave his warning grunt and changed "own" to "clown" in such a way that the "c" changed "lean" into "clean," and the "c" was on a bonus square.

After the game we both owed Wallace. We paid him. Judy yawned and said, "Not another. I know when I've been stomped, pardner. I am going to go stare at a star and then crumple into bed."

"Need help looking at a star?" I asked her.

"You take half the light years and I'll take the other half."

We went by the dancers. They seemed unaware of us. We

29

went down the stone stairway and out to the end of the left wing of the dock. Judy kept her hands shoved deeply into the big patch pockets of her wool skirt and scuffed her heels, shoulders a bit hunched against the night chill. There were almost too many stars. The red mat she had been sunning herself on was wet with dew. I flipped it over to the dry side and moved it near the edge. We sat down, dangling our legs toward the water. I lit her cigarette and turned and looked up over my shoulder toward the high terrace. The music was faint. Sometimes I could see them as far down as the waist when they moved near the edge of the terrace. Other times they were back out of sight.

"Pretty fancy tumbril to ride in," Judy said.

It took me a moment to follow her. "How sharp is the knife?"

"Sharp enough. People have heard it being sharpened. So I got canceled out of a couple of guest spots on summer shows. And the gang is beginning to break up. Can't blame them. They need a warm spot come fall."

"Don't you?"

"I don't know. I'm just so damn tired, Paul. I can always grow a new head. I've done it before. I'm a rough girl, Paul. I'm a fighter. So I keep telling myself. I could get a Vegas deal. But I'm just pooped. I don't know. I've made it and I've kept more than most and it's stashed where I can't touch it, thank God. I'm supposed to react, I guess. Maybe she wants a down-on-the-knees response. I can always act, if it'll keep her happy. Me for bed." She got up. I stood up beside her. She put her fists up and began to wobble around the end of the dock, rubber-legged, lurching, snarling, "Yah, you never touched me, ya bum."

I was suddenly aware of the very special quality of her courage. I took her by the arms, holding her arms tightly just above the elbows. I shook her a little. I said, "I like you, Judy. I like you a hell of a lot."

"Leggo, or I'm going to cry right in your face."

I stood out there and watched her walk back to the shore, up the steps, out of sight across the terrace. I finished another cigarette and then went up. It was after one. Steve and Wallace Dorn had disappeared. Wilma and Gilman Hayes sat on a low couch. They stopped talking when I came in. Hayes sat with his big arms folded, looking at the ceiling. He looked sullen and stubborn.

"Mavis went to bed," Wilma said. We said good night. Hayes gave me a vague nod.

Mavis, just a shade unsteady on her feet, was getting ready for bed, humming one of the Latin numbers. She gave me a warm moist smile. We went to bed. She was very ready, with swollen and eager readiness that completely ignored our increasing coolness toward each other. There was nothing flattering about it. Gilman Hayes had readied her, and the alcohol had primed her, and the music had quickened her. I was merely a convenience. A perfectly legal and uncompli-cated and available convenience. There were no words of love. It was all very sudden and very tumultuous and very mean-ingless.

Afterward I heard her breathing deepen and change into the breathing of sleep. The music was gone and the flood-lights were out. There was a sound of water against the twin piers. She had managed to kill something. I did not know precisely how it was done. But I lay there and looked at the light patterns I could make when I squeezed my eyes shut, and I searched through my heart and could find no love for her. I was certain there had been love. But it wasn't sup-posed to go away, like throwing away the pumpkins after Halloween. I looked for fondness, and found none. I looked for respect, and found none.

She slept beside me, and she was just a big, moist, nubile, healthy, sycophantic young woman, too damn selfish to start bearing the children I wanted, big in the vanity department, small in the soul department, a seeker of sensation, an expert in the meaningless, a laboratory example of Mr. Veblen's theories. I wanted to be rid of her, and I wanted to cry.

Saturday was bright and hot and still. Breakfast was served in sections on the terrace as people got up, an affair of rum sours, *huevos mexicanos*, and Cuban coffee that was closer to a solid than a liquid. The combination melted mild hangovers. As people began to come to life it became pretty obvious that this was going to be one of those electric frantic days, with everyone galumphing about, working muscles, short of temper, drinking too fast, and playing too hard.

Gilman Hayes put on a pair of trunks of jock-strap dimension and was hauled up and down the lake on water skis by Steve at the wheel of one of the runabouts. Hayes looked like one of the lesser inhabitants of Olympus. Mavis

ahed and cooed from the end of the pier. I guess Steve got
tired of it. He made a bad turn and put slack in the towrope
and yanked hell out of Muscle Boy. Muscle Boy got indig-
nant. Steve told him to go to hell and stretched his stocky
body out in the sun and yelled to José to make with the
Scotch. Randy, at Wilma's request, took over the towing job.
Hayes instructed Mavis on how to stay up on the skis. There
was much giggling and shrill yelps and the support of an arm
like an Atlas ad.

I swam a little and drank a lot. Judy Jonah went through
a regular conditioning routine, knee bends, back bends,
holding one leg straight up, handstands. She had a trim figure.
I enjoyed watching her. Wallace Dorn paddled around in the
water between the two docks, looking as if he were enduring
this indignity for the sake of mingling with the herd. Noel
Hess sat fairly near me, ordering her drink freshened each
time I did. I wondered about her. She's dark and small and
quiet. You never feel as if you know her. She seems to be
watching you all the time. Yet you get a feeling of a lot of
slow dark fire burning 'way down underneath all that placid-
ity. She wore a yellow swimsuit and I noticed for the first
time the almost textureless purity of her skin. The way she
was built seemed to emphasize the ivoried intricacy of ankle
joint and wrist and shoulder, making you conscious of the
human form as something of delicate and vulnerable design.
Wilma swam for a time, with a lot more energy than skill,
and then waved in the trio off the lake and whooped up a
game of croquet. She appointed Randy scorekeeper and
referee, and the rest of us split into two teams of four.

I was teamed up with Judy, Wallace Dorn, and Noel Hess,
with Hayes, Mavis, Wilma, and Steve as the competition.
Wallace, playing with bitter concentration, and Noel, with an
unexpectedly good eye, kept up our end of the score. Judy
clowned it, and I was getting too tight to be much good.
There were ground rules. If you captured a ball you could
hammer it into the lake. The person knocked into the lake
had to chugalug a drink, retrieve the ball, replace it on the
edge of the parking area. Whenever one team had gone the
length of the course, everybody had a drink. It got pretty
blurred for me. They kept knocking me into the lake. The
voices started to sound funny, as though we were all in a
tunnel. The stripes on the wooden balls got brighter. The
grass got greener. I remember Judy pleading on her knees,

32

hands clasped, while Steve took a gigantic swing and, losing his footing, knocked both her ball and his own down the cliff into the lake. I don't know who won. I think I had some lunch.

Then, in some mysterious way, I was in the living room, weaving, trying to focus my eyes, and Judy Jonah was supporting me.

"Come on, now," she said. "One big fat foot after the other."

"Where's everybody?"

"Out being mad and gay. Banging around in the boats. Churning around in the water. Come on, lamb. Judy won't let you fall on your head."

There was another blank and then I was in bed, and Judy was looking down at me, shaking her head. She walked to the foot of the bed and took my shoes off. I was still in my swim trunks. She floated a blanket over me.

"'Preciate it," I said. "'Preciate it."

"Poor old bear," she said. She leaned over me, kissed me lightly on the lips, and then she was gone, the door shutting softly behind her. The bed started to veer dangerously around a circular track. I grabbed hold of it and steered it carefully into sudden sleep.

When I woke up it was dark. I looked at the window. The outside floodlights were on. I heard laughter. Somebody was running water in our bathroom. The door opened, and through the dressing room I could see Mavis outlined against the lighted bathroom as she turned in the doorway and clicked off the switch.

As she moved quietly through the room I spoke her name.

"So you aren't really dead after all, dahling?"

"What time is it?"

"About nine. It's quite warm. We're all swimming. I imagine you feel dreadful, I hope."

"Thanks so much."

"You made a spectacle of yourself, you know. Stumbling around like that. I hope you feel stinking." She swept out and banged the door shut.

I drifted off again. When I woke up I had a feeling it was much later. I felt a little better. I drank three glasses of water, put on a bathrobe, and went out into the living room. Two small lights burned. The music was FM unattended, some asinine disc jockey who said, "And it's thirty seconds to Cinderella, cats, so I guess that winds up the ball game. Sorry, Eleanor, we didn't get to spin that Julie platter for you, but ..." I found the right knob and cut him off. I walked out on the terrace, to a warm night of a billion stars. Somebody came up the concrete steps with reckless speed. The hurrying figure rushed to the switch box and the banks of floodlights began to snap on, one section at a time, dimming the stars. I blinked at the lights and saw it was Steve. The others were down on the dock.

Steve grabbed my arm hard. "Paul, Wilma's gone."

I was fogged by long sleep. I stared stupidly at him. "Gone where?"

"We think she drowned."

Chapter Three

I KEPT THINKING the whole situation could have used a better script. Heaven knows I'd become an expert on bad scripts during forty weeks of Judy-Time. That was the inane name the agency stuck on my half hour of frenzy.

It was so damnably disorganized, everybody running around and bleating, and Paul Dockerty the only one who made any sense. He got the phone calls placed as soon as he realized what had apparently happened. It was clear enough, all right. Her stuff on the end of the pier and all of us staring at the emptiest, blackest water there ever was. Sure, we'd been paddling around in it, very happy-time, floating and star watching and feeling that little thrill of danger that night swimming gives you. But after we knew what had gone on, I don't think six strong men could have hurled me back into that water. Paul got Gil Hayes and Steve out there with him, diving in the area where we thought she had been. Wallace and Randy couldn't swim well enough. So Randy handled the boat and shone the big flashlight down into the murk of the water. It was very still. We'd hear them cough and gasp when they came up. That fool of a Mavis Dockerty sat near my feet as I stood watching them out there. She made an interminable messy bleating sound as though her insipid little heart would break right in two.

We heard the sirens coming. It sounded as though they were riding across the black hills. Paul called in to me, asking me the time. I took my watch out of the pocket of my robe and held it so the bright lights were on the dial. "Nearly quarter to one," I shouted.

I heard him say, "O.K. That's enough. The experts are coming. It's too late anyway, even if we had luck enough to find her. If it isn't some kind of a stunt of hers, and if she

35

isn't sitting down the shoreline, laughing like hell, she's as dead as that mackerel in the moonlight."

His voice carried well over the water. "Don't talk about her like that!" Mavis shrieked, and then started a more furious round of bleats.

There were two big young troopers in one car and a fat man with a dull, kindly face in the other. They came down and made a rough count of noses and stared out across the water. One of the troopers couldn't seem to stop looking at me. It gave me an insane desire to burst into a routine for him.

Paul said, "I hear boats coming."

The civilian was named Fish. He said, "I told the phone office to get the boys out of bed and have them come over here. They'll drag for her."

"She's dead now," Paul said. "Why don't we wait until morning?"

"Well, we always start right out, soon as it happens. We always do. She couldn't be playing one of those jokes now, could she?"

"I doubt it," Paul said. "She would have heard the sirens and come in."

I walked away from there and left them talking. I belted my robe a little tighter, lighted my last cigarette. I sat on the stone steps and looked out at the lake. Bugs beat their furry brains out against the nearby floodlights. I sat and thought of several ways I would have liked to hold Wilma under the surface, and started giving myself the creeps because I knew I couldn't have.

Oh, she'd saved it and planned it, and even though I told myself I didn't care, when she finally gave it to me, she had certainly done it in her own unique way. She made a habit of leaving you nothing. I decided I would stop thinking about it. It wasn't any good to think about it. There wasn't a hell of a lot that was good to think about.

I watched boats arrive, saw the grappling irons and hooks, looking like medieval torments, rigged under the lights while they split up the area. The officials were in a huddle at the end of the pier where Wilma had parked her things.

After a time Paul came slowly up the steps toward me. He stopped and shivered and said, "Stick around, Judy, while I get dry and get more cigarettes, will you? I want to talk to you."

36

"Sure."

He was back quickly and sat on the next step below mine, rubbing his wet hair with a towel. He said, his voice muffled, "That deputy sheriff named Fish found that two-piece suit of hers in the pocket of her robe. What was going on? Was she wearing a different one?"

"Nope. We were being naughty. Practically a group bacchanal, unless you can think of a more clinical description. By starlight."

He turned and frowned at me. "You too, Judy?" It struck me as odd that the first question hadn't concerned the tepid Mavis.

I pulled the top of my robe apart. "You will note, kind sir, that I am still clad in my old blue serge swim togs, the ones with the shine on the seat. For me, cold lake water has a strange lack of aphrodisiac appeal. And if I am to be groped at by starlight, I want some firm footing underneath. You may mark me down as a spoilsport."

"How about Mavis?"

"A lady would say she didn't know. But your lady is remarkably nude under that lush robe of hers. And a remarkable figger of a woman, I might add. The other spoilsports were Randy, who doesn't swim well enough, and Wallace Dorn, who possibly couldn't bear the loss of dignity."

He was still for a little while and then said, with shock in his voice, "Noel, too?"

"Consider us both nonplused, Paul pal. I lay it to brandy. Or to atavism. Or obscure revenge on hubby. Or urging by one Steve Winsan. In any case, I say to hell with it. I feel like this is a conversation we should have over a back fence while hanging out the wash. There was chatter about getting back to Mother Nature. Though I am used to appearing before the public without benefit of dignity, I'm still a shy girl at heart. I draw lines. I get all crawly. I think about the decadence of modern society. See, I'm a thinker, said with no trace of a lisp."

"Where were you when it happened, Judy?"

"I really don't know, because no one seems to have any precise idea of when it did happen. Somebody started calling her. I think it was Mavis. Then we all listened. Then Gil Hayes started bellering her name so big it echoed off the other side of the lake. And we all listened. No Wilma. So

37

Steve came roaring up to put on the lights, giving his playmates very little time to get decent. I heard the mad scrambling. Steve must have donned shorts while at a full gallop. You entered the scene at that point, from the wings, looking like something pried out from under a stone. And then your executive talent asserted itself. Order out of chaos."

"My God, I wish Mavis would shut up."

There was no answer to that. I wished she would too. I looked at the back of his head. I liked the funny boyish way his uncombed hair grew in a sort of swirly thing on the crown of his head. Poor bear. Great big guy with an integrity you could sense. Maybe his claws and teeth were sharp enough in the world of business, but in a setup like this he was a toddler. Types like Steve and Wallace Dorn and Randy and Wilma and—go ahead, admit it—Judy the Jonah could disembowel him with a flick of the wrist. I guess this is the difference: We learn, maybe too early, that the deadliest battlegrounds are the cocktail parties, the dinner parties, the theatre parties, the quick drink before lunch. For a man like Paul Dockerty such things are supposed to be relaxation. So here he was in the midst of wolves, burdened with that silly wife who has—I should say *had*—that severe crush on Wilma, that silly wife without enough experience of the world to even sense the subconscious reason for that crush, though Wilma certainly knew the score. And, had she lived, I wouldn't have put it past her to lead Mavis just far enough so the girl would one day get a pretty godawful look at herself and her motivations.

Poor bear. Poor decent bear. Nice guy with a rugged face, bewildered by his lady, and more than half disgusted with her. Judy, my girl, it is a luxury you can't afford, but oh, how nice it would be to take off the mask once more and hold the big bear in your arms, hold him safe and sweet, because it's a long, long time between loves.

"They seem to know what they're doing down there," Paul said.

There did seem to be a sort of orderliness about it, in the sweep of the boats back and forth, up and down. The wind began to come up and it was unexpectedly chilly. My robe began to feel thin.

"I'm going to go put clothes on," I said.

"Good idea. They aren't going to find her in a hurry. They keep getting hung up. It must be a rock bottom."

"Do they go . . . right to the bottom?"

"I understand they do. Then, if they don't find her, after a few days decomposition creates enough gas to bring the body to the surface. They used to fire off cannon to bring the body up. I'll be damned if I know why."

It made me shudder so hard my teeth chattered and I got up hurriedly. Noel and Randy had the next room. I heard his voice, harsh and high-pitched with strain, saying over and over, "Omigod, omigod, omigod." Then I would hear her voice, softer and lower, quieting him. There was a boy with a problem. A juicy one. Nor did I envy Noel.

My suit was still sodden. I peeled it down and stepped out of it, took one of the big thick luxurious towels, and rubbed until Judy glowed. It made me feel so good that I heard myself humming a little thing in time to the toweling. Like a damn pussycat, I thought. Everything gone thoroughly to pot and all of a sudden you feel just dandy. Pot made me think of pot, so I sucked in my midriff as far as it would go and turned in profile to the mirror. It made me stick out upstairs and protrude in the cellar, but tummy was nonexistent. Hell, I could hum, couldn't I, if I had my health? Twenty-nine, and I took off on my first road trip at fifteen. One more year of it and it would be half my life. At fifteen I'd looked eighteen. At twenty-four I'd looked eighteen. I got a good many good years out of that eighteen. A stupid lovesick fifteen, lying about her age, traipsing off to sing with a real tired band just so she could be near Mose, who could tear such sweet notes out of that battered horn.

Whooo! All the years of fried food and riding the bus all night, and the well-cockroached hotels, and the booking agents with one fat hand on your knee. Golly! Those prom stands, and the big-wheel collitch lads, and Mose finally marrying me, and stepping up from tea to horse, keeping it quiet, cutting his throat in Scranton after Mitch dropped him, leaving me the legacy of one battered horn and three songs he couldn't get published. That weird winter in Chicago on a sustaining show, and that crumby room shared with that Janet character. Came back and found her in jail for fishing out the window, for God's sake. A borrowed rod and scraps for bait, and hauling the yowling alley cats up to the window, three flights up, selling them for two bits apiece to the medical school. Baby, baby, you were 'way, 'way down before you started up, before Dandy Adams, bless his black

39

soul, saw the capacity for comedy and started you on those first good routines. A long way down there, and, knocked off the top, you can't fall that far, can you?

But I'm just so tired.

I want to curl up with a nice bear.

I patted old friend—old flat tummy. I got into a pleated Irish tweed skirt and the floppy frayed old cardigan that goes everywhere with me for luck. I thought of how cold it was and so I headed for the other wing, for the kitchens. I found José and used some of the kitchen Spanish I picked up during that season in Mexico City. It seemed to please him. He knew the señora was dead. The fact had been examined and accepted. I didn't think any one of the three of them would do any major weeping. I told him the men would be cold. I suggested he make a lot of coffee and take it down there. He said he would.

I went out the back way. Paul came across the gravel toward me. Window light touched his face as he walked through it. Good sober face. I felt as if somehow I had been hung out in space for a long time away from a lot of good things. He was the trunk of a tree. I wanted to swing so I could reach him and untie myself and climb down to where there was a place to plant your feet.

I stepped out of the shadows, startling him. I put my hands on his arm. "Look, Paul, I've been running in mid-air. It's a good trick. It's a clown trick. You make your feet go like crazy and ... you make faces and ... "

Then something broke behind my eyes, and damned if I was going to cry, so I shut my teeth hard against it because there was no reason to cry, and out came this thin terrible sound from between my clenched teeth, a sound that came up through my throat like files. He took hold of me. I felt his uncertainty as I kept making those inexcusable misery noises, just going sort of "nnnnn nnnnn nnnnn" through my teeth, thinking, My God, Judy, you sing because a towel feels good and now you stand out here going crazy. He turned me and led me toward the cars. I walked along bent over, because crying without making noise, without making much noise, sort of doubled me up. I stumbled but his arm was around me. He got me into a new-smelling car and got the doors shut and rolled the windows up and put his hand on the back of my head, pushing my face against his jacket, and said, "Now let it go."

With those words, he kicked the bottom out of the dam.

40

A hell of a lot of water came roaring down the valley. A mess I was. I clutched and slobbered and ground my face into his coat and moaned and yelped and blubbered, not knowing where it was all coming from or why. There was a good big chest and a good big pair of gentle arms, and a comforting murmur whenever the sound track gave him an opening. It all blubbered away and for a long time I was just nothing. Just yesterday's leftover spaghetti. A sodden mass that, at increasingly rare and unexpected intervals, would give off an explosive snort. As awareness slowly returned, so did pride. I pushed myself up and away, and hunched over to the far side of the seat. There was a cleansing tissue in the cardigan pocket. I blew a nose that I imagined now looked like a radish. I dropped the tissue out the car window, rolled it down farther, and asked in a very marquise voice if I might have a cigarette. He provided same. I spoiled the first inhale with the terminal snort and nearly choked.

I resented him. Who was he to intrude on my privacy? What did he think he was doing, anyhow? Who wants *his* pity?

"I seem to have got a bit out of hand," I said.

"You did a thorough job."

I whirled toward him. "I'll have you darn well know, friend, that I'm not crying because I've been licked."

"How long since you've cried like that, Judy?"

"Oh, gosh. I can't remember. Five years, six years. I don't know . . . why I did."

"If I had to guess, I'd say it was just hydraulic pressure."

I had to laugh. In laughing I saw how ridiculous I was to resent him. Poor guy. A female had fallen wetly into his arms and he'd done the best he could. And I thought of the black lake and stopped laughing.

It's a good thing to cry like that. And even as I was enjoying the floating, drifting feeling of release, my mind was nibbling at the situation, trying to turn it and twist it into something usable, something that could become a routine. Perhaps a thing where I'd do three or four women, the way they cry . . . a duchess, a lady wrestler, an actress from the old silent movies, with different background music for each one.

How fake can you get? Can't you even cry honestly? I wondered what was left of me. Just a strange device for turning everything into the grotesque. Like a machine that eats up tin, paper, and beans and spews out an unending column of cans of soup.

41

O.K., chalk it up to sudden death, sirens in the night, black water, and feeling alone. Not the tears. What happened next. Happened his hand rested on my left shoulder. He was behind the wheel. Happened his hand felt good. Happened I tilted my head to the left, laying my cheek on the back of his hand. Happened I turned my head a little so my lips touched the back of his hand. Should have been then an awkwardness. Too many elbows in the way, and noses in the way, and no place for your knees. But it was as if we had practiced. His arms opened up and I switched around so that my back was toward him, and then I lay back into his arms, my feet up on the seat toward the car door, and there were good places for all our arms as his lips came down on mine.

To me there has always been something contrived about love. It goes like a pendulum. I start enjoying myself and then the pendulum swings the other way and I get a look at myself and I want to giggle. Because there is something ridiculous about it, darn it. People pasting their mouths together. People sighing and panting as if they'd been running upstairs. Hearts going poomp-poomp. But this time the pendulum swung over and caught on a little hook and stayed over there and there wasn't anything ridiculous at all.

A very rocky Judy Jonah untangled herself and sat up very straight and stared right ahead at absolutely nothing. I had pins and needles from my ankles to my ears. "My goodness," I said. I sounded as prim as a maiden aunt. He touched my back and I went up on wires and landed a foot farther away from him.

"What's the matter?"

"If you don't know, brother . . ."

"I know. I mean I think I know. Once when I was a little kid my grandfather was up on a stepladder. I kept running up and giving it a little shake and running away, screaming with delight. He got tired of it and flailed away at me with his coat. He forgot he had a small wrench in the coat pocket."

I turned around, my back to the door like Captain Hammer standing off nine Chinese bandits. I said, "I'm going to talk fast and get it all in and don't interrupt, please. In spite of several grave mistakes, I am a very moral-type moral lady. That little kiss tore my wings off and I am highly vulnerable. You touch me and I shall shatter like they do to the wineglass with the violins. But being an entertainer, small print, doesn't mean I play games. You are a married guy and

42

thusly you are poison and so this is something I'd write in my diary if I kept one, but for the record it rocked me, if that pleases you, and now I leave on these rubber legs, full of chastity and regret." I opened the door and got out.

He said, "Something can be done about the obstacle, Judy."

"Don't talk about it. Don't think about it. Give me a ring next Decoration Day, at my apple stand."

I got out of there. I looked back. I saw the red end of his cigarette. I went down onto the pier, onto the one that had nobody else on it. I sat cross-legged in the dew. I heard one of the men say, "Got a hell of a nice bass right there off these rocks three years ago. Went a little over four pounds. Got him on a frog."

And the other man in the boat said, "Can't use frogs, myself. They hold onto the line with their hands. Makes me feel sick, sort of. I use bugs."

"Hold it. Hung up something."

I held my breath. Then I heard him say, "Solid bottom. Rocks again. Swing it the other way, Virg." And after a moment, "O.K. It come free."

I had a hell of a mood. I wanted sad flamenco guitars and Spanish types singing through their noses while I swayed and snapped my fingers and let the big pearly tears roll down my damask cheeks. I sat there a long time and then went up to the house and went to the kitchen and begged a monstrous sandwich off Rosalita, she of the face like a family vault. Emotion gives me hunger.

It was nearly dawn when they got her. I went down to the dock. They did a fumbling job of getting her up out of the boat and they dropped her. I expected Wilma to sit up and give them hell for being so clumsy. But she was dead. Not a messy death. Not like on that South Carolina road when Gabby, in the sedan ahead of us, turned out into the path of the lumber truck. They were a mess. All of them. Mitch went into shock, I guess. I can remember him trotting up and down the shoulder of the road, picking up the sheets of the arrangements that were blowing all over, making a neat pile of them, looking at each one to see if he'd found any part of "Lady, Be Good," because he'd paid Eddie Sauter to do that one for us in between those good Goodmans.

No, this one was a lot cleaner. Noel was there too. I wondered what she was thinking, looking at the body. That body was a trap that had caught Randy and Gilman Hayes

43

without question, and probably Steve Winsan and perhaps Wallace Dorn. And Paul? That thought hit me and it did bad things to the digestion of my sandwich. If Paul belonged on the list too, it gave Wilma a perfect batting average on her house guests. No, I thought. Not Paul. The sandwich subsided. And I wondered why that sort of fidelity had suddenly meant so much to me. It was Mavis' lookout, not mine. I had no claim. A kiss in a car? In Wilma's set a kiss in a car was as consequential as combing your hair. But, damnit, I was not of that set. I was there only because it was bread and butter.

And then I remembered it was exactly the same thing for everybody else. Including Paul.

It was genuine, if feeble, daylight when they herded us into the so-called lounge and the one named Fish made a little speech. As I listened to him say that Wilma had been "stobbed" in the back of the head I wanted to say, "Oh, come now! *Dragnet* does better than this. Your routine is corny. Get some new writers. Get a bigger budget."

And then it hit me that it was true. It wasn't an act. It was murder. The taking of a life. I went cold all the way through. It wasn't any game. The taking of a human life. I looked around at the others. My God, we were pretty people. I could eliminate myself. And Paul. But that was all. Six people left, and six good reasons. And six opportunities. It had been a dark, dark night.

Noel walked out of the room. She seemed so darn calm. If you had to pick a guilty-looking one, you'd pick Randy. He was a jittering shambles. Mavis was still blubbering. I couldn't figure out where she got all the water. Paul looked grave and sobered. Our eyes met. It made warm things run up and down the Jonah spinal column. Wallace Dorn stood there with the disapproving expression of a master of hounds who has just seen a farmer shoot the fox. Steve was talking his way into a PR pitch. That suddenly rang some bells. Judy Jonah guest at murder party. TV comic in nude revel. Wild party ends in murder. Cosmetic Queen Slain. Wow! The networks have a code. I would be cooked like a White Tower hamburg in spite of having been a very good girl. It would be a more effective bounce job than Wilma, living, could have managed. Gilman Hayes sat on the floor reading a picture book.

Apparently we had to wait for the big shots to arrive. The

big trooper sidled over to me, subtle as a hippo. By daylight he was younger than I had thought.

"I've sure liked you on the TV, Miss Jonah."

"Thanks, friend. You're one of the last survivors of a dwindling race."

"I wouldn't say that."

He was big and dumb and honest and sweet. I had pained him. "I'm planning to retire," I said, wondering why I said *that*.

"You are? Well . . . I suppose it's a case of quitting while you're ahead."

"I might get married, even," I said. The conversation was rapidly working its way into a hole.

"That would be nice." Boy, we were sparkling.

"It'll be tough to do. I've done that bride routine so often."

"Hey, I remember that! You did it in that movie. Where you got all fouled up with that long thing in back."

"My train."

"And then you got the hay fever from the bouquet."

"And tried to keep from sneezing, like this."

He watched me with pure delight and laughed and slapped my shoulder and nearly knocked me down. Then everybody was staring at us. The trooper turned bright red and began looking stern. We'd been whistling in church.

It was, all in all, a highly unreal Sunday morning. Vividly unreal. We seemed to be standing around like a cast waiting for the director. When you stay up all night it does strange things to the following morning. But I didn't sag. I was aware of Paul in the room. I felt keyed up. Mavis had finally stopped.

What happened next was purely and simply nightmare. What happened next I do not really believe I will ever pry out of the back of my head. It's still there, in color. Just last week I woke up out of a juicy nightmare about it and Paul held me safe and close, and a long way off a coyote howled. I needed a lot of comforting.

Chapter Four

(STEVE WINSAN—BEFORE)

I KNEW I was going to have to go up there to Wilma's place and do plenty of scrambling. She made that clear when she phoned me. She's cute, like a crutch. "Randy has been telling me I'm dreadfully poor, darling. He keeps going over lists of things and making little check marks. He gave you three little marks. I don't know if that's good or bad. I guess you'll have to ask him."

You never let a client see you squirm, especially if the client is Wilma Ferris. "We'll still have our beautiful friendship, kid."

"And poor Gil will be so depressed if he can't read about himself in the papers any more."

"I guess I can make it all right, Wilma."

"I thought you would," she said a bit obliquely, and hung up after telling me to be there by cocktail time. It meant canceling out some things in town, but nothing too special. She phoned me on Wednesday. I managed to keep telling myself everything was fine until late Thursday afternoon, and then I hit bottom. Dotty came in and stood by my desk and asked me if there was anything else and I growled at her to go on home.

After she left, banging the reception-room door behind her, I took a yellow pad and a soft pencil and tried to figure out just where the hell I was. I figured it out in the most pessimistic way possible. I assumed I'd lose all three of them. I had already figured on losing Judy Jonah. Willy, her agent, had given me the confidential word on the trouble he was having trying to place her show. It was, of course, too expensive to operate to take any gamble on sustaining, even if a decent half-hour spot could be opened up for it. And the way the rating had skidded, he had a big problem interesting any new sponsor. We agreed that it was highly unlikely that Ferris would go along with her another season.

A thing like that you can stand. But three at once makes a hell of a hole. I had to keep paying on the tax deficiency they'd nailed me for, and keep sending Jennifer her five-hundred-a-month alimony so she could sit on her scrawny tail out there in Taos, and keep paying the rent on the office and the apartment, and keep paying Dotty, and keep up the personal front. I'd built the list up to twenty-one hundred a week. And with a six-hundred drop it just wouldn't add up. I couldn't make it come out. And new clients don't jump up out of the brush in the summer.

But all the time I knew I was worried about more than the six-hundred drop. This is a rumor town. What the hell has happened to Steve? Hear he lost Hayes and Jonah and Ferris. Guess he wasn't doing a job for them. Just the faintest smell of failure and it would make it an awful lot tougher to plant a release and then maybe the remaining ones would get nervous, and then Steve would be really sunk. And there wasn't a PR firm in town that would take me on. Not after the way I set myself up in business back there in '48, walking out with the clients in my pocket. They've been waiting for me to fall on my face. Hell, a man has to take care of himself. They would have kept me on coolie wages until I was seventy, and then invited me to buy in—maybe a big two-hundredth part of the business.

I sat there and I was really scared. I knew who would be the fourth one to go. Nancy, my Big Author. I'd run out of angles as far as she was concerned. It didn't seem to occur to her that maybe she better get another book published. I'd even run out of panel shows I could get her on. All I had to do was mention her name and the columnists I laughingly call friends would groan.

I sat there in the dying city and wished I'd been a little smarter. The cream is in the industrial accounts. A few of those and I'd be set. But my people are individuals, most of them in the arts or entertainment. I suppose that's natural. That was my beat when I was on the paper. Clubs and galleries and theatres, radio stations, concert halls.

I sat there and I began to feel artificial. Something that had been made up. Packaging is everything. They don't seem to give much of a damn about the contents any more. Make the outside pretty. Give it that glamour look. The hell with the product. The public will buy. And that was what I was in. The packaging business. Dressing up personalities.

I went into the small bathroom off my office and turned

47

on the fluorescent lights on either side of the mirror. It is not a kind light. If I squinted a little, blurring my image, I was still Steve Winsan, that fabricated product, that All-American tailback type, bluff and hearty and confident as all getout. The man to see. But with my eyes wide open, my face under the naked lights looked like the face of a tired character actor. That was it, maybe. I'd been playing the part of Steve Winsan so damn long it was going stale on me. I was sick of Steve Winsan and of a world full of things that didn't work quite right any more because they weren't making good products any more. They were fudging. Filling the armpit salve with air bubbles. Making nail polish guaranteed to flake off in twenty-four hours. Publishing books guaranteed to stand only two readings before the pages started to fall out. Putting fenders on cars you could dent with the heel of your hand. Make them stand still for the upkeep. Put crumby steel in their razors, weak thread on their buttons, waterbase paint on their walls. Keep them coming back. Hooray for enterprise. Hooray for Stephan Winsan Associates, which vends a product nobody ever heard of thirty years ago, and practically anybody can do without right now. There was nothing wrong with me that a double orchidectomy couldn't cure.

So I went home and changed clothes and went out on the town and I was gay as hell and got home earlier than usual and quite alone and set the alarm, and by eleven o'clock I was being a Fancy Dan in the parkway traffic, tooling the MG in and out of the lanes and wondering why the hell I owned a car when I used it not more than three times a month and why I had three suits ordered and why I'd given Dotty a raise, and why Jennifer couldn't fall off one of those New Mexican cliffs, and what the hell I was going to say to Wilma that would make her pat me on the head and call me back into the fold. And I wished that I had never clambered into that nine-foot bed of hers, because all it had done was use up a weapon that might have come in handy this week end. Wilma is the sort you do not gain ascendancy over by pouncing on. Her only involvement, ept though it may be, is physical. All you lose is your dignity, and all you gain is the responsibility of coming on the run should she crook her finger again. Much the same loss that Dotty had suffered with me.

I ate a late lunch on the road, a heavy lunch to put a good base under the drinks that would be flowing. I arrived a bit early and thought I might be the first. But the Hesses' car was there, between Wilma's and the station wagon. Just as I got out of my car, Judy Jonah came boiling down the drive in that Jag of hers. She swung in beside me.

She got out of the car and put her fists on her hips and stared at the house. "Wow!" she said.

"First time you've seen it?"

"Uh-huh. Looks edible, doesn't it? How are you doing, Steve?"

"Medium. Did Willy say anything to you yet about that Millison thing?"

"It sounds great," she said with a look of disgust. "He'll have something real gay lined up. Like catching a custard pie in the puss. Something subtle like that."

"A thousand-dollar pie, my lamb."

"Not by the time I get it, it isn't."

"He's a replacement. They've got the hell budgeted out of him. That's all he can do."

José came out to get our luggage. For once he seemed almost mildly glad to see me.

"Don't think I'm not grateful, Steve. Willy told me that you found out about it and sicked him onto it." She smiled at me but there was a little bit of frost behind it. We used to get along a lot better. And then I made a mistake. One of those things. It wasn't even very important to me. All she had to do was say no. But she said no and, at the same time, gave me a wicked smack across the mouth. It cut my lip and I came within a tenth of a second of really hanging one on her, I was so mad. She told me she would stay on as a client merely because she thought I knew my business, but my professional services were the only ones she required, or would ever require. Hence the little suggestion of coolness.

"Where is Willy, by the way? Come on, we go around this way."

"Absent by request. Wilma says this is social."

"Wilma says."

She gave me an oblique look, a quick flash of those expressive blue eyes. "I should have at least brought a writer, I guess."

"I'll feed you some lines."

"Brother, this is really a place."

Wilma and the Hesses and Gilman Hayes were on the big terrace just outside the lounge. Hayes was dressed for the water, standing, talking to them, and I wondered why he

49

didn't have spangles on his trunks. He said hello to Judy in a bored way and gave me the shallowest possible nod. Wilma did her normal amount of gushing. Randy gave me a nervous cold hand and Noel smiled. Judy was in a rush to get her suit on while there was still sunshine. I was in a rush to get Randy off in a corner somehow, but I couldn't be obvious about it. Wilma said she'd given me the same room as last time. I told José what I wanted as soon as he came out to the terrace bar again. Hayes went down the steps and out onto the big dock. I hate the big arrogant muscular son-of-a-bitch. I made him and I hate him. I would like to unmake him. Do a reverse PR job on him. But he's Wilma's playmate, and if I want to cut my throat I can borrow a straight razor someplace.

Judy came hurrying out in her yalla swimsuit and went running down and out the left-hand side of the dock and off in a flat dive. The next time I looked down they were both spread out in the late sun. I didn't get my chance to cut Randy out of the herd until after the Dockertys arrived and Wilma took them in to show them their room.

"Let's take us a walk, kid," I said to Randy.

He looked uneasy, "Sure, Steve. Sure."

We went around the wing of the house and out to the tables near that croquet layout. We sat down there and I rapped a cigarette on the tin tabletop and lighted it. "Wilma gave me some yak over the phone Wednesday, Randy. Something about saving money."

"My God, she has to, Steve. She had to borrow to pay taxes. This thing put her in the hole when she built it, and she's never got well since she built it. I've been after her and after her. Now, for the first time, she's beginning to listen."

"I'd hate to think for even one minute, Randy, that you'd want to do any cuts in my direction."

"Now, don't try to get hard with me, Steve."

"Look, you call yourself her business manager. You're more of a personal secretary, aren't you?"

"I manage all her affairs."

"It looks to me more like she does the managing. Now, how about that profile thing? Happen to remember that?"

"I certainly do. You did a good job there, Steve."

I knew I'd done a good job. I'd happened to have a friend on a magazine. He let me get a look at a piece they

50

were considering. It was an article on Wilma Ferris. A girl had done it. It was good work. She was a couple of years out of Columbia, free-lancing. It was one of those snide jobs. The magazine wanted a fairly extensive rewrite on it, but the top editorial brains were excited about it. And well they should have been. Nothing libelous, but very, very tongue in cheek. And it would have done quite a job of blowing the Wilma Ferris myth sky high, the mythology I had created. My friend wasn't placed high enough to clobber it. It was one very hot item indeed. The girl had all the dope. And our Wilma, on her way up the cosmetic ladder, had been one very rough girl.

I had to move on it. I went to a friend on another magazine. I did him a favor once. I had something coming. And he was placed high enough. He gave the freelancer a staff job. She withdrew the article from the first magazine. He lined up a tame seal to do the rewrite, and between us we took all the sting out of it and stuck in some of the usual glop. The deal was that he would fire the girl after the article was published. But as it turned out, she began to work out pretty well on the staff, so they kept her. So nobody was hurt.

"I wouldn't want you going in for any false economy, Randy. Not at Wilma's expense."

"I don't think you realize how serious this is, Steve. She's got to pull in her horns. She's got to take it easy. I mean very easy, or she'll never get her head back above water. I risked my . . . position with the things I told her. She's got to get that Gilman Hayes off her back, let the apartment go—it's too big, anyway, and rent the Cuernavaca house. Since she's going to have to live a good deal quieter, anyway, I see no reason why she should continue to retain you. I told her that. Furthermore, Steve, I see no reason for her to retain you even were she quite solvent."

"And let things like that magazine story go through?"

"The public has a short memory."

For a few minutes there he sounded fairly impressive. I remembered people saying he was a pretty good man before he went to work for Wilma. He had one of those little businesses that do accounting work, personal financial management, and insurance work for their clients. He had built it up himself, and when he took on Wilma she kept him so busy with all kinds of weird errands and services that he started dropping his other clients, and ended up working for her, giving up his office, maintaining a so-called office in her apartment.

"I don't think it would be wise to stop retaining me, Randy."

"And I think it would be."

"So there we are." I stood up. "I better look for somebody else to convince, Randy."

He shrugged. "You can talk to her, of course. I can't stop that. But I'm pretty certain she's made up her mind, decided to take my recommendations. Her attorneys are backing me up. She could get out of the hole immediately by selling her interest in the company, but I don't believe she'd want to give up control."

"Understatement of the year." He got up too, and we started to walk back. He had griped me. I stopped and halted him by taking hold of his arm. "You were kicking some opinions around, Randy. Here's one of mine: I think she needs a business manager like she needs Gilman Hayes. You're just sort of a superbutler, and I bet she could get a better one cheaper."

He looked at me and looked away and he looked pinched around the mouth. He yanked his arm free. I said, "Did you put yourself on that list of economies, Randy? Or are you suffering from the delusion that you're essential?"

He walked away from me and he didn't look back. He carried his narrow shoulders in a funny rigid way, as if he were balancing something on his head. If I was an unnecessary expense, what in the world was he? I laughed out loud. I felt a little bit better. Not much, though. I got the glooms again when I rejoined the group and tried to figure out some way to work on Wilma. She has all the vulnerability of a meat ax. And I very well knew that she was waiting for me to start begging. That would be the end. That would be when she would start to smile and go to work with the knife, enjoying her work. I sat and chattered away at that Mavis Dockerty, a great mass of nothing if I ever saw same, and all the time I was trying to think of some pry bar to use on Wilma. Like attacking the Washington Monument with a wooden spoon. I drank a little too much without intending to, and then made a damn fool of myself by telling Dockerty the score when he got me aside. I cannot understand most of those guys in business. They seem to do all right, but in an environment like this one, they don't even know what's going on. They can't seem to see a knife when it's sticking right out of your back.

It wasn't until dinner that I got the idea. It happened this way:

Wilma and Randy were talking about something in low tones. And Wilma raised her voice and you could hear it all over the room when she said, "For God's sake, stop blithering and dithering!" and Randy turned meekly to his plate. Right at that moment I happened to glance at Noel Hess. I saw on her face an expression of complete contempt. It was a look that included Wilma and Randy and perhaps the surrounding area for a good half mile. She turned then and caught me looking at her, and blushed and began to eat again.

There was no pry bar to use on Wilma. But here was a dandy little brunette pry bar with which I could bring Randy right up on his tiptoes. I had never particularly noticed her before. She was a subdued type, which seldom appeals to me. Pale and a bit thin-faced, with a long upper lip and rather small dark eyes. But as I made a more careful inventory, I saw things about her that I liked. I did a quick review to see if I'd said anything to her or near her that would spoil my pitch. No, the Steve Winsan impersonation had been unfractured. I wondered if Wilma had told Randy that she and I had been intimate. If so, maybe Randy had told Noel. And, if so, that might cancel me out before the starting gate opened. She had given Wilma that sort of look. And she was doubtless all too well aware of Randy's consistent infidelities prior to Wilma's acquisition of Gilman Hayes, aware of the complete range of the services performed. Suddenly, thinking of the whole thing, I felt a little ill. We'd been a bunch of dogs trotting after Wilma, tongues lolling in the country sun. And now I was going to try to complicate it with deliberate seduction. I wondered if, at this late date, I was getting a weak stomach. A man saves himself first. She'd maybe already started an interesting career of getting even with Randy. But she didn't look the type, somehow. She even looked a little bit like a girl I'd once known in the Methodist Sunday School in Deephaven, Minnesota, back in the days when I'd attend with my hair pasted down and watch her for the full hour and wonder how I was going to tell her that I was perfectly convinced I was going to be a famous surgeon and

53

I wanted her to wait for me. Back in the days when I was full of dreams and glories and a girl was a sweet and fragile and precious thing.

I knew the plan wasn't too good. I might get nowhere. And even if I did, it was no guarantee that I could get her to put the pressure on Randy. And if she consented to that, and if Randy told Wilma he'd reconsidered, Wilma could still tell him she'd already made up her mind.

But at least it was a plan, and even if it didn't work, it promised a less boring week end.

I didn't get much of a chance after dinner. Wilma and I got into our usual gin game, noisy and deadly serious. Randy dithered. That silly Dockerty bitch danced with Muscle Boy. The others played Scrabble. And Noel, unfortunately, went off to bed. I watched for some reaction on Wilma's part to the dance team. She didn't seem to notice them. As this was an atypical reaction on Wilma's part, I began to suspect that Gilman Hayes might lose more than my PR representation before the week end was over.

Once when Wilma was shuffling I leaned back and looked around at the shadows and silences in the big room, at the tricky spots on the game boards, at the glass and the dancing and the groomed softness of the women, all of us here interlocked with each other in curious ways in this architectured thing of warmth and careful lights, while outside there were the lake and the contours of the hills, which would not change a tenth of an inch in ten of our lifetimes. Bass would be drifting deep by the rocks, gills straining the cool water, and deer would be bedded down up the slopes away from the lake. But I had walked for a long time on a narrow and dangerous place that grew ever narrower, and to turn around and walk back was a feat of balance beyond my abilities.

"Wake up, dreary," Wilma said. "Take a dull card."

I took a card and I had to look at it longer than usual before I saw that it was a six of spades and that it fitted so neatly with other sixes that I was able to go down for seven.

When I woke up in the morning with a barbiturate taste, it took the usual chill shower and the usual Dexedrine before my motor started to turn over smoothly. This would be, I suspected, muscle day. Wilma likes to exhaust her guests. If she can send them back to the city with aching bodies, she thinks they remember it as a good gay time. It was warm

54

and breakfast on the terrace was fine in the sunlight, and finer still when I was able to sit at a table with Noel. I had given the gambit some careful thought. I had to make her curious about me as a person, and it had to contain a strong hint that I was not like the others.

After a few banalities, I found the silence I wanted and said, "With a few thousand years of selective breeding, Noel, I could really make an improvement in the race. I was thinking about it last night."

"An improvement?"

"We ought to have a setup like the lizards do. After you grow a little older and wiser, then you shuck off your skin and become somebody else. You become a better image of yourself. The way it is now, if you change, the way people inevitably do, you're still trapped in your old life, in the way you've always looked. It hardly seems fair."

I saw the awakening of interest in her eyes and saw at the same time that her eyes were a good shade of brown, a very dark brown that perhaps you could see only in sunlight, with some very tiny flakings of gold around the pupils.

"What do you want to change to, Steve?"

"Undecided. Just something different. I'm sort of a bright young man emeritus at this point. Can't afford to look tired. Got to keep running fast. Sort of maintaining an impersonation. How about you?"

"I guess this is just female, Steve, but I'd like to be big and golden and shiny instead of a sort of . . . brown mouse. I sit in too many corners and watch too much and think too much. Maybe I just want to be part of the act."

I allowed myself a look of contempt. "This act?"

"No, not this act. This one is worn out. I want a better act. New and fresh, with trumpets and drums."

"I'll book that. I'll plant releases. We'll pack the house."

And I looked into her eyes very seriously and intently and saw her eyes widen just a bit before they moved away, saw the faint color of pinkness on her throat, and knew that I had created in her an awareness of me and a curiosity. It's smart tactics to stick pretty close to what you really believe, because that way you can achieve a feeling of sincerity and reality that you can't get if you pick too fictionalized an approach. She wouldn't be difficult. She was too mixed up and tired of her life and Randy and Wilma and herself. It didn't take a trick shot. You could nearly fire blind and knock her off the shelf. For a little while I thought I'd better not, because it was too easy. But a man has to save himself in any way he can.

Later, during the morning swim, after I spilled Hayes off his skis, I had a chance to stretch out on the dock and talk to her some more. Sermon on the emptiness and artificialities of our special segment of civilization. The need to get back to something clean and honest. No honesty any more. All angles. And she gave me all the little clues of a growing recklessness. Even in the way she walked, conscious of herself and of me. She began to glow from the inside, and it softened her mouth and made her laugh more often. And made her tip up the drinks. And Randy was a great help to me, in the feverish way he took care of the little errands Wilma gave him. And she gave him a great many.

The croquet game was a special shambles. Paul Dockerty had got almost alarmingly drunk. And it was evidently the Mavis-Hayes Mutual Admiration Society that had set him off. Noel and I exchanged glances of commiseration, wry smiles, and, with increasing frequency, the reassurance of a light touching of hands. Lunch was late and very liquid and people were folding up gently to gain strength for the coming evening. I had José find me a thermos and I made up a batch of stingers and told Noel there was a place on the lake I wanted to show her. It was the critical move. She agreed readily, almost hastily, and we went down and I took out one of the runabouts and dizzied her with the speed and the curves and the roar of the water along the hull. I took her to the small island and I went over the side and towed the boat ashore and helped her out and up to the grassy bank near the familiar clump of sumac.

She was full of areas of resistance. Some were soothed with words and others were eased with caresses. And a few were melted by the thermos. We were utterly alone, the boat out of sight of the house, the water and mountains in front of us. Capitulation, though delayed, was inevitable. And I found her full of unexpected frenzies, far too many tears, far too many of the broken words denoting a permanence that I had not expected or wanted her to feel. It gave me the troubled, confused, nervous feeling of having taken on far too much. She had never been unfaithful to Randy before. And she was convinced that now we were together forever and ever. I knew it was a rationalization. She could not

56

excuse what she had permitted, and so she had to label it a great love. I knew that I could not keep on being evasive about this forever-and-ever deal. I could see the beginning of suspicion in her eyes. So I had to go along with it. I told her that unfortunately, my fortunes were temporarily tied up with Randy and Wilma and the others, so we would have to be very careful, make good plans, avoid impatience.

"But it has really happened, my darling," she said, smiling at me.

"Really."

"I never expected to find you here. I've waited for you so long. So very, very long, Steve."

"It has surprised me too," I said in momentary honesty. "But we'll be together."

"As soon as we can make the arrangements without knocking my business in the head."

"She can have him. Gladly. I give him up. He's a useless thing, Steve. He has been, for a long time. He blundered into the web and she wrapped him up, and when he couldn't move, she sucked him dry. You're a man, Steve. He hasn't been a man for a long time. Oh, I'm so glad we found each other. Hold me close, Steve. Remember what you said this morning? I've shed my skin, you know. I'm all golden and shiny. I'm not a brown mouse any more."

"The new skin is fine. I like it. It's an improvement. Extra-soft. Extra-fine texture. Guaranteed imperishable."

"Stop staring. You're making me blush."

"Hummm, when you blush it seems to start about here."

"Steve!"

We stayed there until the summer dusk and the end of the sun. And the end of the thermos, our bodies growing heavy and slow-moving with the dragging sweetness of outdoor love. I felt uneasy about entering into an implied contractual relationship for all eternity. But it was fruit on the bough that had happened to grow within reach. And I could create delay after delay, with excuses that at first would be very reasonable, and would slowly grow less reasonable, and eventually it would be a pose that we maintained as a rationalization, the idea of "someday." And it would eventually end, as such things have ended before for me, and as they will end again, because pleasure without purpose feeds on itself until it is finally consumed and the thing is dead.

We went back, her face so luminous with fulfillment that I

was glad it was near dark when I came into the dock and saw Randy standing there, frail and still.

"Where have you been?" he asked in a quiet voice.

Noel laughed in the silence, in the dusk. She gave a rough and unmistakable imitation of Wilma's voice. "Why, we seem to have been on a picnic or something, dahling. Miss me?"

He turned and walked away. He seemed to be spending the week end walking away from me. "A little too rough, honey," I said to her.

"Was I? How can he afford self-righteousness? How—"

"Ssh, honey. Please."

I gave her my hand and helped her out of the runabout. She came up onto the dock and leaned against me for a moment, light as a whisper. "I'm sorry," she murmured. "I feel reckless, I guess."

"Keep it bottled up. Just for a while."

"Of course, darling. Anything you say. Anything."

But I kept an eye on her. The night was warmer than any I had seen at the lake. We ate. The stars came out. We brought bottles and glasses and ice and mix down to the dock. The lake was black and laughter sounded good. Noel had acquired a little drunken giggle. Wilma was the one who suggested we kill the lights and do our swimming the way nature had perhaps intended we should. It seemed like one of the better ideas. Judy, Randy, and Wallace Dorn backed out. I went up to the box to turn off the lights. I turned them off. I waited a few moments and then turned them back again. There were yells of imitation anger. I put the lights off for good and felt my way back down. We were all there except Paul Dockerty. I found someone in the water. It was Mavis and she thought I was Gilman Hayes. We straightened that out quickly. I found Noel. We floated on our backs, holding hands, looking at the stars. She was fish-sleek in the water. All very gay. All very childish. Oh, we were delightful irresponsible people. There was some sort of disorganized game of tag for a time, with the rules getting continually more complicated. Randy, I think, was sulking. There was a bit of hysteria in Mavis' laughter. I had the feeling that we were a pack of circus seals, performing for Wilma's amusement.

I wondered why Gilman Hayes was calling Wilma so loudly.

58

Chapter Five

(WALLACE DORN—AFTERWARD)

I WAS most definitely happy that I did not have to join that undignified scramble for clothing in the dark while Winsan ran to switch the lights back on. I heard their wet panting. And it alarmed me a bit to recall how close I had come to joining their little debauch. I had, indeed, been tempted for a few moments, thinking of the dark lake-wet flesh of women in the night. It is the mood of recklessness that Wilma knows how to develop, going at it quite coldly, for all the impression of warmth that she gives.

I wondered what Wilma had been thinking as the water had closed over her. Knowing her, I would judge that it had been a feeling of vast impatience, of plans interrupted. Not fear, I believe, because I feel that she, like a child, would be utterly incapable of objectively contemplating her own demise. She had a nice knack of making others die a little. Now she had died a lot. Thoroughly. And I found it quite pleasant to think about, actually. For me it was an extraordinarily convenient death. We had had our little chat. Death made her decision meaningless, as I had intended that, somehow, that decision should be made meaningless.

I felt as though now I could begin the process of recreating my own dignity. The years of Wilma had left me precious little. Nothing, perhaps, but the appearance without the substance. Now perhaps I could begin to feel that I could be free of all these other dreadful people. Free of Randy, that husk, that ethicless nothing. Free, of course, of Hayes, and of having to use his utterly talentless blobs in the Ferris program. Free of the Jonah woman, that crude, unfeminine clown. Through at last with Winsan, who is an almost obscene exaggeration of my own loss of self-respect. Of all of them, Paul Dockerty would be the one I would keep, out of necessity. And he is the best of the lot. Perhaps he is the best because, barring Gilman Hayes, he is the most recent. A few more years or perhaps a few more months would have given him over to Wilma in some devious way so that through her control she could despoil him.

I knew I would deal with Paul from now on, and sensed that he would retain our association. I had nothing to fear. I kept telling myself that. Nothing at all to fear.

It did not become quite horrible for me until they were all assembled and went back and forth in their boats, dragging for her body. I envisaged the cruel hooks seeking her flesh. I have always been too imaginative, I believe.

I could not watch it. I had been told by a uniformed and rather officious young man that I could not leave. I went to my room. I wished to ignore the whole episode. I donned my treasured flannel robe and sat in the deep chair in my room in darkness and smoked my pipe and tried to think of the work that would face me once I returned to my office. But all the time I was aware of them out there, with their lights and boats and hooks and their snickerings. I knew that it would be in the papers and that Mr. Howey would feel it necessary to call me in for one of his little chats.

I used to feel that he liked me. He does not seem to like me any more. He cannot claim that I do not do my work. It was, of course, Wilma Ferris who poisoned him about me. That is not fair. I did not seek out the Ferris account. What Mr. Howey does not seem to realize is that I can be most effective when I handle those accounts where business is conducted on the proper plane. You should be a gentleman in business relationships. Calmness and careful thought can be much more effective than all the self-conscious bustling about in the world. A good quiet lunch and a brandy and a discussion of business problems. I never asked for the Ferris account. I have never felt entirely competent to handle it because I was never able to talk properly to that damnable woman. She seemed to be forever laughing at me. And I do not consider myself to be a ludicrous man. I am educated. I am rather well set up. I have health and, I trust, a certain dignity.

I did not ask for the account, and had it not been given to me to handle, I should probably, even now, be on much better terms with Lucius Howey. It is quite clear to me that she poisoned him against me. Deliberately, maliciously.

I do not understand such people. One must have good

60

will. At times, naturally, I have been forced to deal firmly with underlings in order to protect myself. But good will is my credo. If all my accounts were such reliable conservative old firms as Durbin Brothers, life could be very enjoyable. We agree on the media. I never attempt to force them to increase their total bill. We are in complete agreement on the dignity of the copy. And what finer program to support can there be? Their Citizens' Forum improves the mind. The Durbin Brothers consider it a privilege to support the Forum. They are my idea of the business person who is aware of his obligations to the society in which he lives. True, it is a rather small account. But an excellent product. Excellent.

They would never be guilty of the sort of behavior that Wilma was guilty of that hideous day when I took the new copy to her apartment at her request. I had toned down some of the obvious floridities in it. And I had repaired some rather clumsy layouts. She was expressionless as she read the copy. I could not guess her reaction.

And then she had torn it all to bits and scattered them on the floor. I did not know her well. I made some sound of dismay.

She came over to me, her face contorted, and leaned so close to me that I leaned back in alarm. She called me Buster. She said, barely opening her mouth to say it, "Buster, you need some of the facts of life underlined for you, don't you? That was supposed to be perfume copy. With that senile drivel you couldn't sell sachet to your maiden aunt. All you got to do in that copy is to tell the girls that if they smell better they'll be had more often."

"Really, Miss Ferris!"

"Don't boggle at me, you stuffed shirt. I said sexy copy and I want sexy copy. In my perfume line, I'm not selling smells. I'm selling sex. If that distresses you, Dorn, go paddling off and I'll get somebody who can understand what I'm talking about. Maybe you don't approve of sex, you bloodless old nanny goat."

"I cannot permit you to talk to me in this manner."

"I've heard tell you used to write fair copy. Get over to that desk and write something remotely usable or you're going to be known in advertising alley as the boy who bungled the Ferris account."

There was nothing I could do. Actually the woman alarmed me. She kept me there for three hours. Finally I turned out something she liked. I more than half expected the magazines to turn it down. To my astonishment, they took it without comment.

We had similar scenes later. I could never guess how she would react. And most of the time I was off balance because I was wondering why she should give the constant impression of laughing at me. She had to dominate me. I sensed that. And I could not prevent her doing it.

I actually believe that my helpless feeling of being dominated was what finally led me into the ultimate mistake there at her apartment. I really believe that I was finally reversing our roles by regressing to that most basic of male-female relationships. And, believing that, I spent a fool's hour in that ripest of gardens, believing that I was inflicting my will on her, enjoying to the utmost her really remarkable favors and then, to my complete horror, as I began dressing, fully expecting warmth from her, and a certain humility, she sat on the edge of her bed and began snickering and finally collapsed in helpless laughter. For a long time she could not tell me what amused her. When she could speak, she said she had imagined some rather coarse, crude things, most of them to do with my mode of dress and my behavior, though I have always felt that I behaved with the dignity of a gentleman.

So the expected reversal of roles led only to greater humiliation.

I know she poisoned Mr. Howey against me.

I cannot understand a person like that.

I am totally glad she is dead.

I am very glad.

I rejoice.

And I am not afraid.

Chapter Six

I TOLD NOEL that Wilma expected us both for the week end, and that started another of our dry, bitter little quarrels. There is no ranting and raving. Just a sour quietness. It was not always this way. Not before Wilma. My nerves used to be better. My wife and I are almost strangers. It seems a long time since we have laughed together. And that did not matter to me very much before Gilman Hayes came on the scene, six months ago. He displaced me nearly entirely in one area of my usefulness to Wilma. I think of that and wonder how I have managed to give up all pride and decency. And I wonder why I am willing to trade day after day of the humiliating tasks she gives me just for the sake of those brief rare times when she opens her arms.

I think of myself and wonder that I can feel so devoid of shame. I think I used to be a proud man. I have that memory. But it's a memory that seems to belong to some other person.

She is not bad. She is not evil. People make a mistake when they say she is evil and malicious. She is merely Wilma. I remember one time when she talked to me in a voice I had not heard before.

"I was a fat kid, Randy. A horrible fat kid. My bones are big and there was a lot of padding on the bones. My God, I ate all the time. And I hated the way I looked. I was ugly." She spoke quietly beside me in her bed, her profile clear against the red mist high over the city. "I used to dream that a fairy godmother would come along. She would have a wand. She would touch me on the forehead and she would tell me I was beautiful. And, in the dream, I would run, run, run to the mirror, my heart in my throat, and I'd look in and there I'd be, the same fat Wilma. I used to hate my fairy godmother. Maybe that's what started me on this cosmetics thing, Randy. I've wondered about that. Magic wand. Say, make a mental note of that, will you? For the stick perfume. It might be good. I'm too relaxed to think about it right now. I guess it did other things, being fat and ugly like that. You see, I'd see the little golden girls going to their parties. I'd hide. Sometimes, when I was brave, I'd throw mud. There was a boy they all had crushes on. My God, I had a crush on him too. My heart used to go thud-thud just seeing him in the school halls. And it was so damn ridiculous. I told my psychiatrist about all this."

"What did he say?"

She rolled over and up onto her elbows, half over me, one large perfect breast eclipsing half the world. "He said, Randy, that he could isolate the cause for my so-called nymphomania. He says there is absolutely no physiological basis for it. He says there very seldom is. It's because usually a person wanted to be loved so badly. And there's some obstacle. Mine was the way I looked. My God, underneath I was a mess. All a bunch of crazy longings. And that family of mine! Brother. They'd crack you for nothing, just for walking by. Funny, thinking about it, about spending the rest of your life getting even. He said that was what I was doing. That I resented the male. He hadn't noticed me when I wanted to be noticed. He said it was too bad, because now I can't really love anybody. Hell, I guess I don't miss that. I asked him why I needed so much physical love. He said it was just a symbol. He said that given time, he could cure me. And I thought about that and told him I would go along as is, thank you very much. So you see, Randy. I really hate you. Can you believe it?"

And, looking up at her, I could believe it. And yet understand her. Yet pity and love the child she had once been.

And pity myself for having been standing in the right place and time to have been run down by this implacable female machine, and still know that it was no excuse for me. She had merely uncovered a basic sensuality, a masochistic weakness in me that I had not suspected.

She seldom talked that way to me. My role was more generally that of whipping boy.

There was another time. "Does Noel know about this, Randy?"

"I haven't told her, if that's what you mean."

"But she knows?"

"I'm pretty sure she does."

"Doesn't that make you feel bad? Wouldn't you like to give all this up and try to make her happy again?"

"I know that's what I *should* do."

"But you're going to keep on with this, aren't you?"

"Yes. I guess I am."

"Tell me why you are."

"What do you mean?"

"Tell me why you're not going to give this up."

"Because . . . I can't."

"That's what I wanted you to say. Let me tell you about the others, Randy. Don't you want to listen to me?"

"Please don't, Wilma."

"I like to talk about them. Like I talk to them about you."

"Stop it, Wilma."

"I'll stop it. Tell me what you are. Are you weak?"

"Weak and vile and foul."

"And ashamed?"

"No. Not ashamed."

"Should you be?"

"Yes, I should be. What I'm doing is a sin in the eyes of man and God."

"That sounded nice. You must say it again sometime. But right now we'll stop talking, won't we, Randy? Right now, darling, we'll stop talking. Won't we? Won't we?"

And there was no escape, as there never was. As though I needed vileness. As though I sought degradation. As though I had to go on punishing myself for inconceivable crimes, for a guilt that had not yet been explained to me. And I wondered if I would ever kill her. It was the only possible release. She did not tire of the little humilities. The emptying of her ash trays. Sorting her clothes for the cleaners. Taking care of her shoes. Picking up after her. She was a robust animal and she casually littered the rooms in which she lived. She liked to have me tell her about how important I used to think I would become. Sometimes she made me tell her those old dreams while I was making up her bed while she sat at the dressing table, watching me in the mirror.

I knew of her other affairs. She made certain that I knew of them. Ears should be able to be closed, like eyes. But I was not deposed. I had the most of her and that had to be enough. Until she took unto herself Gilman Hayes.

"He's no good, Wilma. You've got to get rid of him."

"We'll have a nice talk about him. As though you were my girl friend, Randy."

"He's no good."

"He's a fabulous artist, my dear."

"Who says so?"

"Steve Winsan says so. I'm paying him to say so in the right places. The places where it counts. Be good, Randy. And be patient. He's a very arrogant young man, and a very splendid animal, and after he has been properly broken to the halter, we shall send him on his way and forget about him."

"He's costing you too much money."

"You nag me like an old hen, Randy dear. Be your sweet and patient self, and Wilma will be back soon. Poor Gil has the absurd idea he's doing me some sort of a favor. That's a little attitude I shall manage to correct. And then, because he's a bit dull, we'll send him on his way, older and wiser."

She had told me the list for this week end. Hayes and the Dockertys and Steve and Judy and Wallace Dorn. There was one small gain in this Hayes affair. It had given me time to go over her accounts. And I did not like what I saw. I had a talk with her on Tuesday. I tried my best to frighten her. I made it strong. She smiled and ticked the things off on her fingers.

"Rent the Cuernavaca house. Check. Get a smaller apartment here. Maybe. Drop Gil and cancel out Steve's efforts for both of us. Check. Stop spending so much on other things. Check. And you know, dear, as long as we're making changes, I'm getting awfully tired of Judy and Wallace Dorn, too. I think I'll make some changes. And wouldn't you say you're an expense to me too?"

"That's up to you to decide," I told her.

"Brave Randy. So very casual about it. Get Mavis on the phone for me, dear."

"Were you serious about ... letting me go too?"

"Now you've spoiled it by getting anxious. You just be a good boy this coming week end. Then we'll see. Get Mavis, and while I'm talking, you can leave for the day. Gil will be along soon. Poor dear, he just detests finding you here. I don't think he likes you at all."

Noel and I drove up on Friday, chatting with the faintly evasive formality of people who meet on a train. She looked very trim and pretty, but for me it was like looking at a picture of a girl I had known once upon a time. There was nothing personal in looking at her. The whole world was dry and vague and flat. The only vividness in the world, the only reality, was a demanding body that was labeled Wilma and in which there would be another time of forgetfulness, of the great blindness that surpasses all regrets.

I timed the trip so that we could arrive early. Gilman Hayes had come up with Wilma in her car. They were there when we arrived. Wilma had told me the room we would have, so I carried our luggage in. I believe that she has told José that I am a person of very small importance and not to help me. He even mixes and serves my drinks with an almost detectable reluctance. It is a typical example of her small methods.

After Steve Winsan arrived I could tell by the way he kept glancing at me that he wanted a word with me. I suspected what it was. When he found a chance to ask me, I agreed. He was fool enough to treat me with contempt. I was firm with him, wishing all the time that Wilma had given him no hint of danger. And then he was shrewd enough to put his finger directly on Wilma's personal threat to me. After vaguely threatening me. He is an alert and dangerous man, perfectly capable of using any weapon he can find. But I couldn't think of any weapon available to him. Wilma had said he was out. And she is not the sort who changes her mind.

Mavis was as gushingly tiresome as usual. Judy Jonah was almost herself, but I sensed tiredness in her. Paul Dockerty seemed rather out of place in our little group. Once upon a time I might have been, also. Gilman Hayes was at his obnoxious best, insulting the ones he didn't ignore. There was a lot of strain in the air. It looked like a bad week end. It made me nervous. I tried to keep remembering what the doctor had told me. Take it slow and easy. Try to relax whenever you can. But my doctor had never spent a week end with Wilma Ferris. She creates strain. She feeds on it. She deliberately creates cross-purposes, misunderstanding.

Wallace Dorn was his normal pompous self. Noel sat as though she had deliberately taken herself out of the group. Wilma is always almost excessively sweet to her. We drank and we ate and they played games. I wandered around and watched, and drank too much. Mavis danced with Gilman Hayes. It was not an entirely pretty thing to watch.

I was glad when the evening ended. Noel went to bed early. She was asleep in her bed when I went to our room. I undressed and lay in the darkness, feeling as if my nerves had poked out through my skin, waving in the night, sampling all the emotions that moved through the big house. I paired them off. Perhaps Steve had found his way to Judy's room. Paul and Mavis would be rightly together. And Gilman and Wilma. All the dark blinding plungings, while I lay bloodless. The rustlings and kissings, while I lay dead. It was all there was. They gave you the big words, the philosophical words. Man's destiny. And then you learned the only destiny was function. Be born, breed, and die. And of the three, there was only one over which you had control. Function of man. And, with us, an empty function. A sterile sensation, creating not. Destiny and function in a dark house, in the nerve-end night while my long untouched wife lay deep in her silver dreamings, deep in the precise and immaculate imaginings of her viscid brain, the unused body composed and still, and the blood moving within her and the oxygen molecules trundling along the crowded corridors. It was a secret I could tell her. There is nothing left but function, my bride. Nothing but that. No big words any more. No pride and no shame. No honor and no dishonor. Nothing but the body and its needs and the forgetfulness of filling its needs. I lie here dead and know that I am dead. And with so little effort I could take Wilma with me. To hell. Why did I say that? If there is only function, then there is no hell. No temptation, no evil. Just the pretenses we build for ourselves in order to make life endurable to a limited extent. Because we need those fictions. Were we ever to come face to face with the ultimate meaninglessness, we would die. As I have died in so many little ways over so long a time that there is nothing left.

And then, astonishing myself, I rolled over and ground my eyes into the pillow and cried with the muted helplessness of a sick child. It astonished me, because I had not thought there was even that much left.

I went to sleep thinking of how Wilma would look were she dead.

Noel was up and gone when I awakened. Most of them had finished breakfast and were down by the water. I had slept long, but there had been no rest. It has been like that for some time now. Sleep so heavy that I awaken in the same position. Dreamless sleep. A little death. But I get no rest

68

from it. And I wonder about the significance of that. The doctor said it could be related to my physical condition. I think it a part of the death wish. There are other indications.

Back in the happy days Noel used to tell me that I made a fetish of orderliness. That was true. The yellow pencils aligned and needle-pointed. The soldierly columns of the figures with their inevitable totals. The gray steel files and the little colored signal tabs. The April report. The stock listing. Staples and the creamy gleam of the file folder, and the appointment pad with each day bisected by the scalpel of the clock. My world was in order. Even to the socks placed just so, and the shoes containing their trees, and the clean scalp and the close shave and the morning moment of elimination. I was clean and I put my heels down with firmness when I walked and I conversed with rhythmic logic, in confidence-inspiring cadence. I was clean and my wife was clean and my life was clean, and I could shut my eyes and reach into any part of my life and put my hand on what I wanted, and I could look through all my prisms into the clean future and see the etched extension of the selected path.

Now I know where nothing is. Even the little business details. I throw the papers in a drawer. Sometimes I crumple them first. I wear shirts too long. I am often able to smell the odors of my own body. I do not walk as I did before.

It is odd, because back in that other life I was aware that there were men who became obsessed with a woman, with the living body of a particular woman. I thought of such men as being closer to the animals, of being more elemental in their heats and furies. I was a cool man. People did not tell off-color jokes in my presence. I had an austerity. And a dignity.

Now I am obsessed, and now I know that it is the type of man that I am that is most often subject to this warm disaster. The man who seems somehow to have skipped childhood, to have been born solemn, the boy who leads scholastically and in nothing else, who corrects papers, is inclined to preach, who has thought dimly of the ministry, who becomes an accountant or a teller or a teacher or an actuary. Such coolness subconsciously seeks warmth. The spirit seeks the body. The ice looks for flame.

Now I sleep in heaviness, and seek disorder and demand cruelty. In debasement I seek an ever deeper pit, a continually increasing darkness. A death wish. For the final function of flame is to consume entirely. I can see myself and what is happening and I do not care. I am nothing but function. And through function I look for death.

The day was warm. They swam. I pulled the water skis behind the runabout for a long time. I kept score and made decisions when they played croquet. They were drunk. Paul was the worst. When they did not like a decision, they ignored what I said. Wilma had changed to a rose-colored denim sunsuit for the game. I watched her body as she would walk, as she would bend and strike the ball, as she would turn from the waist to watch someone else play. Once when I stood too close she swung the mallet back and hit the side of my knee, wood against bone. It was painful. She apologized profusely. Everyone knew she had done it on purpose. They were silent. I felt their contempt and it washed over me and I liked it. Then they forgot. After a time the pain went away. I stood close again, but she had a knowing look and she did not strike me again. Because she knew I wanted her to.

It was later, much later, that I realized that I had not seen Noel for a long time. A boat was gone. I found Wilma and I asked her if she had seen Noel. She said that Steve Winsan had taken her out in one of the boats a long time ago. I realized then how Winsan had thought he had selected a weapon. It made me want to laugh.

I sat alone and watched the lake. No boat moved. I thought of the other man I had once been. A man who, perhaps, would have tried to kill Winsan. But Noel was a girl I had once known. She could do as she pleased. I could warn her about Winsan, as I would warn any pleasant stranger I saw getting too close to him. I pictured him seducing her. I made vivid pictures in my mind, trying to summon some fragment of anger, some morsel of regret, some pinch of pain. And there was nothing.

I was there a long time. Finally I saw the boat coming. It had come from behind a distant island. It was dusk. I wanted to know, out of objective curiosity, so I went down the steps and out onto the dock, and when the boat stopped its noise I asked in a quiet voice where they had been. Her answer was coarse, unlike her, and unmistakable. So I knew. Even in semidarkness Winsan had the uneasy look of guilt. I walked away before I laughed in his face. I heard him hush

70

her. It meant nothing to me. So one more thing had been taken from me. And I had moved one step closer to death.

They swam that night. They were all there, except Paul, and all quite high again. Noel, in her new freedom, laughed too much and with an odd note in her voice. I did not wish to swim. I sat on the dock to be near them. They decided to swim without suits. Steve went up to turn off the lights. Moments later, playfully, he turned them back on for a second, freezing all of them there in a blinding whiteness against the night. Noel was in the act of stepping out of her suit. Then her slimness was gone, fading slowly on the back of my eyes. It gave me a strange feeling. It is difficult to describe. Very much like that feeling you have when you are starting out on a trip and you slow your car because you are certain you have forgotten something. You think, but you cannot remember what it was. And then you shrug and push down on the gas pedal and tell yourself that it was nothing important, nothing that cannot be replaced wherever you are going.

They swam and shouted with the daring self-conscious boisterousness of people who mistake silliness for boldness.

I got up and went silently, quickly, breathlessly to the very end of the dock and my eyes were used to the night and I could see the white body of Wilma, almost luminous in the water, in the faint starlight, and I wondered if she could see me outlined against the stars. I could not reach her throat. But . . .

71

Chapter Seven

(MAVIS DOCKERTY—AFTERWARD)

IT WAS the most dreadful thing that ever happened. She was the most wonderful woman in the world. No one else understood her. They didn't know what she was like. None of them. The way they acted, they might as well have laughed or something. Like they were glad. Like nothing had happened at all.

I scraped my hip getting up on the dock and for a minute I couldn't find where I left my robe. I knew the lights would go on. Honest, I was terrified. I don't mean of the lights on me, but just of its being so dark and not finding things, that feeling of things coming after you out of the night. But I found it and I just pulled the belt tight when the lights went on. Those lights can make you go blind, when you've been in the dark. When I could see I found my suit and wadded it up and wrapped it in my towel. It had to be some kind of dreadful joke or something, but I guess all the time, deep in my heart, I knew that something had happened to her and she was dead. I knew it because that was my luck, because that was the way things always are for me and always will be. If a wonderful thing happens, I know it will go bad for me. The way I used to think Paul was wonderful before he started making my life a hell with his insane jealousy.

Right when we'd been having such fun, this had to happen to Wilma, the best friend I've ever had on earth or ever will have. I thought of her, floating around under that black water, and the tears came right up. They were wrenched right up out of me, thinking of her like that. It was worse, even, than when my sister died so sudden. They didn't even know she was real sick. She went to bed with a headache and in the morning she was right there dead. It's like Wilma said once. We've both had hardships and that's why we're so much alike. It is funny, being so much alike that we could almost wear the same clothes. Hers were just a little bit loose

72

around the hips and bust on me. But then, she's older. You got to expect that a little when you're older. But she isn't fat. Just firm. And honest, you'd have thought she was younger than I am that day we were giggling around and I was trying on her clothes that time.

It's like I said, I'll never have a better, truer friend in all the world.

I stood there like my heart was going to break and pretty soon Paul had to come down and start ordering people around. It's like he gets some kind of a big boot out of that. They went out in a boat with Randy holding a light and the three of them, Paul, Steve, and Gil, started diving for her, as if that would do any good. It had been too long and I knew she was down there and I knew she was dead. I said it over a lot of times. Dead, dead, dead. I couldn't make it fit Wilma. She was the most alive person.

The sirens came and the people who know about such things came and they made Paul stop all that silly diving business. By the time there were a lot of boats there all going around in circles dragging things and trying to hook onto her, I just couldn't stand it any more. Anyway, I was getting cold. Crying like that cuts down your resistance, I guess. I went to the wonderful room she had given us and when I walked in it made me remember how she had been, so sweet, when she had shown it to Paul and me, and it started the big tears all over again. I had got down to little tears, but it brought the big ones on again. I just dropped across my bed like some kind of a dishrag and the tears made me sort of roll back and forth and for a time it was like I stood beside the bed and watched myself rolling back and forth in agony.

It took a long time to work the tears back down to little ones. Then I went over and looked at myself in the mirror. My hair was a mess. I opened the robe and looked at my hip where I'd scraped it getting out of the water. My skin is very sensitive. Everything makes a bruise. There were three little parallel scratches, like a cat had done it, and a big bruise was getting dark all around the scratches. I even wished for a minute that it was much worse, so I'd have some kind of a scar on my body to remember by, but that was silly because I certainly wouldn't ever forget it. Or her.

I was the only one she *really* liked. Out of the whole bunch of them. They never knew her. Gosh, what was I before I met her? Just a nothing. Just a dumb girl. She taught me how to be *myself*. I used to dream all the time.

73

Real crazy stuff. Ever since I was a kid. Always pretending things. I used to have regular parties with my dolls. Little dishes and real food, but I had to eat it all myself. I used to play by myself a lot. I guess I started pretending because I didn't like the way things were. I mean that neighborhood, with every single house just alike, and six kids so I never did get to have a room of my own. If they'd known I was going to do better than any of them, maybe they would have given me a room of my own. Look at that bum Harriet married. He looked good in uniform, but after he took it off, he was just another bum. I used to pretend so much that I'd forget to do things I was supposed to do. I'd walk to the store and then have to walk all the way back and find out again what I was supposed to get. We never had a phone. So they used to be at me all the time. Mary this. Mary that. None of them can order me around any more. But there's just four of us now, and the old man. I knew all the time that I was going to have a wonderful life. Better than the others. 'Way better.

I got out of there just as soon as I could, believe me. I got out of business school one day and the next day I had a job and an apartment of my own. Not really an apartment. More like two furnished rooms, and sharing the bath with three other girls who just took hours and hours in there in the morning until I was almost frantic every morning.

But I was out of that mean little house in that street I grew up on, and I certainly wasn't going back, not after changing my name to Mavis. I left Mary Gort right back on that street where she belonged. I told them if they wanted to see me they had to come to my place. I wasn't going back there, and the only one who ever did come more than once or twice was Mom, and she came regularly until she died.

I really worked hard at my job because I couldn't afford to lose it. I got sort of control over the pretending and dreaming during working time, but afterward I would really let myself go. For a time there I was spending all my money on Oriental stuff for one of my rooms. I bought a kimono with a dragon on it. There was incense and I'd sit cross-legged and read that book of Chinese poems until my legs went to sleep. I finally gave it up. I can't remember why. Oh, yes, I do. It was on account of the Affair. I think of it as having a capital A. I thought it was all so wonderful, and then that funny little woman came and called me all those names and told me to leave her husband alone. The next time I saw him he was all changed. He'd been glamorous and

74

all of a sudden he was just a sort of funny-looking man. It all went poof. That can happen from doing too much dreaming. Like Wilma said, you don't see things the way they really are.

Anyway, he was the only man in my life before my marriage, because nobody in his sane mind would count that Beecher boy back in the neighborhood and the day his family was away. That was only like kids do all the time.

I fell hard for Paul. All the girls were after him and I was the one who got him. We used to talk in the girls' room about how he looked like Randolph Scott, sort of. That seems funny now. Just a couple of weeks ago a woman said that to me again. I'd almost forgotten it. I can't see it. He looks like Paul Dockerty and that's all he looks like. Nobody in his sane mind would say he looks like anybody else.

After I got married and we came back to New York, I guess I thought I was happy. Wilma said I only *thought* I was, because the proof of it was that I'd kept right on dreaming silly stuff. She said that if I was genuinely happy I would be so contented with what I was that I wouldn't have to pretend I was somebody else. Anyway, he used to laugh at me. He doesn't any more. Like we would be walking somewhere and I would pretend we were rich South Americans who had fled to New York to escape a revolution and then I would say something with an accent and he would laugh at me. Sometimes he would try to play my games, but he would always spoil them. That's because he has to be a big wheel all the time.

When he took the better job I thought it would just mean living a little better and saving a lot more, because he has always been one for saving. But then Wilma started being nice to me. At first I couldn't hardly believe it. What did she see in me? A woman like that. But being alone, not having much to do with Paul working all day, I got so I saw a lot of her. She would talk to me. I'll never forget some of the things she would say to me.

"I don't believe Paul wants you to express yourself, Mavis. He seems to have a Victorian concept of womanhood. You have a distinct personality, and it is up to you to express it and not be satisfied with being a satellite of your husband with your whole world revolving around him."

That made a lot of sense. He'd been keeping me shut up. I began to express myself, all right. And we began to have a decent standard of living.

"That figure of yours is a deadly weapon, Mavis. You must use it as such. You must display it properly, give it good care, use it as a weapon, both offensive and defensive."

And that made it easier to get the nice things I wanted Paul to buy me. It was a lot better game than all that pretending.

"I hope you don't mind, dear, if I do some intensive work on you. I want to correct your way of speaking and your voice level. And the way you walk, and the way you get in and out of chairs. And I'm going to introduce you to a really fine beautician."

I didn't mind. It didn't hurt my feelings. A girl should improve herself, and I'd been sort of blind to myself. I saw right away how I could be improved a lot.

"Mavis, dear, a lot of your ideas are so dreadfully provincial. There's more to you than someone's sodden, dull little housewife. Your instinct was right about children. They would be the final trap, of course. But you still have a soap-opera attitude toward unfaithfulness. Darling, it isn't a tragedy. It's entertainment. Of course, some people, like poor dear Randy, get too terribly morbid about it. I wish you could be more Continental in your attitude. Goodness, the bloom *must* be off your marriage by this time. A lover would give you more self-confidence. Make you feel much more alive."

I sort of agreed with her, but it scared me a little. It sounded as if it would make things so complicated. And anyway, it is a sort of private matter, and I was seeing so much of Wilma whenever I could, whenever she wasn't busy, that it just didn't seem as if I had time to make an arrangement like that. Enough men liked me, but I didn't think much of them. I decided it couldn't be so sort of cold-blooded with me, the way it was with her. Maybe in that way we were a little different. It would just have to sort of happen, and when it did happen I was going to let it happen, because, like she said, who wants to be provincial and sodden?

Paul would make a big gloomy fuss about going to her parties. He's just dull. He doesn't like all those interesting people, writers and poets and musicians and people who are out in the real live world, not shut up in a dreary office over in Jersey. He can't ever get interested in anything outside himself. Like when those people brought all those drums to her party, the kind you beat on with your hands, and we

76

danced. He acted like it was something disgusting. Like Wilma says, he has a typical Rotarian-type mind.

Well, it finally happened and it wasn't at all the way I thought it was going to happen. It was scary and kind of messy. She told me on the phone she would be in. I went to the apartment and went up and Gil opened the door and he told me she was gone for the rest of the afternoon. He told me after I got inside. I hadn't liked him. Except when I had danced with him a few times, he had always looked on me like I was dirt or something. But I guess he looks at everybody that way. He's a famous painter, Wilma says. He started kissing me, and I guess, without thinking, I started acting provincial. Then he stopped and I had time to remember what Wilma had told me and then I told him Wilma wouldn't like this and he said if I thought she wouldn't like it or would even give a damn, then I didn't know Wilma very well. He took me back to a bedroom and I got provincial again and he acted bored with me. I couldn't imagine anybody getting bored with Wilma. So I tried to be Continental again, and then it happened. But it wasn't like love. It wasn't like people loving each other. It was just people doing something as if they were sort of cross with each other.

I told myself I was getting some experience of the world. He was certainly awful strong. He hurt me. Then I got dressed and he yawned and he told me to go home, he was going to take a nap. He shut his eyes. I stood there and looked at him and then I went home. Wilma told me the next morning I could come over. I had to tell her about it. She was rubbing some kind of a new cream into her face. She just kept rubbing away and half-smiling. I told her I was sorry.

She told me not to fret about it because Gilman Hayes was sort of like one of those toys you wind up and put down on the rug. It just goes and that's all. She said he would go after anything in a skirt and she used some pretty rough language talking about him. She said she was getting tired of him anyway and she was about to get rid of him. She rubbed the cream off her face and told me that there was nothing to forgive. She stood up and kissed me to prove it. She kissed me in a funny way. It made me feel all flushed and silly. Then she told me to run along.

I went like she said, even though I'd wanted to ask her about something. About why, on my way home the day before, after being with Gil, I'd started to cry on the street like a ninny. But I guess I knew what her answer would be, anyway. That provincial thing again. The next time I saw Gil he looked at me as if he didn't know me. And I guess maybe he didn't. I didn't feel as if he did.

But going home that time I didn't cry the way I've been crying now. After a while Paul came in. It started me off again. He stood over the bed and just said in a disgusted voice, "Oh, for God's sake." Then he went and got a different jacket and went out again. Like he was a big wheel. Like he hadn't got so filthy drunk that same day that Judy Jonah had to practically carry him to bed. None of them knew Wilma. They didn't like her. Maybe Randy is the only one who did, but that isn't like liking her. Not the way he felt about her.

Now she's dead and I can't face thinking of how boring my life is going to be.

I sat up then and stopped crying because I thought of what I would do. It was what Wilma would have done. If I stayed with Paul, I'd be trapped. I couldn't stay with him. Not any more. Wilma would want me to leave him. Since she changed me, an awful lot more men have been interested in me. And Paul makes good money. So he can darn well afford the divorce and some decent support for me. I'll go where people are alive. Someplace like Miami or Las Vegas or Paris. There won't be a single darn provincial thing about me. Not any more. I came off that crumby street out of that crumby neighborhood and I knew right from the beginning that my life was going to be wonderful. I guess I will look back and be grateful to Paul for being the one who got me in touch with Wilma. But that's all I'm grateful for.

He never looked the least damn bit like Randolph Scott.

I don't think I want to marry again. They want to put you in a box and turn the lock. They want you always doing things. Where did you put this? Hey, find that for me. Hey, clean up the place. Hey, come to bed. Like a slave. If you're a provincial type, that's all right. Maybe you can even get to like that sort of thing. But I'm not going to get trapped again. Look at how Noel is trapped. In a different kind of a way, she's a sort of pretty little thing. But I'd say she was pretty shallow. I bet there's never anything going on in her head the way things are always going on in mine. She just sits and sort of watches the world going by. She probably doesn't even know that Randy had more than one way of earning the salary Wilma paid him. She's that stupid, I bet. But what Wilma ever saw in Randy, I'll never know. He's so jumpy and skinny and nervous and kind of sloppy. The only man here with any dignity is that nice Wallace Dorn. He speaks so nice. He wouldn't be cruel and snotty like Gilman Hayes. But I liked dancing with Gil. While they played their silly games.

No, sir, Paul Dockerty, last night was the last time you're ever going to touch me. That was the end, even if you don't know it yet. It's silly, when you think of it, a little piece of paper giving a man the right to do that to you until you're such an old hag he doesn't want to any more.

I got dressed and I stopped by the door and thought about her real hard. I thought about her until I started crying again. And then I went out. It was pretty dark in the living room. Noel was there talking to a big trooper. They didn't see me. I turned around and went out through the back. I was sort of looking for Wallace Dorn. Then I saw the cigarette light in our car so I went over. Paul was sitting in there alone. He jumped when he saw me. I guess I startled him. He said, "I want to talk to you."

I was going to say that, but he said it first, so I just gave him a look and turned around and walked away. There wasn't anything he could say to me. Nothing. I was going around the house when I stepped on something that rolled under my foot so I nearly sat down. I felt around and picked it up and took it over to a light coming from a window to see what it was. It felt like some kind of a smooth stick. It was the striped stick from one end of the croquet game, the stick you have to make the ball hit after you roll it down through the hoops. But the end you stick in the ground was gone, broken right off. I guess somebody fell over it in the dark and broke it off and got mad and threw it. I threw it back over onto the court.

I was restless. I went to my room again and then I wandered around some more and then there was yelling and people running toward the lake and I heard somebody say something that sounded like "Got her."

I didn't want to go down there, but I had to. I'm always doing things like that. I have to see things. Once on Madison Avenue there was a crowd of people looking at something and dumb me, I had to push my way through so I could see

79

too, and what it was was a fat female person who had fallen out of a window. I nearly lost my lunch.

I had to go down and see, but I walked slow. I wasn't going to run like the rest of them. Even so, I was in plenty of time. They had her in a boat all covered over with a dirty canvas. They lifted her out and they dropped her. I was crying again. I hated to see them drop her. I wished there was some way I could make her come alive again. Some magic words to say, like in the stories.

I thought if I could make her come alive again, I would devote my whole life to her. There would be just the two of us. We would go away somewhere and there would be just the two of us forever and ever. And there wouldn't be any men around us.

Then I stopped and wondered why on earth I had thought a dumb thing like that. Well, if all the men were like Gil, I certainly wouldn't want any around. Afterward it was sort of by accident that I saw Steve pull Noel Hess into his room and shut the door and I heard the lock go click. Still waters certainly run deep, I thought. I had her all figured out for being provincial. It just goes to show you. Never judge a book by its cover. I wanted to listen by the door but I was afraid somebody would catch me.

Then they called us all into the living room again after they had a chance to look the body over or something. We had to sit there while a man named Fish made a speech. Everybody looked solemn. I was crying sort of to myself and I wasn't even listening very much. Then he said a dreadful thing about her being stuck in the back of the head with something. Killed! Somebody had murdered my Wilma. Just thinking of it made me feel like a tiger or something. I would gouge their eyes right out. I'd jump up and down on them. And we all had to wait around for big shots to come. I kept trying to remember where we'd all been in the water. But that wasn't any good because we'd been moving around a lot and I didn't know exactly when it had happened to her. Noel left the room, saying she had a headache. I bet! I waited for Steve to follow her, but he was busy trying to talk them into something about reporters that would be coming.

I just sat there. I stopped crying. I kept thinking about who had murdered her. Judy Jonah was talking to a trooper. She glanced at me and then she sort of frowned at me. Not really at me. . . .

I wonder what the trouble is. She looks sort of funny. Somebody is behind my chair. There is a hand. Nobody should touch anybody like that, put his darn hand on my breast reaching around from behind me, right out with people looking. If this is Paul's idea of a joke....

Chapter Eight

(GILMAN HAYES—BEFORE)

EVIS HAD PHONED from the gallery. He wanted to know when he could have more work. He said he could sell it. People were waiting for more to come in. I told him I wouldn't work for a time, maybe a month, maybe two. He said it might be smart to get some work in before his customers cooled off. I told him I didn't like the implication. I didn't like the hint that I was some sort of a fad. He apologized to me. But there was a practiced smoothness about the apology that I didn't care for. I hung up on him.

The world is full of drab inconsequential people like Evis. Living half lives. Afraid to grasp. The world gives to the ones who take boldly. People like Evis are there to be kicked.

But his manner had bothered me. Even though I knew I shouldn't let it. I went to see Wilma. It was midafternoon. She let me in and then went back to the phone. She was talking in Spanish. Finally she hung up. "I was talking to José," she said. "Telling him how many were invited."

"To what?"

"Did you forget, dear? This coming week end at the lake."

"I guess I forgot."

She sat beside me and took my hand. "What's the matter?"

"Evis asked for more work. I didn't like the way he asked me."

She shook her head, almost sadly. "When will you learn what you really are, Gil? How long is it going to take you? Grimy little people like Evis don't matter. He's a parasite, feeding off your strength. Humility doesn't become you, darling."

I could feel the strength coming back into me. She is the only one who can do that. Sometimes I feel as though she created me. But that is wrong, of course. She merely brought out what was already there, hidden behind all the weaknesses and uncertainties I used to have.

I had wasted so much time before I met her.

I want to laugh when I think of the pathetic thing I was. She saw what was there.

I've never made friends. You do or you don't. It seems that easy. I never knew why. She told me why. The less gifted always sense the difference. That's easy to understand, isn't it? She talks about mutations. The inevitable change in humanity. To become bigger, stronger, quicker, more ruthless. A survival thing, she has told me.

And I used to crawl and beg. Oh, not obviously. But thankful for the little jobs. Lifeguard, counter boy, usher, dance instructor, model. Little people throwing scraps to me, and hating me because they could sense that I was better. Women were easy. They have always been easy. Wilma says that is a clue. I should have been able to read it. They are easy and meaningless. Except Wilma. Because of what she has done.

It was always a dream. From the time, I guess, that Sister Elizabeth, in the Home, said I could draw. She put that picture on the cork board in the big hall. Of trees. I drew every leaf. She told me what I had to do. Study, work, study, work. She should have known better. Where is there time for that? They let you go when you are old enough. When I was little they thought I would be adopted. I was out three times. But I was sent back. They wanted kissings. I could not do it. I stood and looked at them. Unresponsive, they said. They let me go when I was old enough and they found me the job and the place to live. How can you study and work to be an artist? The books were too hard. I learned the words so I could say them. And lessons are expensive. I would take some and then I would quit because they would not let me do what I wanted to do. Sit here, they said. Draw this pot. Draw that apple. You could go on for years drawing the dull things they put in front of you. That is not being an artist. I took them the things I did myself. All the colors swirled together. They always laughed and pursed up their mouths and tilted their heads on the side and used the words I had learned. Little people, refusing to see what was better. Hating me.

So I did very little of it. And I didn't show it to anyone

any more. But on Sundays I would put on my good clothes and walk where there were the best-dressed people and walk among them and pretend all the time that I was an artist, a very good one. And on those Sundays I would usually find a girl. That was never very hard. As Wilma says, that should have been a clue.

I am ashamed of the way she found me. It was a job for Gherke. Sometimes he would use me. Not often and not for much money. I would have to lean, sweating, over some meatless girl, trying to look charmed and devoted to her, while Gherke fussed with hot lights and camera angles, always complaining about my wooden expression. The ad she saw was for Ferris perfume. She asked at the agency and the agency sent her to Gherke and Gherke told her where to find me. She sat at a stool. I had to wear that monkey hat behind that counter. Ridiculous. She knew my name. She waited until I was off. I thought it was just more of the same. I did not care. She was older, but not too old, I thought.

That night was what made everything different. It was not what I thought. It was at first, but not later. Not with those lights low and with her asking me the questions about myself. She knew when I was lying. I have always lied. Usually I say things like coming from a rich family and my people killed in a plane or something. But she kept asking and after a little bit I found I was telling her everything. Sister Elizabeth, drawing every leaf, how it was easy with girls, everything, and after a while I was crying. I couldn't remember crying before. She told me later it was like psychoanalysis. Releasing tension. It all took a long time, because I could not express myself well. It was dawn when it was over and I felt as if I had run as fast as I could all night long.

Then she told me what I was. I had never known it before. She told me how the world always tries to suppress the best.

That was the beginning. After that came the clothes, and how to treat people, and getting the studio apartment for me, and her there all the time while I painted, doing pictures very quickly, and Wilma telling me all the time to be bold about what I was doing. Not to try to paint something, but to paint a feeling. With big sweeps of color and spatters of paint.

She introduced me to Steve, and it didn't matter to me that he didn't like me. She said he had his job to do and he would do it. We went to good places and were seen there

84

and after a while I was in the columns and then that man did the article on my work and then the gallery took me, and then there were all those arguments in the art sections of the papers and people began to buy the paintings and talk about me.

But she had taught me how to act. To always remember that I am better. That they are all slobs. Treat them as such. They like it, she said. They come back for more. It is really very easy to do. I had always acted sort of that way, but it was an unnatural shyness. I mean it just looked like arrogance.

Wilma made everything come true, but I know now that even without her it would have happened anyway. It might have taken longer. That is all.

There is still a weakness in me. Like when Evis acted that way. I had to go to her again because she could make me feel strong and whole again. But I am going to get over that. So nothing can disturb me. I am, as she has explained, a mutation. What the race of men will one day become. She is a little bit that way, but not so much. The ones who are that way, they are big and strong and quick. I have always been bigger and stronger and quicker than the others. I can walk down any street and look at men and know I can knock them down. And look at women and know I can have them. That is the way I look at them. So that they know it. They have always hated me anyway. They have always rejected me. So it makes no difference if I give them more cause, does it?

At first Wilma bullied her friends into buying my work. She knew it was good. And then strangers started buying it. At first I would read something. It would say, "Weak, amateurish, exhibitionistic. A monstrous joke. A triumph of press agentry." It would make me uncertain.

But she would have another clipping. It would say, "Gilman Hayes exhibits a truly startling growth in his latest work. His dynamic approach to space relationships, his iconoclastic attitude toward traditional concepts of design, his daring use of color have burst open new frontiers in subjective art. We predict that..."

I keep the good ones in a scrapbook.

I go to be with Wilma, and in that she is very demanding, but for me it is not like the others. It is like a comforting. Like being protected from outside things that

85

want to hurt you with sharp edges. A warmth around you. Sometimes we laugh together at Hess. He is such a ridiculous man. So helpless. So futile. I think of how insignificant he is and how strong I am and I want to put my fist through his skull. I know I could do it. It would be like tearing brittle paper. As if he were not really there. As if he were not really alive. The way I am. The way Wilma is. I am strong enough to put my fist through the world. It would tear like paper, too. As easily subdued as that Mavis was, walking around trying to be Wilma. And can never be.

Once I remembered the party at the lake, I was glad. I like it up there. I remembered Amparo Loma. Perhaps this time.

Wilma and I left very early on Friday morning. Her driving frightens me. I do not let her see that it does. She was quiet on the way up, intent on her driving. On one straight stretch she made the little car do 110. It will go faster. She laughed when we were going the fastest. I could not hear her. I saw her mouth and knew she was laughing. She has done a lot of living. She is older. She can go fast. I have a lot left to do. I thought of the car overturning, and of my skin and muscle and bone sliding and grinding over concrete. It made me feel pale. But I could not let her see it.

It made me feel pale like that time in the Home. There was a concrete fire escape. It had an iron railing. I was small. One of the big boys took me out on the top landing. He held me over the railing. I could not even scream. I saw the bricks down there. There was nobody to help me. He brought me back over the railing and dropped me. It hurt my head. I started to cry. He slapped me. Then he turned his back. He leaned on the railing. He ignored me. I wasn't there any more.

We got to the lake at two o'clock. There was nothing there but the old station wagon José uses. She walked in and checked everything and gave orders. What to serve. Where to put people. She sent José to the village for more things. I swam and rested on the dock in the sun. I let the sun unwind my nerves. I could hear her yelling at them in the house. In Spanish. She treats them like dogs. They don't seem to care. I guess it is because of the money.

The others came. Randy and Noel Hess. Judy Jonah. Steve Winsan. The Dockertys. Wallace Dorn last of all. They all drink too much. I have never enjoyed drinking. It dulls things. It spoils things. I make a drink last a long time. I did

86

not pay much attention to them. I almost laughed at myself. Once upon a time I would have thought this was the greatest thing in the world. You get used to nice things quickly. I have always liked nice things. Clean smells. The feel of silk. Long showers. Now I had them, and would always have them, and I knew it was meant that way from the beginning.

I sat with them and listened to the foolish talk they made. I played a game. This was my place. I was a baron. Wilma was my aging lady. Soon I could be rid of her. And rid of her empty friends. And I could live here alone, with the brown Amparo. And beat her severely when she displeased me. When I had a party, it would not be these people. It would be people who depended on me, who needed my strength. I would tell them what to do. And when.

Usually, when we were in a group, Wilma would look at me from time to time, and there would be a quick understanding between us. But she had acted strangely on the way up. She had acted strangely ever since we had talked about Evis. I could not catch her eyes. I wondered if I had displeased her, and then I made myself stop thinking that way. It was the other way around. It was up to her to please me. We had changed status. Inevitably.

They played games. I have never cared for games. I danced with the Dockerty woman. She was a little drunk. I dance well. I knew her husband was aware of us, and I knew that the dancing excited her. It gave me pleasure to make him nervous. I knew, when we danced on the terrace, that I had only to take her wrist and lead her out into the darkness away from the floodlights. It was that easy. But I did not. It pleased me to tantalize her. She meant nothing. I knew the others were aware of our dancing. All of them watching us, pretending not to. All of them envious of me. Or of the Dockerty woman. That was pleasant too, to feel the emotion of them, of the weak ones watching the strong.

Wilma had put me in the same room as before, the one with the door that connects with hers. But when I tried it, it was locked. I raised my fist to knock, then lowered it. That would be a loss of dignity. It did not matter. Not at all. I went to bed. There was the flush of the sun on my body. It felt good. And the faint weariness of much dancing. And the smell of rich things around me.

I slept. I have never, in my whole life, dreamed. They talk about it. I don't know what they mean. Of that one thing I am envious. It must be nice. Little stories that go on in your head when you are asleep. I make up dreams sometimes, and tell them to women. They always seem interested. They like to tell me what the made-up dreams mean. It seems to excite them to tell me what my dream lies mean.

I was up early, as I always am. I was the first. Amparo brought my breakfast. She moved quickly away when I tried to touch her. I knew what this day would be. They would be drunk. But there would be sun and some good exercise. That was enough. I could wear my trunks all day. They look at me. It is good to be looked at, when you know that all of you is brown and strong and well formed. I liked posing for the life classes. Back then, in my stupidity, I thought their drawings of me were good. I know better now.

The others got up. Steve drove a runabout, pulling me on the skis. The fool let the towline go slack. Instead of releasing the bar, I tried to hold it. When the line came tight it felt as though it would yank my arms out of the sockets. It hurled me through the air and awkwardly into the water. I was certain he had done it on purpose. I would take his throat in my hand and bang his head on the concrete pier. But by the time I swam in, the redness had faded away. Hess drove the runabout. I taught Mavis how to stand up on the skis. She is a giggler. A fool. But her co-ordination was fair, and she learned and became very proud of herself. Again I knew her husband watched us warily.

That may have been the reason he got thoroughly drunk, stumbling around while we played croquet, disappearing finally to pass out. It turned into a sleepy afternoon. People disappeared, reappeared. I tried to find a chance to talk to Wilma, but she avoided me. Mavis lay beside me in the sun on the pier, talking inanities, sweating rather unpleasantly.

It was dark when I finally had a chance to talk to Wilma. She called me over to her. We went up and sat on the edge of the steep bank near the croquet layout. I watched them down there in the floodlights, swimming. And I heard them laugh.

And Wilma talked to me.
And talked to me.
And talked.

Chapter Nine

RANDY DID NOT LOOK directly at me when he told me we were going to Wilma's place at Lake Vale for the week end. We do not look at each other very much any more.

I was given a present once. The woman next door brought it over. I had been sick. I was sitting up in bed. My mother was there. I took off the paper. There was a wooden box, just a bit smaller. And another. And another. My breath came faster. The last box would contain something tiny and exquisite. It had to. It had to be something very small and delicate and lovely and precious to merit all the boxes, one within the other. The final box was empty. I looked into it for a long time and felt as if somebody had been there before me and stolen whatever it was. I cried. My mother was ashamed of me. The woman smiled and said it was perfectly all right, but her eyes did not smile.

For a long time I tried to find something good enough to put in that box, the littlest one. There was nothing good enough. I stole a ring from a girl in my class. It had a red stone. I took it out of her desk. I hid it in my shoe. It hurt but I didn't limp. I took it home and put it in the smallest box. Once it was in there I saw it clearly. One prong was broken. The silver was turning yellowish. It was not good enough. I had stolen. I had to be punished. I held a wire in the gas flame on the stove and put it against my arm. I did not cry. After the scab came off there was a thin white scar. It lasted for years. Now I cannot find it. I threw the ring into tall grass. I never liked that girl again. Once, during fire drill, I pinched her—hard. She cried and told on me. I was punished.

I am a lot of boxes. All going down, down to a tiny one. And nothing in it. Anything so intricate, so difficult to construct, the corners glued so carefully, needs something valuable inside. I am intricate. I am well made. To enclose emptiness. So it is a feeling of not being used. And of having been most carefully planned for use.

How must a woman be? Full of things to give, perhaps. Giving of love and work and loyalty, living in sensitivity and awareness, making a nest of love. I am that.

So I think of this thing that has happened to me, and look back along my life and try to discover how, at thirty-five, I am empty. My father died. My mother had to work. I was too little. So I went with cousins. Five of them, racing and yelping and talking loud and fighting over food and games. There I found my strength. In waiting and planning and working. They were all so disorganized. I wanted orderliness. And I made it for myself. And I liked it when I had made it, aiming myself like a careful arrow at the things I wanted. The high grades, the poems memorized, the clothing I made, the neatness of my bed. Perhaps I was a prude. A solemn dark-headed child, full of herself. And liking the clean clear things. The scholarship attained, the degree achieved, the research job secured.

And I met Randy, who seemed to be what I was. Determined and ambitious and quiet and orderly. Clean and precise. I was virgin. And so was he. It was not without magic. It was a spiritual love. It was full of high thoughts. But on the physical side, we differed. He seemed always to be distressed by the very mechanics of the act, shy of the indignities of it, gingerly about my very femaleness of function, appalled by fervor. And I found that, unlike my husband, I wanted abandon, a careless wildness, a lushness about it. Yet, sensing his wishes, I practiced the restraints he wanted, so that we made love to dignified formula, in precisely scheduled asceptic dignity, considering the soul and ignoring the inescapable body, making it a thing of silence and controlled breathing. Yet I knew him, and thought I loved him, and not too infrequently I was satisfied. Perhaps if there had been children . . . I wanted them. I went to doctors. He would never go. And so I was labeled the infertile one.

There was not much joy in him. And little spontaneity. But in our fashion we were happy.

And then Wilma went to him as a client.

The change did not come quickly. It makes me think of something that happened when I was little. A boy had taken a fuse apart. There was a disk inside, of mica, I believe it was called. By being very careful we could peel off the thin sheets. Each one was transparent. But the whole disk was almost opaque.

And that is the way it was with Randy. I did not notice the first few transparent sheets that came between us. And by the time I became aware that he was on the other side of something that misted his image, there were too many of those sheets in the way. It was too late to break through. I knew he was dropping other clients. He stopped talking about his work. He stopped asking my opinion. One day he said he was giving up the business, that he would work exclusively as her business manager. He named the salary. It was a good one, though not so much as he had made before. He gave up the office not long after that. He worked at her apartment. He no longer touched me. Ever. And the scent of her was on him. In his clothes, in his hair, on his skin. He slept like death. We lived more expansively. We dipped into savings. Until they were gone.

I was stupid. I had no experience with that sort of thing. He would not talk to me. We had sour quarrels. I thought he had started taking drugs. Or something equally vile. Then the next time I saw them together, I knew what was between them. It was not something I had to reaso̶n̶ ̶ ̶ ̶ ̶ ̶ ̶ ̶ ̶ ̶ to me, out of some primal intuition. And it̶ ̶ ̶ ̶ ̶ ̶ ̶ tually and physically. For days I would vom̶ ̶ ̶ ̶ ̶ ̶ of the two of them together. She was rep̶ ̶ ̶ ̶ me. She has no morals. She has no soul. S̶ ̶ ̶ ̶

Then it began to mean something else to m̶ ̶ ̶ he had told me that I was not enough—th̶a̶ ̶ ̶ ̶ meager. I would sit and look at myself. Lo̶ ̶ ̶ grotesque length to my upper lip, an appallin̶ ̶ my eyes, a scrawny raddled look to my bod̶ ̶ ̶ ̶ think he had every right to go elsewhere.̶ ̶ ̶ change all around and I would be full of ̶ ̶ ̶ had never permitted me to be what I cou̶ ̶ ̶

And then all that would go away and I w̶ ̶ ̶ For what he was doing to himself and all hi̶ ̶ his austere dignity.

And then there was nothing left to do but̶ ̶ ̶ him. There is a fascination in that. I canno̶ ̶ ̶ People run to fires. There are newsreels of whe̶ ̶ big chimneys down, and dynamite cliffs. You̶ ̶ ̶ thing being broken. And you cannot take your̶ ̶ ̶ knew he was seeing a doctor. He would not tell̶ ̶ I watched him acquire his soiled look, and his ne̶ ̶ ̶ nervous self-deprecation—like the manner of a dog that, locked too long in a house, has made a mess on the rug, and seeks to avoid punishment with hectic affability.

I believe I could have refused to go up there with him. But it was part of the old disease. Watching disintegration. Examining decay. And so I went. On the way up we talked as strangers talk. The traffic seems light today. It must be much warmer down in the city. Yes, I could eat any time you want to stop.

Sitting there, being carried along at fifty miles an hour in the car we did not own, with clothing not yet paid for, wearing our unloved bodies, which flexed and jiggled to the road's irregularities, his hand on the wheel, mine demure in my lap, driving through our special and personal wasteland toward no place at all.

Randy got increasingly nervous as we neared the place. We parked behind the house. Randy carried our luggage in. Wilma was on the terrace. Gilman Hayes was coming up from the dock. Wilma slipped easily into the part she plays with me. The affectionate older sister. A sort of we-girls thing. A sweetness that is patronizing. I have never let it

let it bother me.

out. It just how it was so typical of her
sickened me. Ac- dinner and then
it when I thought s and went off to
ulsively sweet to n, some dogmatic
he is an animal. vapid imitation of
me. By his action mments by Wallace
at my gifts were Randy in some odd
ok until I saw a vant. He had some of
g squintiness in he would have looked
y. And I would ed over his arm. I got
Then it would
indignation. He be able to eat breakfast
ld be to him. all when Steve Winsan
ould pity him. there was no point in
plans and all ash young old man. The
gles, always balancing too

sit and watch
t describe it. rted talking about improv-
n they knock then I heard him saying
watch some- of sense, at least for me. It
eyes away. I use it was so close to what I
me about it.
w manner of

had been thinking ever since my marriage started to go bad, started to spoil. About being able to become somebody else. About changing from what you are.

I looked right at him, and it was looking at him for the first time. His gray eyes were surprisingly good. Gray and level and honest, for once. I asked him what he wanted to become. And he told me he was tired of running, tired of impersonating himself.

He had been honest with me and it became something very special between us. I do not know how to describe it. Perhaps this way: Suppose you are at an ancient movie, all jerky and black and white and no sound track. Then, right in the middle, it turns to good color, and there is a sound track and you become interested in the plot and you sit forward on the edge of the seat. It was like that. The week end suddenly came alive. And I couldn't remember anyone else in my life ever looking at me in exactly that way, with that special look of understanding, of personal concern. It occurred to me that he knew what was happening to me and he had seen it all, and it troubled him. And he liked me. Maybe that was it, most of all. He liked me for myself. Because, of all of them there, I was certainly the one who could do him the least good. With me there could be no angle. Nothing to promote. Yet I was the one he had chosen to talk to about the things he was really thinking.

After it was over I knew I wanted to talk to him some more. I wanted to hear his voice. I looked at him from a distance. There was a pleasing look of reliable strength about his shoulders.

Later we had a chance to talk on the dock, stretched out in the sun. It made me feel shy to be so near him.

I remember one thing he said. He frowned down at his knuckles and he said, "Noel, don't you get the feeling that everything is going to go bang? Not to everybody. Just to people like this group. My God, look at us. Could any setup be more artificial? Take a look around. Every human being should have some purpose, some good purpose. Look at this crowd. Is there a single person here worth a damn? Outside of you?"

"Including me, Steve. No."

"It's got to go bang. There has to be a purpose. I don't want to sound like a Sunday school, but it has to be a clean and honest purpose. Not a PR kick, not cheap comedy on

TV, not making people smell better, not selling more gunk, not kidding the public with phony art."

"Where do I join up?" I asked him, smiling at him.

"You and me. We'll form an association. Onward and upward, or something." And then he looked sad. "Maybe it's just too damn late for us, Noel. Maybe from here on in all we ought to look for is kicks. Like in that glass you just happen to have in your hand."

"You mean this?" I drank it quickly. I had a funny feeling of recklessness. It *was* all going to go bang, and soon. And all I was doing was waiting around for it. There should be better things than waiting. And I had the crazy thought that maybe Steve would be one of the better things. At least he was honest about himself. I felt as though I were glowing, as though I had become prettier every minute.

During the croquet game I was aware of him all the time. Aware of the way he was watching me. And I wanted to be pretty for him. More pretty than I was. There had been a lot of sun and too many drinks and I felt careless and dizzy. And very contemptuous of Randy.

After the game and after we ate, people had stopped running around in circles. Steve came to me and told me there was a place on the lake he wanted to show me. I made myself say yes before I could think about it too much. We took one of the runabouts. He had a big thermos bottle. He said it was a picnic. He drove the boat fast, scaring me when we went around corners, laughing at me, his teeth white in his face. And then he went slow and we were near an island. He went over the side and pulled the bow up and gave me his hand and I jumped down onto the sand.

It was very quiet there. There was a grassy bank. I felt myself growing scared. I felt the drinks oozing away. He kissed me with a hard confidence that was frightening. I drank from the thermos cup to make the fright go away. He caressed me. He was confident in the way he touched me. I kept trembling. I had the odd feeling that I had seen a man doing that before, murmuring and applying firm hands to quiet a restive horse. We were very much alone there. The grass was deep and soft. Somehow, without actually meaning to, I let him take me a bit beyond the point where I could turn back without making myself look entirely ridiculous. There was just something about his confidence.

And then he took me and I knew that it was exactly what

94

I had wanted all my life, and knew then that I loved him and would always love him, and I told him so, many, many times. And he told me that it was a good thing that had happened to us, and we would have to be careful about the plans we made. But my word had been made whole. Nothing else mattered. I felt a shyness when he looked at me. It seemed so incredible to have found him there, at this place, at this party. To have found the Steve I love hiding behind that brash city mask. When it started to get dark at last, we put our suits on and got in the boat and went back. Randy was standing on the dock when we came in. I wanted to laugh at him. I was finally free of him. I wanted to tell him what had happened to me, and exactly how it had freed me.

When the motor stopped its noise, Randy said, "Where have you been?"

I imitated Wilma. I felt reckless and brave. "Why, we seem to have been on a picnic or something dahling. Miss me?"

He walked away. Steve shushed me. I couldn't get mad. I felt too good. I felt full of light bulbs and cymbals and fur. And I drank some more. And stayed close to Steve. Let anybody in the world see I was staying close to Steve. I wanted to have them see it imprinted on my face, in the way I walked, in the tone of my laughter. For I was not only free of Randy, I was free of other things, of dry constraints, of shy imaginings. I was free to be a woman and love the way I wanted to love, without a book of rules.

I was glad when Wilma suggested we swim without suits. That was the way I felt. The lights came on for a moment after I had taken my suit off. And I did not mind. I did not mind being seen by anyone. That, too, was an indication of my new freedom. I went into the water and waited for Steve to find me. He did. We floated. We held hands. I turned into his arms. We kissed underwater. I felt sleek and alive. I felt brazen. I laughed at nothing. At just being alive. Then I was with him again after a silly game of tag.

I heard Gilman calling. "Wilma! he yelled. "Hey, Wilma!"

I was telling Steve how much I loved him. He told me to shush. It hurt my feelings. I pouted. Then I started listening too, waiting for Wilma to answer. I wondered why she didn't.

And all at once the water seemed to turn cold. My teeth began to chatter. I swam toward the dock.

Chapter Ten

(Paul Dockerty—Afterward)

After Steve told me he thought Wilma had drowned, I stood there for perhaps ten seconds. Your mind works slowly after the kind of sleep I had. I had to dismiss the idea that it was a gag. Steve couldn't act that well.

"Have you phoned?" I asked him.

"Phoned?" he said blankly.

I remembered where I had seen a phone. I went in and it rang at least ten times before the sleepy operator answered, a trace of indignation in her voice. I spoke sharply.

"This is the Ferris place. Wilma Ferris. Know where it is?"

"Yes."

"Miss Ferris has drowned. We're looking for her. Get hold of whoever can get over here with the necessary equipment. Can you do that?"

After a pause she answered in a voice that had forgotten sleep and annoyance. "The troopers, the sheriff. Right away, sir."

I was still in swimming trunks. I went down to the dock. They were milling around, staring at the cold unfriendly water.

"Where was she last seen?" I demanded. They talked and argued and interrupted each other and the net result was that no one knew. I got Steve and Gilman Hayes into a runabout. I went along. Randy Hess handled the boat. He had got a big flashlight from the house. I pushed off and let the boat drift out a way. We took turns diving from the bow, following the flashlight beam down. It was damn deep. Only once was I able to touch rock at the bottom. Hayes claimed to be able to get to the bottom each time. He probably could, with that chest on him. I knew it was a wild chance that we'd find her, but a chance worth taking, even at astronomical odds. Each minute that ticked away lessened her chance of survival, even if we found her. And there was another thing. For my own sake, I had to do all I possibly could. Because I knew that I could not be genuinely sorry she was dead. Any slackening of effort would give me almost the feeling of being an accomplice.

Each time I came up, gasping for air, clinging to the boat, I could hear the ridiculous sounds Mavis was making. They weren't genuine sounds. There was a bit *too* much heartbreak. I felt a digust for her that seemed to me to be unnatural.

Steve clung to the runabout beside me and said, his teeth chattering, "What's the point, Paul? Hell. Needles in haystacks. My God, there's a lot of lake here."

I heard the distant sirens then.

"A few more times, Steve. Come on."

"Then you'll be looking for me, too."

But we kept on. And then we went in, and I knew that no matter what anybody did now, it was too late. Too late for Wilma. The urgency was gone. Now it was the routine of recovering a body. Nothing more. I talked to the troopers and to a man named Fish and heard the boats, far across the lake, converging on the Ferris place. I'd dropped my robe on the shore end of the dock. I put it on, found the nearly empty cigarette pack in the pocket. The terry cloth of the robe dried my body and I began to feel warmer. I wanted to talk to somebody and it certainly wasn't Mavis. I glanced up toward the stone steps and saw Judy Jonah sitting up there, looking small, huddled, a bit forlorn. My cheeks got a little hot as I remembered leaning heavily on her, drunk, maudlin, silly. Yet of all the people there, she seemed to be the only one who— to use an old tired phrase—was my kind of people. And that in itself made no sense. A famous comedienne, and a business type. And I had seen the look on Fish's face when he'd found Wilma's swimsuit in the pocket of her robe. Fish and I had been equally appalled. So here was Judy Jonah, who doubtless had been a part of the so gay, so mad swimming party, and maybe I had better plan on relaxing with types like Fish, who shared my Victorian hangover.

I asked her if she'd stick around for a minute while I got a towel and some cigarettes. She said she would. I couldn't read anything in her voice.

I made it fast, and went back. I asked about the swimming party. And I found out that she and Randy and Wallace Dorn had kept themselves clothed. I don't know why it mattered. But it made me feel good. And I didn't give a damn about Mavis. So it could be Macy's window as far as I was concerned. And so Mavis had managed to kill something that had been a long time adying. Killed it dead.

And there's nothing so damn lonesome. How do you say it? There has to be somebody who cares how you get along. Just somebody. Somebody really involved with you. Somehow it's all a big kindergarten and you trot home with a gold star pasted on your forehead, to be admired. Or go home with a bruise, demanding intricate bandages. The world is a great cold place. Men die in strange cities. Obits are on back pages. The ball of mud keeps spinning, and the parades line up on all the holidays. You have to have somebody. Maybe it's really dead and gone when you at last realize that she *doesn't* give a damn, that she would make traditional bleating sounds for you, but with that same trace of corn in her voice that I could hear, sitting there with Judy, sitting on the step below her. It made me feel cold and lonesome.

I had the ridiculous thought that Judy had warm arms and I wanted them around me, and wanted her telling me that I was safe and important. Yet, of course, I couldn't get to her. Not while she kept on being Judy Jonah—because that was as though she were a juggler. She kept busy keeping the parabola of shining things spinning around her, and if you tried to reach they would all fall and break and the act would be spoiled. But it seemed like an act that went on out of forlorn habit.

She said she was cold and wanted to go get dressed. The wind was getting a bit stronger.

I went back to our room. Ferris products on the dressing table. Smell of Blue Neon heavy in the room. My bed rumpled from alcoholic sleep. I stood there in the room and I felt something happen to me. You go along on momentum. You have been set in a track and wound up with the key in the back and you run along. A good key and a good spring and you run for all your life. But the spring slips, or maybe there weren't enough turns on the key. And suddenly you find that you have run down and stopped. That was it. I stopped right there. Maybe it's a point of decision. Or of evaluation. I don't know. But I was motionless in my track, nothing turning any more, nothing pushing at me. And a damn funny thing happened. I felt free. By God, I could wind up my own spring and turn the wheels and find a new track. I was glad everything had stopped. No more of this whipping myself along in order to achieve ends and desires that had become meaningless. No more running like Sammy. Health and reasonable intelligence and good digestion. I could chop wood, sell cars, plant corn. Any damn thing. Liquidate myself along in order to achieve ends and desires that had pleased, and I wanted it to start with walking along a country road into places I'd never seen before.

I stood in this bedroom I'd shared with a stranger and I wanted to laugh. I dressed and combed my hair and went out and around the house and out toward the back. I didn't want to see anybody. I wanted to be where it was dark and give myself a careful going over and try to find out just what had happened to me. I walked around for a time. My shoes crunched the gravel. It was cold and I went back for a warmer jacket. Mavis was on the bed bleating and snuffling. I could have been a hundred miles away.

I went back outside, and from the shadows near the house Judy spoke to me, startling the hell out of me. She said something that made no sense about running in midair, and then she began to make the darnedest noise I'd ever heard a woman make. A sort of keening sound, through clenched teeth, a sort of spasm that bent her over at the middle, and it took me a few seconds to realize she was trying to keep herself from crying. I steered her to our car and got her inside and got my arms around her and her face against my chest and told her to let it go.

She let it go. All the misery in the world. Crying like a child. Over a thousand parties she hadn't been asked to. Over a hundred broken dolls. Over a dozen lost loves. She wasn't Judy Jonah any more—face on the glowing tube, backed up by brass and strings, prying yaks out of the studio audience. A girl in my arms, crying. A hell of a thing, actually. It made me think of those guys, those unknowns—doctors and agents and writers—who marry the big-name screen stars. Do they have this? Holding warm the helpless tears? It's such a big glamour kick, so much beating of drums, that you forget they're women. Women in the tears sense. Women with sniffles and headaches and lotions and fears. Women who burn fingers, break straps, curse runs in new hose, snore when they sleep on their backs, watch their weight, cat-talk their sisters, sweat in the heat, chatter in the cold, blow noses, covet dresses, get the blues. They must. They are human and they are female. And being human, they share that sense of being dreadfully alone.

I held Judy until it was all gone and she fought her way

99

up out of it, subduing the snifflings, blowing her nose lustily, moving away from me, getting her chin up, and, I suspected, beginning to resent me for being there and seeing it happen.

We talked a bit. I felt her stop resenting me. I put my hand on her shoulder. Casually. She rested her cheek against my hand and then, turning her head, brushed her lips lightly across the back of my hand. She came quickly into my arms as I reached for her.

I remember the first time I ever kissed a girl. I think I was almost thirteen. It was that traditional game. Post office. Her name was Connie and she was on the timid side. Her voice shook when she said she had a special delivery for Paul. I damn near died. Girls! Good Lord! Girls! I was filled with lofty male contempt. But I had to go through with it. I was trapped. The post office was at the dim end of the front hall. She waited there for me. Head bent. I had every intention of one quick harsh peck in the general direction of her face. Remember how it was? The perfume of them? The first awareness? Those lips of that astounding, incredible softness? There was a concept in your head. Girls! Miserable things. And those lips took that bitter concept and flipped it and it landed the other side up and all of a sudden there were a hundred mysteries to be solved. From despicable things they suddenly became the source of all fevers. You are not supposed to relive that first kiss. Ever. But somehow Judy's lips became the first, turning concepts upside down in the same old way. Blotting out everything known and substituting a full new range of unknowns.

Then she moved and twisted and was gone. Leaving exactly what she was and the hint of what she could be firmly imprinted on my mouth. Indelibly. And I was stupid enough to think that it had been meaningless to her, as meaningless as it was meaningless to me. Too much male suspicion. Too many times burned, maybe. Not realizing that it must be mutual impact to be any impact at all. And something not too often used, too often given away. A kiss. My God, how many wet and furtive ones are exchanged at the club on any Saturday night? Or in your kitchen the last time you had a party? And how many of them move along from kissing to fondling to motel, culminating in an act that achieves its nastiness merely through its meaninglessness? Old-fashioned?

I guess. Practice and familiarity and shallowness dump you off the end of the porch, right into contempt and self-disgust. And if you eat spiced foods, you can drink one hell of a hot cup of coffee.

This was honest, and she put her back against the car door and told me so, and told me it was the end of this particular bus line, and got out and went away from me. But not before I made a feeble comment about canceling out Mavis. Knowing, as I said it, it was too fast and too ridiculous. She looked back once. Pale face turning, light catching it.

I sat alone.

Now be a big boy, Paul. Act like a grownup. You just kissed a famous female. It rocked you both—assuming she wasn't acting. (I know she wasn't! I know it!) You're both upset about this Wilma thing. (No. We're upset about other things. And we can be the answer for each other because I know we want the same things.) And this is a crazy environment. You do silly things in a setting like this. (But it would have been the same on a ten-cent ferry ride or in a public park or on a picnic or sitting in a balcony. Exactly the same, wiping out everything that has gone on up to now.) And you're an incurable romantic, Paul. Always looking for the rope of hair hanging out of the high stone tower, always ready to tie colors to your lance. (But never finding *her* until now. Always looking at the wrong tower windows. Wearing the wrong hues.) And she is a busy gal and next week if she met you on the street she'd look baffled for a moment and then, maybe, remember your name. (It happened to her the way it happened to me.) Anyway, Paul boy, you're married and that's something you work at. You don't give it up all of a sudden because you happened to marry somebody who, at times, manages to be a remarkably silly woman. (Silly, vicious, shallow, and phony. Too selfish for motherhood. Predictably unfaithful, if not already, then soon. Woman who doesn't give a damn for you except as a meal ticket.) So skip it, Paul. (And what if you can't? What if it's something beyond the exercise of will?)

Skip it anyway.

So up came Mavis and she startled me and when I saw who it was I told her I wanted to talk to her. She

101

turned around and walked away. At least she'd stopped blubbering. She walked away. I wanted to jump out and catch her in three strides and see how heavily I could hit her on the back of the neck. Then I wondered how many people go around with crazy thoughts like that popping into their heads. Like, on the way up, when we had quarreled, I kept looking at the front ends of the oncoming trucks. One yank on the wheel. How often does that happen? Car out of control. Wife goes yammer, yammer, yammer. Man sits there, shoulders hunched, hands tight on the wheel. So maybe lots of times the yammer has a chance to turn into half a scream before the explosive crunch, followed by the long scrapings and tinklings, and they both die mad.

Yes, I wanted to talk to her and I was going to talk to her. And she wasn't going to like what I was going to say. Because, Judy or no Judy, win, lose, draw, or default, I had had enough. Enough of Mavis, Manhattan, Management. I had a Daliesque view of myself. I sat in a big tin tub in the middle of the desert while a big brush scrubbed me clean, inside and out. Then the brain would be taken out of the white suds, rinsed gently in spring water, and popped back into the skull.

The spring was winding up and the wheels were aimed in a new direction. There weren't any road signs. I spent a long time with myself there. When I got out of the car I felt cramped and stiff, as though I had spent a long time under tension. I was watching the way the mountains were beginning to show in the first gray of Sunday morning when I heard the shouts. All the lights went on again, killing off the look of morning. I hurried down to the water.

They had her. Steve and a trooper lifted her up out of the boat. They had her wrapped in a tarp, but they fumbled it and dropped her, so she rolled naked out of the covering. I looked at that body and decided right there I had no tendency toward necrophilism. Objectively, I suppose it was a fine lush body. But it was very, very dead, and I turned my back and heard Judy yell at them to cover her up. I knew she felt the same way I did about it.

Officialdom took over and shooed us off the dock. The

102

boats began to head for home, toward the women who would indeed cherish this morsel.

I tell you, Helen, I just knew there was a lot of things going on over there. A regular orgy. All those city people, romping around stark nakid. Dope fiends too, I'll bet you. Well, they say you shouldn't speak bad things about the dead, but I can tell you, Helen, I'm sure not sorry trash like that isn't going to be coming up here any more. I hope some real nice people get that house. You know, that Judy Jonah was over there too. If she comes on again in the fall, I'm not going to let the children watch her. I'm going to write to the sponsor. I say if a person don't live decent, Helen, they've got no right to put themselves up in front of the public.

I looked around for Judy but I couldn't find her. I guessed she had gone to her room. I was heading toward the kitchen, thinking vaguely of hot coffee, and it was some time after the body had been found and the world was full of murky daylight when we were all herded into the vast living room. Mr. Fish had a few words for us.

I guess I was staring at Judy like a lovesick pup. I wanted to check on how she looked in daylight. I wanted to know what she liked for breakfast, how long she'd owned that beat-up sweater, what books she read, what sort of things made her cry, what size shoes she wore.

And I heard Fish saying something crazy. I stared at him and finally caught on. Not an accident. Not just a drowning. Not a fatal combination of alcohol, darkness, and lake water. But a hole in the back of her head.

So instead of a drunken scandal, we had us a nice juicy murder. Brother! I started thinking of a million things all at once, relating it all back to the job I was trying to do. Effect on the market? What approved advertising programs would be in bad taste now? Who would be running the whole thing now?

We were warned to stick around pending the arrival of more important brass. I surrendered my car keys to a trooper. Noel Hess had walked out on the group. People had begun to mill around. The other trooper was talking to Judy. I was thinking of some good way to break it up and get her off where I could talk to her. Just talk. Just look at her. She made the trooper laugh. Beyond Judy I could see Mavis, not crying, her face unpleasantly bloated

103

with too many tears for too long a time. Mavis looked shocked and angry.

I saw it start to happen and at first I didn't understand and thought it was some sort of game in poor taste, and then when I did see what was going to happen, saw Judy turning to stare too, there was a moment when I felt as though I stood neck-deep in glue, unable to move or speak. It went on in slow motion. In horrid slow motion, with descending glint of brass, and nothing in the world could stop it. And nothing did.

Then the trooper and I got there at the same moment. Too late.

Too late. I saw the oiled blue arc, heard the bite of impact, the face turned up and still and away for a moment before the falling. And all of us there for a moment, a tableau, stillness, with the memory of a scream clotted against the high walls, so that in turning, so as not to look, I saw Judy's eyes, saw them on me, clear and real and known, and took a half step toward her.

The young doctor knelt. I saw his face when he looked up. It is all the same to them. Always they meet the same adversary, though he may wear many masks. It's an adversary that always wins. And the doctors, those fighters of delaying actions, must wear closed faces.

It was ended, of course, and nothing would ever be the same again.

Chapter Eleven

(Judy Jonah—Before)

THERE WAS a special expression the photographer wanted for the still that would be a part of a testimonial, and after it was over I walked up Madison to Forty-sixth, feeling as if somebody had used a sponge on my face. I told myself it would keep me young—maybe. Muscle tone or something.

Hilda smiled and said Willy was alone and I could go right on in. He got up from behind his gray steel desk and patted my shoulder and looked at me with the concern of a family doctor and patted me into a chair.

"Judy, honest to Gawd, you look nineteen."

"Good old Willy. Boy of my dreams." Willy is built close to the floor. He has no hair, a size twenty neck, and a pair of big soft damp brown eyes, like an abused setter's. Several generations ago he did songs and light chatter and a soft-shoe routine on the Keith circuit. Now he agents. He's a fighter and he's sharp. And he stays as honest as he can and still keep his self-respect.

"This I will get over with quickly, Judy. Carlos and Jane want out. Now understand. They're good kids. I can keep them tied down. You know that. They'll stick. But it looks like a break for them."

"Let 'em go, Willy. No. I'll talk to them. I'll do it. They're good. They ought to have their own show."

He leaned back and laced fingers across his tummy. "I knew you'd say that, but I sort of wished you wouldn't. If you were tougher..."

"Tough like you, Willy?"

"The wrong business, kid. Both of us. But if it breaks right, I got people. We can put something together that will knock them dead."

"It's been a long time, Willy. I think you better let me have it between the eyes. I think you better stop kidding Judy. I think you owe me that, Willy."

105

He fumbled with a yellow pencil. "O.K." He picked up the pencil. He wrote down five names. He slid the piece of paper across to me. I read the names, nodded. He said, "Big-time they were. In 1951. Their own shows. Nice ratings. Fat. This damn medium, it eats you. It's like this: Suppose a guy likes pickled beets. So for a year his wife feeds him pickled beets twice a day. Then what? He never wants to see another beet. Radio, you could last. Tough, but you could last, given the writers. But this damn thing, they see you and hear you. Judy-Time has had what? Over a hundred weeks. Better than the ratings is ticket requests for the studio. They go by that. Those five on the list, where are they? One is singing in Paris for peanuts. One is on radio sustaining out of Chicago. One of them in a casino in Brazil, for God's sake. And the other two, they could find work, but it isn't good enough work for them. They think they're still on top, but they're dead. This thing, it eats you up, and then it's a hell of a long drop to the next thing because ... right between the eyes like you said ... people get damn sick and tired of looking at you. Pickled beets."

"One more season, Willy?"

He shook his head. "I doubt the hell out of it. You could put a show together. Put it on the market. See who you could get by paying scale, and it would still eat up your bankroll before you could find any kind of sponsor. And the odds are you won't. The word is out."

"How about a new kind of show? Situation stuff."

"I know you could do it. I know it would be good. But it's a hell of a gamble. Take it this way: Why gamble? You've got it made. It's tucked away. How much living have you done lately?"

"Not much, Willy. Not much at all."

He made a lunge across the desk and grabbed my hand. It startled me. His voice got hoarse. "Look, Judy. Like an ad. Switch to Willy. Not easy on the eyes, but easy on the nerves. I haven't got anybody any more. We can get a place maybe in Connecticut. My God, grass. Trees. I can commute. I mean you don't have to be in love with me. That, maybe, would be a good trick. But we talk the same. We think the same. We could make it work."

Those brown eyes nearly got me. But he saw the answer on my face. He released my hand. He said spiritlessly, "Well, it was a try."

"I'm sorry, Willy. I mean that. I wish it could be."

He smiled. "I guess you do." He sort of shook himself like a fat dog coming out of the creek. "Now, what's all this thing with that Ferris woman?"

"She wants me up there. She says it's purely social. But she let me know Dorn would be there. And the sales manager, Dockerty. And Steve Winsan."

"My word to you. Drop Winsan. A luxury at this point. Look, girl. The standard advice, no commitments, is out. Because up there you get no offer. I can smell that. This is the hatchet."

"I think so too. Just a question of how she does it."

"That woman, she's a sadist. She gets a sexy bang out of squashing people like bugs. You got to go up there with a special attitude. You got to go up there saying to yourself, I couldn't care less. Can you do that?"

"I can do it without even pretending, Willy. I'm just . . . so damn tired. I think I want the hatchet."

"Then what will you do?"

"Get out, Willy. Get rid of all the junk. Load the wagon and head west. Change this hair to black so I don't get stared at. I want a mountain cabin twenty miles from no place, with a stream in the back yard and a grassy bank to lie on, and a bunch of books that will be tough to read. Hard books. There's things I want to do. Learn the constellations. Learn to cook. You know, all I can do is fry stuff. I just want to slob around, Willy, and take walks and turn into plain Jane Jones."

"Take me along."

"We've been through that, Willy," I said, smiling.

"O.K. Look, don't let that bitch unravel you, Judy. Ride with it. I don't know Dockerty. That Wallace Dorn is a chunk of nothing. Steve will be on your side, just to save his fee on you, but he won't be able to do a damn thing. Don't let her get you sore. She's the kind who'll ask you to do some routines for free to entertain her guests. If so, you got a headache."

"A brute of a headache."

I said good-by to Willy. I went to see Carlos and Jane. They were shy and apologetic and they acted ashamed. But it wasn't hard to see the joy and excitement when I told them I'd release them. Then they kept interrupting each other telling me about their chance. It sounded hot. It made me

107

feel old. It made me feel as if never again would I be able to hoke up that much enthusiasm over anything.

Friday morning after I packed I phoned the garage and had them bring the white Jag around. When I leaned out the window and looked down, it was parked right in front, and Horace, the doorman, was talking to the garage man, who was unhooking his little delivery motorcycle from the rear bumper. The Jag was pretty in the morning sun. From up there at the window, it looked like a boat. I took the two bags down and Horace helped me stow them in the car, one in the tiny luggage space and one in the spare bucket seat beside me. To Horace I'm a riot. I ask him what time it is and he goes into helpless laughter. It's very wearing.

As I drove north on the parkway, I pretended it was all over and this was the first leg of my trip west. But it didn't feel right. Because, I decided, the car was part of the window dressing. Part of what I would be leaving behind. I loved it, loved its fine response, but it was just too damn gaudy for the mood I was going to be in. And not enough room in it for a girl to carry along everything she had left in the wide world. Nice as it was, there was something a little phony about it. A little bit too too.

So this was going to be the hatchet, and I couldn't care less.

Or could I?

Hess had mailed me a marked map, so I had no trouble finding the place. Steve was getting out of his car when I drove in. The place wasn't exactly a cabin. It looked like an outpost of the United Nations. Steve and I talked a little business.

Every time I talk to him, I keep remembering how I had to set him back on his heels. Guys like that. The town is loaded with them. That big palsy approach with the hand that wanders. I busted him across the chops. That public eye. Rumors and rumors. Snicker and smirk. Now you take that Judy Jonah. Man, oh, man. Hot pants. Dirty little men and it makes them big in the bars when they can give that reflective leer and lip smack and thusly label you round of heel. Round enough so the other dirty little men who hear them have to make their try at you. You smack them down, but their vanity won't let them admit it to the brethren in the bars. Then they, too, add themselves to the mythical list of your lovers. It's the same with any other presentable gal in show business. We all have to stand for the same thing. Rarely, very rarely, there will be one who tries to live up to the billing she gets in the cocktail lounges. And, in trying, will fizz out of the business like a wet rocket. The fringe gals, who end up by calling themselves models and paper the town with their uptown phone numbers. And collect pictures of ex-presidents. By the time they work their way down to Grant, they're still around. But by the time they get down to Hamilton and Lincoln, they've moved their base of operations. Juárez or Troy. Milwaukee or Bakersfield.

But the myth persists, and I won't say that Steve had been suckered by it. I'll say only that he's the type that always makes the automatic try. Though seldom belted as hard as that. He had to wrap an ice cube in a napkin and hold it against his lip. Poor lad.

He led me around the house. I could see that he had the jitters, even though he had anointed himself liberally with ersatz confidence. Wilma and the Hesses and Gilman Hayes were on the terrace. Hayes nodded at me with his normal cold-eyed contempt. Three times I have met him. I started out with a violent dislike, and each time since I have liked him less. But a chunk of male. Biblical movies he should be in. In the Roman arena, with shield and sword and one of those metal dinguses around his biceps. Everybody says he's good. I saw one of his things. A bunch of black lines like a wrought-iron fence after a tornado, with some big blobby things behind it. It had a title. "Reversion." I gave it my rapt look because the owner was damn proud of it. But it meant nothing to me. It could be good. That's one of the things I'll take along some books about.

My room was plush and the weather was fine, so I skinned quickly into my suit and trotted down to the big twin docks. Hayes was prone in the sun. The water was blue. With eyes shut against the glare I felt as though Wilma, up on her terrace, were watching me, with some mental licking of chops.

I concentrated so much on keeping my guard up that I sort of blinded myself to what was going on around me. Steve and Hayes and the Hesses and the Dockertys and Wallace Dorn were just part of the scenery. I suppose I nodded and spoke in the right places, but I was as aware of Wilma as is the mouse of the cat.

I didn't begin to react to people until after we had dinner,

109

and I got snared into a Scrabble game with Paul Dockerty and Wallace Dorn, while Mavis Dockerty danced with Gilman Hayes, and Steve and Wilma played rabid gin. Wallace Dorn, whenever it was his turn, took a great deal of time. I sat and smoked and listened to the Latin music while Randy jangled around like a bride in the late afternoon. Noel Hess, mild, dark, watchful, and pretty, had gone to bed. She seemed to me like a toy I had once. A girl clown standing on a drum. You wound her up. She whirled around and around and the music was inside the drum. Then I wound her up too tightly and the spring snapped. No music and no more whirling for Noel. Randy had snapped her spring. It's sad. It's something that happens. It's the reaction one sort of woman will have. Another would pack her bag and take off. Another would bend his skull for him. But the Noels sit around with snapped springs. I'm more the skull-bending type.

I watched Mavis Dockerty. Her dancing was pretty clinical. Paul Dockerty sat at my left, studying the Scrabble board. What is that word? Empathy. Yes. That's what I had then. For Paul. A nice big decent-looking guy with a very silly lady. And said lady under Wilma's dark spell. I had the feeling they could have gone along indefinitely with a fair to middling marriage. But Wilma was steering it firmly toward the rocks. Using Hayes, perhaps, as one of the rocks. Maybe at one point in the past Paul would have got up and broken up the dance act. He had enough reason to. But they'd gone by that point. So he had to sit and sweat it out. I could see by the little glances he'd flash toward them that he was edgy about it, and didn't know what to do about it. And maybe he was close to the point of not wanting to do anything about it. I saw Hayes dance her out onto the terrace. I guess Paul didn't see the change of dance floors. I saw him look around and saw his face harden and change and saw him start to get up. I put my hand out quickly and stopped him and jerked my head toward the terrace. He looked through the glass and saw them. He relaxed a bit as he saw them. Then he looked at me. Grateful. I gave him a public-property-type grimace.

Dorn beat us both badly and we paid off. I wanted some fresh air. Paul surprised me by asking if he could go along. I didn't want to be any part of one of those husband-wife jealousy gambits, but I sensed right away that he wasn't trying to pull anything like that.

We went down onto the dock and he flipped the wet mat over to give us a dry side to sit on. There's a funny intimacy about sitting in the night under stars. And I always talk too much. I'd wanted to keep my guard up all the way, but I found myself gibbering on about being tired. He was that kind of guy. The safe, kindly breed. The kind that always disarms me.

Once upon a time a drunken psychiatrist told me, at a party, what makes Judy tick. He said, "Your spotty emotional life, dear, is the result of trudging through the world looking for the father you never had." And it was just right enough to make me self-conscious. Just right enough to chill me.

So it is with the Paul Dockertys that I find my hair coming down. I had yakked too much. It was late. I felt ashamed of myself, so I got up and clowned it, doing my Kid Jonah, the Boston Butcher Boy.

So what does he do? He grabs me by the arm and sort of shakes me and tells me he likes me. I don't know how I got off the dock without blubbering. I said some stiff-faced good nights on my way through the big room, and I got my door shut and draped myself carefully across my bed and said go. But no dice for Judy. No tears. What can you do with a girl like that?

I know what I did with her. I scrubbed her face, brushed her teeth, put her in pajamas, and put her into bed. I managed one muted and unsatisfactory sniffle, and then I went to sleep.

There was one dream that was a beaut. Like they say, significant. They had shoved me in front of the cameras. Something experimental. But not the cameras I'm used to. No booms, no dollies. A room shaped like the inside of a beehive, and the inside of it was all camera lenses. All looking in at me. I tried to make up lines, and when I would say them, all the echoes would get in the way. I danced and there wasn't any music. Then all of a sudden I was in Delcy's office standing and yelling at him, telling him I never was any good on ad-lib stuff and I didn't like this new idea of his, and he just kept smiling at me, his eyes goggly behind those thick lenses of his. And he told me that it came out well, no matter what I thought. I asked him what he meant. And he said I was standing on it. I looked down and the floor of his office was all new linoleum, like a kitchen. Big squares. And in each square there was a naked photograph of me, in color. Then I

111

suddenly realized that he'd tricked me. They hadn't broadcast it at all. And each camera had made one square of linoleum. So he had no more use for me, because there'd been enough cameras to cover his whole office. Wall to wall. And he said in a voice that echoed around, "Look closer. They move. Look closer. They move. Look closer. . . ."

And I woke up and the sun was out and my heart was trying to jump out of my chest.

I ate much breakfast, swam some, and then went through my body-building routine on the dock, while the rest played. Midway through the routine I became aware of Paul watching me with unmistakable approval. I also noticed that he had started drinking bright and early. Mavis seemed pointedly unaware of him. She was busy shrieking and giggling and preening herself while Hayes taught her how to water ski. In a swimsuit she was a remarkable hunk of woman. I wondered what sort of sickly brawl the Dockertys had arranged after shutting the door behind them.

I think that if Paul had been leering at me, or had even been sly about staring at me, I would have knocked off the exercises right there. But the big lunk just stared at me with such warm and wistful approval that I even added a few exercises I don't normally do. Old Judy the Jonah, exhibitionist.

During the croquet I saw the drinks catching up. Not that he was alone in making a fool of himself. There was one particularly nasty little scene when Wilma whonked Randy with a mallet. And Steve and Noel were getting that look in their eyes. And Gilman Hayes was bunching his muscles like a health ad. And Wallace Dorn is a fool all the time. Poor Paul was just honestly drunk. And getting worse.

When he disappeared after being unable to eat anything, I looked for him and found him in the corner of the living room, sitting like a punished child, licking his lips and swallowing hard, eyes not focusing too well.

"Upsy-daisy, baby," I said. I got his hand and tugged him up. He was a weight. "Come on, now. One big fat foot after the other."

"Where's everybody?" he said, with a ghost of the party fever.

I got him into the hall, down to their room, and into his bed. I pulled his shoes off and covered him up with a blanket.

"Preciate it," he said. "Preciate it."

112

I looked down at him. Poor guy. Out of his league. 'Way in over his head. All mixed up. "Poor old bear," I said, and, on impulse, leaned over him and kissed him lightly on the lips. Then I went out and shut the door behind me.

I went down and took what I thought was enough sun. Steve and Noel, in one of the boats, had disappeared behind a distant island. That was sad too. Everything was sad. I was depressing myself. What wasn't sad was nasty. Jude the Prude.

I thought of old days, old places. The boys certainly got wild enough and weird enough, and, from certain angles, nasty enough. Thumb-in-the-eye nasty. Broken-bottle nasty. Tear up the joint, smash the mirrors. Take advantage of dumb little music-struck girls. Hit the tea and steal liquor and take a quick hack at the wife of the guy who owned the particular joint where we happened to be playing.

But at least, with all that, they were doing something. They were making some music. Giving that horn a high wild ride on top of that fat beat of the bass. Lordy! Blue smoke and people thumping tables and that wild horn riding, riding, glinting the yellow brass lights, the rapt eyes half shut. Sure, a rough and nasty crew, but making something. And this crew was nasty in subtler ways and they didn't make anything. They just stirred each other with sticks.

I went up to my room. As I went by Wilma's half-open door she said, "Judy, dear?"

I shrugged and went in. "Hi, Wilma."

"Are you having a good time?" She was sitting at a dressing table doing something with her nails.

"A dandy time," I said.

"Please sit down, dear. It's time we had a little talk."

"Isn't it, though!"

She gave me a glance like a scalpel and looked back at her nails. "I've been thinking about you, Judy. Trying to find some answers. You see, just out of loyalty, I'd like to be able to use you again this coming fall. I hate to let people go."

I wanted to tell her that at no time had I been aware of exactly working for her. But I remembered Willy's warning and so I just sat.

"I've wondered what made you so popular for a time. I think I know now. You're a rather pretty woman, Judy. There's a certain amount of sensitivity in your face. And you have a pleasant little voice."

113

"Thanks," I said a bit darkly.

She rode right over me. She frowned. "Humor, I suppose, is really the unexpected, isn't it? So really there is something grotesque and, I suppose, amusing, about an attractive girl throwing herself around and trying to look her worst instead of her best. Goo running down your face and all that. And it will charm the public for a while. But it isn't anything you can continue indefinitely, now, is it?"

I had news for her. She had a few things to know about timing, emphasis. How you can smell the audience and underplay when you should and underline when you have to. How you work on the show, adding stuff, throwing stuff out, picking what's best for you.

She put her tools down and faced me squarely. "You have to face the fact, dear, that as far as the public is concerned, you've ceased to be funny. All you had was a certain shock value. I've told Wallace to try to find a replacement for you. But, you see, I take a personal interest in your future. Have you ever thought about taking acting lessons?"

I lit a cigarette and huffed the smoke in her general direction. "Back up a minute, sis. I'm through. Is that what you're saying?"

She smiled. "Quite."

"You, milady, are a rough apple. You're rough as a cob. But leave us restate the case. I sold you my services through my agent and through your advertising agency. Your opinion of my future, or lack of same, interests me about as much as does spherical geometry. So let's knock off the personal approach, shall we?"

"I'm sorry I hurt your feelings, dear."

"You haven't," I said, trying to match smiles, but my hand trembled and I knew, damnit, that she saw it.

"I don't care if you despise me, Judy. I'm just saying this for your own good. You're young. You're at a dead end. You *must* start thinking of what you're going to do with your life."

"I'll do fine with my life."

"You've had the sort of publicity that can go to a person's head. You people fall into the trap of believing what other people are paid to say about you. You know that, don't you?"

"It happens to some."

"I didn't want to do this through middlemen, Judy. I thought we could talk nicely to each other."

114

"We're talking."

"Smart promotion made you queen for a day. That day is definitely over. You must face that, you know."

I got up. They don't call it a retreat any more. They call it shortening your lines of communication. A big one-legged Marine told me that. "I appreciate all your advice, Mrs. Ferris. Miss Ferris. Whatever it is legally. I can scoot off right now, or stay through to the bitter end, whichever you please."

"I wouldn't *think* of your leaving now."

I looked into those eyes. I wondered how her nail scissors would look sticking out of her throat. "Like I said, thanks."

"You're more than welcome, Judy."

I didn't start really shaking until I got to my room. Even if the Judy fad had faded, I'd still had one thing: pride in being a workman. A trooper. A pro. And, damn her eyes, she's picked that one thing to work on. Fourteen years of show business didn't mean a thing. I was a girl they threw goo at, for shock value. Maybe everybody thought that. Damn her! So poisonously sweet, and taking an aimed kick at your best prop. Well, she'd wobbled me badly. Put a few fracture lines in my supports. But I'd last. I always had.

But I was going to spend a lot of time thinking of ways to kill her. Acting lessons! For God's sake. Be a willow tree. Be smoke rising from a fire. Be a sad grasshopper. I'd see Willy and I'd put a show back together, and find a sponsor and shove the show right down her throat.

But . . .

I sat there on the bed and looked at my hands. I sat and felt as if she'd poisoned me. Rejection. Something you put in the blood stream. It dulls the reflexes, waters down hope, hamstrings pride.

I had been going to change. Instead, I put on a robe and headed back out. I wanted a highball that would look like iced coffee. I wanted a fist fight. I wanted a chance to make a big gesture. Any kind.

When it was night we were splashing around. Then they had to take off their suits and turn off the lights and be real bold. Steve called me chicken. I told him I'd got over being childish when I'd got over being a child. I told them about Hash. About how all of us came in on the train into Penn Station and Hash made his bet and I held the stakes. One hundred and twenty bucks he bet. He had to get from

115

the train to the taxi stark naked. He made quite a stir as he went through the station, running like the wind, suitcase in one hand, tram case in the other. Would have made it, too, but his bare feet slipped and he hit his head when he went down. He was fined a hundred bucks. I told them anybody could swim thusly if it was his inclination. But it took a different kind of mind to Minsky your way through Penn Station.

Randy, Wallace, and I were the conformists. I swam around at a safe distance. Randy stayed on the dock, I think. Much giggling and splashing and games. How gay in the wilderness! I wondered what the loons thought. And the perch. I thought, so help me, of how enjoyable it would be if friend Wilma floated down the creek at the end of the lake and on down the river and out to sea.

So when the shouting began to make sense and I suddenly became aware of trouble and made the dock and scrambled up and found out Wilma was gone, it gave me a feeling of nightmare. As if my wish had been too strong. A feeling of guilt. I got my robe on. Come on, Judy. You're a comic. Say something funny now.

Chapter Twelve

(STEVE WINSAN—AFTERWARD)

THERE IS an old, not so funny Hollywood story about two studio heads walking down the street trying to think up a good sequence for a picture in process. Every time one of them gets an idea, he acts it out, with gestures. And the other shakes his head sadly. A safe is being lowered out of an office window. The rope breaks. The safe lands with damp finality on one of the two executives. The other one looks at the scene in eye-bulging horror and then yells, "Too gruesome, Sammy! We can't use it!"

There I was. Idea boy. Standing on the dock and thinking I should call Wilma and get her back in. Too gruesome, kid. We can't use it. It isn't a good PR pitch. The public won't go for it.

And then the night got bigger and blacker. The hills got older. The sky got farther away. The lake got deeper and darker. I shivered. You live in a place full of light bulbs and chrome and rare fillets and box-top contests. But when you die, you die in a place of mountains and sky, earth and fire, stars and the sea. I felt tiny as hell. I didn't like the feeling. I felt like a pasteboard man on a dock somebody built with a toy kit, looking at the real world for the first time.

Up until that moment I had a fighting chance. I might have been able to wiggle things around so as to save my own bacon by retaining at least one of the three sagging accounts. And that one was going to be Wilma. At least, working through Randy, with Noel working on him, I seemed to have the best chance there. I stood there and I saw an imaginary office in an almost first-rate hotel, and me in the office on a stinking salary beating my brains out trying to fatten the guest list with almost first-rate people, with the fractured nobility and with Texans who didn't know any better, and trying to angle the name of the house into the columns of those big warmhearted columnists who would crucify their dear old mothers if by so doing they could add one more paper to the string.

And then that lovely vision faded as I suddenly saw what was being handed me on a platter. It kindled a little fire of excitement in the pit of my stomach and then roared up through the flue. I felt twice life size. This was going to be it. When they recovered the body, I wanted to kiss the stone-cold forehead.

It meant I had to do some very fancy operating. I had to be light on my feet. While I was still thinking, Paul enlisted me to go out there and do some futile diving for the body. I hoped we wouldn't find her right away. Because it might be possible to revive her. This was going to be Steve's big chance. I dived on order, but I did damn little hunting. I was too busy thinking.

The tabloid boys were going to try to turn this into a sensation. There was all the raw material there. When the body was recovered, it was going to be awfully bare. And the house full of lintheads who would talk too much. We had to have a plot, a better one than the one we were stuck with. And the brass that would swoop down on us had to be handled. I would have to coach the people in the new plot and make it consistent. And keep the working press off their backs until they had it clearly in mind. The thing that seemed to make the most sense was to say that we'd all come up here to work out an idea for a new fall show, headlining Judy Jonah. Hayes could be worked into the idea somehow. Maybe sets, costumes. O.K., so we had the sales manager, the account executive, a public-relations consultant, her business manager. If it was handled right, it might generate a lot of public interest in the fall show, and might even make it worth while using Jonah again. The deal on the swimming was what would make it tough. It was too sweet a tabloid angle. What I should do was get to her room and get hold of a suit and smuggle it out and rip it a little and get it into the water. They would probably drag for the body. If I could get the suit on one of the grapples, the whole thing would look better.

If I could cool it all off, if I could give them nothing to chew on, then Steve Winsan would be known around town as the bright eyes who saved the ball game. And that would mean new people on the list.

I was getting pretty pooped with all the diving. Paul had us knock off as the officials arrived. I hung around to see

118

what would go on. Cold as I was. Then the one named Fish caught me flat-footed by finding Wilma's suit in the pocket of her robe. I went up to my room and dried off and changed and went back down, thinking hard all the time. I wanted to get them apart and tell them what I had cooked up. But Fish intercepted me on the dock.

"What's your name again?"

"Winsan. Steve Winsan."

"O.K., Mr. Winsan. Get in that boat there. That's Will Agar. Got to have two men in a boat, one on the oars and one on the grapple."

"But . . ."

"Suppose you co-operate, Mr. Winsan."

"I've got some phone calls to make."

"I already told the operator not to take any calls from this number unless I make them, so you don't have to worry about it. Just get in the boat there and Will will tell you what he wants done."

What could I do? I got in the boat. Will was all teeth, Adam's apple, and adenoids. Somebody yelled from the dock. "You, Will, go make your sweep to the north of Bobby."

The grapple was a crude thing, a piece of pipe on a heavy line with gang hooks fastened in a row.

Will said, "Now if she comes fast, pull slow and easy. If it's the body, it'll come up slow. But if it goes tight, we got bottom. Then we got to work it loose."

I looked toward the shore in complete despair. They'd turned out some of the floods, the ones that were in our eyes. I could count fifteen boats. Holding the line, I could feel the pipe bumping along the bottom, dragging the hooks after it. Every once in a while we would catch. Each time it happened, it would give me a feeling of shock. Will would clamber back and test the tension of the line. "Hung up again," he'd say. He'd circle back and work it loose. I was trapped out there in full view of the house, with no way of knowing what the damn fools there were saying to the officials. The house lights were on. I could see people moving around once in a while. And sometimes they'd wander out on the dock, alone or in pairs, and look out at us. Will wasn't scintillating company. The long slow hours passed. My hands were getting raw from tugging the rough line loose. I had no cigarettes left. We would finish a sweep and then somebody would tell us where to go next. I could see a night city editor

119

someplace. "You know, that Ferris woman. Lake Vale. I don't give a damn if you don't know where it is. Somebody knows where it is. Get one of those guys who fly fishermen around in float planes. I'm lining up somebody for pics. Phone your stuff in to Saul. He's got all the stuff out of the morgue on her."

And I was afraid that while I was still out in this stinking rowboat I'd start seeing flash bulbs popping. With me out here fishing. Everything was a dull milky gray when Will said quietly, "O.K., pull it up, Mr. Winsan."

I asked him why. He didn't answer. I turned and looked at him. He was looking at a boat about forty feet away. That boat had a kerosene lantern on one of the seats. There were two old guys in it. They were gingerly pulling in a line, hand over hand, both staring at the surface of the black water. For a few moments there it looked like one of those old paintings. The two old guys with the light orange on their faces, and the light making a flickering path on the water. Other boats had stopped moving. The world seemed very still. I saw the heavy whiteness break the surface, and then one man yelped and the other made a lunge, nearly upsetting their boat. The lantern rocked dangerously.

"Here she is, boys," a cracked old voice sang out.

They got together and worked her up over the side. She came over the side, white and heavy, the lanterns making wet highlights on her, her head loose, black hair pasted flat. I heard the thumping as she tumbled onto the bottom of the boat. They covered her up and we headed in and the other boats came along.

People were coming down from the house. I got out onto the dock. A big trooper and I were the nearest when the two old men came up beside the dock. We knelt and reached down for her as they strained and lifted her up. We got her. My God, she was heavy. She felt as heavy as two women, with that tarp wrapped loosely around her. The trooper tripped and half sat down backward and I couldn't hold the weight, even though I tried. All I got was an end of the tarp and she rolled out, flaccid. In the lights she was a funny color. One eye was open. The other was covered with her black hair, wet and covering half her face. We fumbled to cover her up again, and I heard Judy Jonah yell at us to make it quick.

I had forgotten my earlier feeling of coming too close to reality, and this brought it all back again. There was some-

120

thing immutable about that silent shape. You couldn't tell it to go away. There were no lamps to rub, no incantations to say. It was there and undeniable and dead.

There was a room. They took me to a doorway. A strange woman took me to the doorway. There was a stink of flowers. She gave me a little push. "Go in and say good-by to her, Stevie." I went in. There was satin and silver handles. It wasn't my mother. They had made it out of wax, and my mother never was so pink and still. And her hands were not like that. Not like white sticks with blue nails. Not so still. They had been busy hands. Busy with soap and towels and brush and broom and quick caresses.

I turned and ran and the woman caught me and tried to hold me against her and I hit her with my fist and I guess I hurt her because she slapped me and then I cried and we both cried.

It had been a long time since I had remembered that. I stood very still. They were telling us to get off the dock. I looked at a slim dark-haired woman. I couldn't remember for a moment who she was. Noel. Like meeting someone on the street. You haven't seen them for a long time. And I remembered, but remembering did not chase away any ghosts.

I went to my room. I rolled up my sleeves. I scrubbed my hands. I wanted to scrub the skin off them. I wanted to get rid of the skin that had touched the heaviness of the body on the dock. I walked slowly toward the door to the corridor. And I heard someone coming. A woman. I opened the door. It was Noel. I spoke to her and took her hand and pulled her into the room and closed the door again. She would know where Randy was. I wanted to talk to him first. He could split the job with me. Maybe we'd have time enough.

She said he was still sleeping. I looked at her. She was a stranger. But there are times when you need the closeness of a stranger. I put my hands on her slim waist and pulled her close to me, and kissed her hard, with a sort of defiance, trying to kiss away all this tarp and flowers and grapple business. But even as I was kissing her, I remembered the afternoon, and remembered that it hadn't gained me anything. I'd just got her emotionally involved. I had to find out where she stood. And, from her attitude, figure a way of untangling myself. She certainly wasn't a hell of a lot to look at. And she looked at me with a discouragingly glazed and sappy expression.

121

So I delved a bit, cautiously, and found out, much to my relief, that she was off on a noble-wife kick. Standing bravely beside the unemployed husband. All very soap sales. It was an easy script to follow. I took my role. The disappointed lover. But not too insistent. The last thing I wanted to do was talk her out of the noble-wife part.

"Then," I said bravely, "I'm to consider this the brush-off?"

It shows you how wrong you can be sometimes. I thought the little minx had been all loaded with sincerity. And what do I hear? One of my own lines, usually used in the brush-off scene. "We *are* a couple of adults, aren't we?"

My surprise showed. And she told me it didn't mean as much as we said it did. I tell you, with that acting ability, she could have landed a part.

I ruffled her hair and made with the "just grateful for knowing somebody like you" gambit. My kind of people. That's what she was. I had a twinge of conscience about all the time I was losing, but suddenly I wanted her again. Maybe whenever there is death and violence around, you start wanting somebody. Maybe nature does it to you. Like affirming that you are the one who is alive. And we sat on the bed. But before it could become particularly interesting, the maid tapped on the door and said we were all wanted in the living room.

I decided right away that was for the best. It broke it up and kept me from wasting any more good time. We made some fast repairs and got ready to go. I checked the hall and it was clear. I was amused at the way she had fooled me. Fooled old Steve, the expert. And I felt affectionate toward her. So as she moved by me in the doorway I gave her a little love pat.

Once I was at a zoo. A human-interest thing, I think it was. Baby zebras or something. Can't remember. But I remember the big tawny cat. It was asleep. One big paw was through the bars. A typical linthead tourist had picked up a little stick. He leaned over the railing and he was jabbing at the exposed paw, showing his cretin children what a big brave guy he was, poking at a lion.

One minute the lion was asleep. The next minute that big paw flicked by the guy's face so fast that he jumped back long after it had gone by. His kids started crying. His complexion was like spoiled library paste.

I just patted her and she whirled and raked me. Her face was all twisted up and she hissed as she did it. And then she was gone. I stood and called her every name in the book and then went in and looked at myself in the mirror. Two long deep ones, with blood gathering slowly. I washed them. I found iodine in the cabinet, and some tape. I patched myself up. She had no damn reason in the world to do that. Not a reason in the wide world. Nobody does that to me. I decided right then and there that I'd get her apart from the others somehow. I'd get her out beside the house and back her up against a wall. I wouldn't mark her, but I'd damn well teach her a lesson she wouldn't forget in a hurry. A couple of good solid thumps in the belly teaches them some manners. It knocks the wind and the fight out of them.

I was the last one to arrive in the living room. I got a cold stare from everybody, and I saw the flicker of speculation as they looked at my taped face and wondered. I saw Judy glance at the tape and then look immediately at Noel.

Even the servants were there, and the young doc with the sideburns. I sat as far away from Noel as I could get. I caught her eye and gave her a hard look.

Fish started talking, and as soon as I got the sense of what he was saying, I forgot all about Noel and my plans and everything else except the fact of murder. For a time my mind was just a damn blank, with a great big red M printed across it. And then the damnedest thing. If she drowned, it was an accident, and something like that could not happen to Wilma. She had to be murdered. My God, she had been born to be murdered. Pushing people. Always pushing. No truth or sincerity in her. Everything an angle. Everything had to be used for her benefit. It was just a case of which damn worm had turned.

And thinking of worms, I looked at Randy Hess.

We got our orders, and we were told that the big brass was coming. I jumped at the first hunk of silence that came along, asking permission to handle the working press on this whole thing. Fish was dubious. I oiled him a little and saw him lean my way. Noel took off. It began to break up into little groups. Fish and the doctor got me aside. I was explaining how I would operate.

I looked over the doctor's shoulder.

Ever since that moment I've been explaining it to myself. Here is what I say to myself: There is something inside you that goes 'way the hell back. Primitive. Atavistic. I keep telling myself that it was just as automatic as yanking your hand back when you put it on a hot stove. Nothing you can control. No part of guts or lack of same. Just a reaction. One minute I was looking and I saw it, and the next second I was running like hell in the opposite direction. I went through the door so fast that my hands slapped hard against the corridor wall as I made the turn. And I ran all the way down to my room before I stopped. I stopped and I listened.

I keep telling myself it was just an instinctive reaction. I mean nobody has given me a bad time about it. They've looked at me in a funny way, but nobody has given me a bad time. I'd suspect that they've talked. You know. Good story over a five-o'clock shot. But what the hell.

I wish I could stop thinking about it. It comes up at the damnedest times. When I ought to have my mind on what I'm doing.

This isn't a bad job, and I'd like to keep it. But if I keep goofing off, going 'way back there and thinking how I ran, I'm going to flub stuff, the way I messed up the timing yesterday meeting that train. And lose this job.

It isn't a bad job. There are twelve theatres in the chain. But now Mr. Walsh has got this idea I should dress up like a damn Martian and walk up and down in front of the Times Square house for this 3D horror thing. I keep telling him it's a job for an usher or one of the assistant managers, but he keeps telling me I'm the publicity guy, aren't I?

It was just like the way you'd snatch your hand off a hot stove. You don't stop and think about it first, do you?

I'd argue more, but I keep thinking about that Sunday morning.

Do you?

Chapter Thirteen

(WALLACE DORN—BEFORE)

Years ago I put my foot down. Firmly. It isn't that I do not love Florence. She is my wife. She has carried and given birth to my children. But I had to forbid her presence at any of those social functions that are connected with my position at Fern and Howey.

I could not function properly while I waited in sick dread for her to put her foot in her mouth. And she always did. Invariably.

It isn't as though I keep her in a locked room. We have our own circle of friends and, thank God, none of them has anything to do with advertising, publishing, or the arts. They are plain people. There is nothing brittle or self-consciously clever about them. And I am very glad that most nights I am able to catch the five-twenty-two out of Grand Central Terminal.

Florence is a comfortable woman. There was a time, of course, prior to and for about a year after our marriage, when I thought she was an enormously exciting woman. It is easy to see now that what misled me was her great vitality. Her hair is red and her skin is very white, and her looks faded very quickly. She seemed to turn, in a few short months, from girl bride to heavy-set matron. But, though I was disappointed at the time, I would not have it otherwise. She knows my wants. She keeps the home neat, cooks well, is good-humored, and very pleasant with the children. They are healthy children.

Florence is not an intelligent woman. She has a certain native shrewdness, but no mental equipment with which to cope with the people I must deal with each day. I am the head of my household. I have seen to it that there is no doubt about that. Someone must command. Otherwise there is fuss and disorganization.

125

I have made it a point not to mention her or the fact of my marriage and my children to my coworkers. Thus many of them are astonished when they learn that I am married. They try to include her in invitations. I say she is not well. That, of course, is a lie. She is as strong as a good horse.

I have been, I believe, a good husband to her. My salary has increased steadily, though it has never been, and perhaps will never become, spectacular. Except for Ferris, the accounts I handle with Fern and Howey are small. I have an even temper around my home. I give Florence a rather generous allowance. Though I have been unfaithful, I consider those lapses as being, perhaps, an inevitable by-product of my occupation, and commend myself on the fact that there have been so few such episodes. No more than nine, I believe, during sixteen years of wedded life.

Each morning she drives me to our small rustic station and I get on the train, and during the forty-minute ride I compose myself for the work of the day and prepare the face I will show to the world. I pledge myself to go through each day with quiet dignity, with as much honor as is possible, with affability and understanding of the problems of others.

And it was with that same attitude that I arrived at Wilma Ferris' place at Lake Vale. But despite all vows, sometimes one finds oneself in a situation where dignity and honor are denied you. I despise such people, every one, except, perhaps, Paul Dockerty. He retains some of the instincts of a gentleman. Though, in a few more years, he too will be lost. I can save myself because I have a retreat. Each night I can go to my home, to my chair and pipe and robe, to the relaxation of a modicum of excellent Scotch, to quiet conversation, to a game of chess with my neighbor.

I knew, of course, that Wilma had poisoned Mr. Howey against me. And I knew that in inviting me she undoubtedly had more unpleasantness in mind. I even suspected that she wished to tell me that she was shifting her account to some other firm, perhaps to some brash outfit completely lacking in the dignity that has characterized Fern and Howey dealings since the establishment of the agency in 1893 by the elder Mr. Detweiler Fern. But I could not allow myself to think of such a contingency seriously. The implications were ghastly. Though Mr. Howey is, I trust, a man of honor, I believe he would feel that he should chastise me severely for the loss of the profitable Ferris account.

Though I did not care for the people, I enjoyed the opportunity of playing games. It took my mind away from the continual problem of what to do if Wilma did what I thought she might do. Scrabble is hardly a challenging game from an intellectual point of view. There are none of the clean rhythms and sequences of chess. I found Dockerty and the Jonah girl rather dull at it, and won handily.

When I said good night to Wilma, just as her game of gin rummy—infantile occupation—was breaking up, she gave me a glance as shrewd and alien and darting as the glance of a snake. It chilled me. After I was in bed I still felt cold. How have I offended her? I want nothing but the security of my job. Am I not good at my job? The Durbin Brothers, and Massey, Grunewald, and Star, and Bi-Sodium and Tichnor Instrument—they have always been satisfied. Every one.

The croquet game the next day was almost pleasant. It would have been far more pleasant had the others kept their minds on the competition. They seemed to have no great urge to win. They clowned grotesquely, and I was most disappointed in Paul Dockerty, getting as drunk as he did. I figured the proper angles, and the odds, and played crisply and well, finishing my circuit first, but avoiding the stake so that I could range back out across the court and aid the laggard members of my team as best I could. Wilma walked close to me at one point and put me badly off my form by murmuring, "Talk to you later, Buster."

Of all the possible names she could have selected for me, she picked the one most calculated to distress me. It is a name completely without dignity. While still tense and worried about her, I played badly, and my ball was captured and driven into the water. I retrieved it and, setting it down in the parking area, I regained the playing field with one stroke, and hit the stake firmly with my next stroke after seeing that my further efforts would not aid my teammates. I was pleased to see that we won.

Wilma saw me in her room before lunch. She had me sit down. She had a cigarette and she walked back and forth, from the door to her dressing table, walking in silence as my tension mounted.

"Miss Ferris, I . . ."

"Please hush, Buster. I'm thinking." That is typical of her. No form, no courtesy. Striding back and forth, ranging like a big cat in a cage, wearing that naked-looking sunsuit, the long muscles in her legs pulling and tightening with her strides, her dark hair bouncing.

Finally she stopped and faced me, looking down at me. "O.K., I've decided there's no nice way to tell you. Dockerty is doing a job as far as he can. But that creepy agency you work for is dead weight."

"Fern and Howey are one of the—"

"Hush. You've never come up with anything either good or original. You just submit to me a lot of fancy presentations of my own ideas. Watered down, usually. I've given you every chance. I thought that in spite of the people you work for, you might come through eventually. Dorn, you haven't had an idea of your own in fifteen years. So you're an expensive luxury. I need a younger, hungrier agency. Somebody with vitality and imagination. You people think you're in something a little like banking. Suits by Brooks Brothers. Dark paneling. Hushed voices. You bore me."

"Miss Ferris, I . . ."

"And you are the dullest man I've ever set eyes on. An imitation limey from Indiana. What are you trying to do? Inspire confidence? I am uninspired, Dorn. When I'm in town Monday I'll phone that unctuous Mr. Howey and kiss him off and pick myself something new. You can cancel out all that stuff they're working on over there that they laughingly call a campaign. My God, stop goggling at me! I can do this, you know."

"I wish you would reconsider," I said weakly.

"I have. Too many times," she said. I looked at her. Nobody knew it but Wilma and me. So far. I could see myself sitting across Mr. Howey's desk, his eyes like little swords.

I wished she would fall dead. I wished she would drop dead on the floor. And I could go to the office and be very upset and tell Mr. Howey that she had told me that she had decided the advertising appropriation should be increased, but had died before she could take steps.

I looked at her throat. I saw a pulse there. I stood up slowly. I couldn't permit this disorderly and ridiculous woman to put an end to a quiet and satisfying and honorable career. Advertising has become a respected profession. I am a respected man. She was doing this to me out of restlessness, out of whatever it was that was driving her. I stood up and my arms and hands felt heavy and powerful. She turned her

128

back on me and went over toward the dressing table. I took one silent step, my arms half lifted. She craned her arms up behind her in that graceful-awkward way of woman and worked at the snaps of the sunsuit top. She said in a flat bored voice, drained of emotion, "Now run along and play games or something, Dorn."

She released the top and took it off and sat down. I let my arms fall to my sides. They felt heavy, but no longer strong. I felt old. I felt as though I should totter as I walked, as though my voice should crack and quaver as I spoke.

I shut her door quietly behind me. I could smell food. Saliva flooded my mouth in sudden sickness. I went to my room. By the time I reached the bathroom the nausea was gone. But my face was sweaty. I dried it on a towel. I looked at my face in the mirror. It is a reliable face. Florence says it is easy to see the character expressed there. I was pale. The color came back slowly, darkening to customary healthy ruddiness. One side of my mustache looked a bit ragged. I took my shears from my kit, and a small comb, and clipped carefully. I stepped back and smiled at myself. That usually comforts me. It did not work. Because I did not know what I would do. I did not know where I would go. Next year I will be fifty. With my usual bonus I make nearly eighteen thousand dollars a year.

And I thought again of what I wanted to do to her. Of the brutal and exquisite pleasure of digging my fingers into the soft pulsing throat until her face darkened and her eyes went mad.

And the thought brought the nausea back. Perhaps because I am a fastidious man. Nausea and sweat and the pallor. What do you do when They want to take everything away from you? When They want to smash you and grind you down and take away everything? But why They? It was Wilma. Why, in her eyes, am I a figure of fun? What is there ridiculous about me? Hayes and Hess are ridiculous men. I did not ask for that account. They gave it to me because they knew she was difficult. Mr. Howey gave it to me because he was afraid to handle it himself. She has prepared him for this by poisoning his mind against me, so that lately I have felt unsure of myself when speaking with him. It is not fair.

Suddenly, almost without warning, I was sick. Afterward I felt faint. I washed my face and rinsed my mouth and lay down on my bed.

129

. . . George, you are just going to have to do something about those dreadful boys. They chased Wallace home again from school today. He was screaming with fright when he ran up on the porch. They were hitting him over the head with their books. They could hurt him seriously. They could deafen him, George. George! Put that paper down and listen to me.

. . . No, George. That's not right. You don't have the right attitude. Wallace has never been physically strong. He's not like those boys. He's sensitive and delicate. George Dorn, you listen to me! I won't have it. Wallace has told me who they are. And I have a list here of their parents' names and where they live, and you are going to get out of that chair this minute and put your coat back on and we are going to go call on those people.

. . . It will *not* make it worse for Wallace. You can make it quite clear that it will be a police matter if it happens again. And if you keep referring to him as a crybaby, I am definitely going to become annoyed with you, George.

And, lying there, still tasting the acid in my throat, I remembered the small boy, huddled at the top of the stairs, listening. And how I sneaked back to my room. Mother would take care of things. She'd make my darn father do something about it. A lot he cared about what happened to me. I hoped the police would put those kids in jail.

I need her now. And she had been gone from me for a long time. Leaving me alone. Leaving me in a world where I had no defenses. They do not leave you dignity and honor. They run after you, banging your head with books, jeering at you, as if you were a nobody.

It was midafternoon when I left my room. It was very still. Some were napping. Some were limp on the dock in the still sun, over mirror water. I felt far back in my head, as though my eyes were tubes I looked through, destroying side vision, so that I had to turn my head slowly to change the direction of my glance. And I went back to my room. On rusty knees. Squatting far back in my head.

I felt as though I waited for darkness. As though darkness would provide some unknown answer. I lay on the bed again and tried to play the game I often play when going to sleep. White pawn to king four. Black pawn to king four. White queen's knight to queen's bishop three. But I could not go further. I had lost the power to visualize. I could not see the board. The words were just sounds. Half remembered. There was no board. No look of ivory on the squares. No slant and rhythm and precision. My mind was a muddy thing awaiting darkness.

It knew that darkness would come. It squatted back there, diverting itself with obscene imaginings.

Chapter Fourteen

(RANDY HESS—AFTERWARD)

SHE WAS DEAD.

I will try to say what I felt. How it was. Once when I was little there was a hypnotist on a stage. Somebody took me there. I remember the boy who went up, scuffing his feet, trying to swagger, giving swift looks at the audience. It was done so quickly.

You are a chicken. And the boy hopped and clucked and flapped his arms. You are a dog. And he scampered and barked. Oh, there was a lot of fun! Oh, they laughed! Wake up! Wake up!

The boy woke up. He stared stupidly around. They were still all laughing. I was laughing. He fled in confusion from the stage.

She was dead.

I woke up. I looked stupidly around at the world. Who am I? How did I get here? Why do they laugh? By what strange road did I get to this place?

I remember another time. A summer camp where I was very lonely and unhappy. They taught us first aid. A man who looked like an ape demonstrated a tourniquet. Roger and I were alone in the cottage during a rest period. It was a contest between us. We knotted huck towels and each used a drumstick to tighten the tourniquet on our own leg, midway between knee and thigh. Nearly as tight as we could get them, and then bet a dime about who would loosen it first. It was very tight. At first my leg throbbed and it was painful. It looked swollen. It turned a lot darker. And the pain went away. It felt quite numb. The contest went on for a long time and then the look of my leg and foot and the numbness began to frighten me. I said we should both loosen them at the same time. He would not. More time passed. I loosened mine. He yelled that I owed him a dime. The towel had cut

132

into my thigh, marking it deeply. For a moment nothing happened. And then I screamed with the pain of returning circulation. I thought my leg would burst, would split open like something that had spoiled. But it did not. It felt weak and strange for a long time. I paid him my dime.

She had died and it was like cutting a tourniquet that had bitten deep, numbing me. The circulation came back. My soul could burst like something spoiled.

But it is more than that. A friend told me of something that had happened to him. Long ago. Back in the days of parachute jumps at the fair grounds, of wing walking, of slow barrel rolls. He had been young then. And madly, helplessly, hopelessly in love with the young wife of the star jumper. A lovely girl, he said. And one day, under a high Kansas sky, he stood with her by the grandstand while the biplane circled higher and higher above the fair grounds, buzzing and circling like a lazy insect. And while they talked she kept her eyes on the plane, and talked without nervousness. Her husband was to make his famous delayed jump. High, high over the hard earth the tiny plane waggled its wings and the drummers in the band began to long roll. Then, he said, the girl ceased talking and he saw her swallow once, her white throat moving convulsively.

The figure dropped, the tiny figure coming down and down through the clear air. He said there was a smell of fall in the fields, that there had already been warning of frost. And the wife held his wrist and she said, "Now!" And the figure still fell. And she said again, "Now!" And the figure still fell and the drum roll broke into a ragged silence and all the crowd breathed at once like some great beast, and the doll figure hit the autumn earth and rebounded from its hardness, and the great beast made a sound half scream and half roar. And my friend said that through that sound her ice fingers were still hard on his wrist and she was still saying, in that cadence, "Now—now—now." And then she turned toward him with her eyes clear, unblinded, and with a pretty and bewildered half-smile, half-frown of puzzlement, she said, "But he . . ."

And then, he told me, her face changed and broke in a way that was quite the most horrible thing he had ever seen.

He lost track of her and then heard from a friend, about a year later, that she was with another show, that she was wing-walking again. He caught up with that other show at the Herkimer County Fair in upstate New York a week later, but found that she had turned slut and her trailer was a very public place indeed. It sickened him to see her like that.

And I was both. Not only the body falling, but the one who watched without true comprehension. And it was not yet clear to me what had happened to me. I was filled with a dreadful and aimless terror. It was good when Paul ordered me into the boat with the big flashlight. We went out onto the lake. It was one of those lights that contain a big square battery. The water looked like black oil. When I held the lens above the surface, the light rebounded. By touching the wide lens carefully against the surface, I could send a murky beam down and see motes drifting through it, like dust in a path of sunlight. I do not know what good it did. Sometimes I would see a flick of arm or leg in the beam as they fought their way down. I could hear the others talking on the dock with that peculiar tone of repression in the presence of sudden death. The side of the boat bit into the flesh of my upper arms, but I held the light steady, pointing down. I was aware of the timeless stars over me, the ancient hills around me, and of my own peculiar meaninglessness, a soft thin white creature in a boat he could not build, holding a light that he could not understand, while others dived, looking for the body of a woman he had never known.

Then I heard the sirens, rising and falling through the hills and the night, crying of lost things, a thin beast message of alarm and regret.

And Paul clung to the side of the boat, shoulder muscles bunched and gleaming in the starlight, and said we would stop looking, that too much time had passed.

They tipped the boat wildly as they came aboard. Hayes grasped a paddle and thrust us strongly toward the dock. I sat holding the dead light, trembling with exhaustion as though I too had dived hopelessly for her, straining lungs and muscles. When I got up onto the dock as Steve tied the runabout fast, my knees started to give way and I nearly fell before I caught myself.

They came out, walking heavily in their official manner, asking questions in voices calculatedly harsh and bored, asking names. And I stood there and heard the boats coming down the lake toward us, outboard motors out of cadence, bright lights moving closer.

I found Noel and I stood close to her. Close to her

134

strength and her contempt, and I felt the helpless shame of a child caught in a nasty act. An act for which there are no amends, no excuses, no explanations. A child with that new awareness of evil in itself, and aware for the first time of the strangeness of the world and all that is in it, aware of the inevitability of loneliness.

"Noel, I . . ." I could not continue, because I had to close my throat against sobbing. She turned and looked up into my face. Her face was still and white. In that light it had an Egyptian look. A still face in a temple frieze, classic and cold.

I moved apart from the others and she followed me. I had not expected her to. "Yes?" she said in a low voice.

"Everything is . . ." And there was no word. Lost? Broken? Gone? Maybe in olden times men had words and were not ashamed to use them. Back when language was permitted to be dramatic. Before we muted ourselves with odd shame. We say, "I love you," and suffix a nervous laugh, taking comfort in a diluted form of drama. We never declaim. It is all underplayed. Little Sheba never comes back. And we stand on no cold towers in the rain and talk with ghosts.

So I had no word.

Yet she knew how close I was to breaking. She touched my arm and we went up the curving concrete steps to the big terrace and in through the glass doors and to the left and down the corridor and to the room Wilma had given us.

Once the door was shut I lay on the bed. I looked blindly at the ceiling. For a time I was able to withstand the self-pity. And then I let it come in a sour flood. Taking sour comfort from it. No savings, no job, no pride, broken health, and a wife I had degraded. While the hypnotic focus had existed, all that had not mattered. I had been content, almost eager, to slide down and down and down. Now that shameful meaning was gone from me. So self-pity came, in all its tormented weeping ugliness. And she sat on the bed beside me and put her hand on my forehead. It was the gesture of a nurse. A starched white gesture performed without meaning, while the nurse counts the night hours and thinks of the laughing intern. And the knowledge that I did not even deserve that gesture of clinical comfort increased the spasms of self-rejection.

I was two people. One rolled and gasped and wept weakly on a guest-room bed, cursing God. And the other stood behind Noel and looked down at the figure on the bed and

135

grinned in an evil way and chuckled silently and thought, Not enough, not enough, not nearly enough, you excommunicated priest, you filthy choirboy, you self-dramatizing fool. You threw yourself back and you know it's too late. Baby wants candy. Buddy wants a bike. Roll and choke, you hopeless son-of-a-bitch.

"Here!" she said. "Here!"

And I propped myself up on one elbow and took the three round yellow pills from the palm of her hand, washed them down with a swallow of the water.

"Drink all the water."

I did so, obediently, and handed her back the glass and lay back. I heard her in the bathroom, running water. She came back and stood by the bed.

"You ought to sleep. Will you be all right now?"

"Noel, we've . . . we've got to talk."

For the first time she showed expression, her face twisting in something like pain. I saw that sometime during my unpleasant scene she had changed to skirt, sweater, and jacket.

"Maybe we don't have to talk, Randy. We never have."

"But I . . ."

"Just try to sleep. That's all. I'll be here. I'll sit here in the dark until you fall asleep, if that's what you want."

I nodded. I was glad when the lights were out. When my face was in darkness, unseen. She had moved a chair close to the bed. I held my breath and I could hear her faint breathing. I began to feel the quietness of the drug. It moved out from the middle of me, crawling slowly down the marrow of my bones. It deepened my breathing.

Once when I was eleven I was very ill. Big faces loomed over me and moved back into shadows. Days and nights were all mixed up. And I would awake in darkness and hold my breath and then I could hear my mother in the big chair near my bed, breathing softly.

I knew what I wanted to ask of Noel. I flushed in the concealing darkness and then I made my voice as matter of fact as I could. "Would you mind very much holding my hand, Noel?"

"I wouldn't mind."

She found my hand in the darkness. She held it in both of hers. Her hands were warm and dry. And very still. Why should it matter? They are hands. Tools for holding, lifting, grasping. Why should there be comfort in a touch?

136

The sleep of the drug began to come. I could feel it. It is like walking along balancing yourself on a curb that gets increasingly higher. You fall off and step back up, and fall off and step back up, and each time it is harder to step back up until you finally fall all the way off.

When the maid awakened me by banging on the door, I had absolutely no idea of where I was. The drug was still strong in me, deadening my mental reactions. I had the idea that I was on some sort of a business trip and this was a hotel room. I sat on the edge of the bed. It was early daylight. I stumbled into the bathroom, ran the cold water, cupped it in my hands, and scrubbed my face hard. It was coming back. Not all in a rush. Bit by bit, each inevitable piece fitting into the previously assembled pieces.

There is always an aspect of hope in awakening. It is a little like birth. A new day of life ahead. But each increment of memory destroyed a portion of that vague and feeble hope until there was none left. I stood alone in a gray place. The maid had called out something about everyone going to the big room. Maybe they had found the body. That fierce bright body, tumescent, full ripened, vigorous, and voracious. It could not be flesh, as other bodies are flesh. It could not die as others die. Not that thing of gloss and firmness, delicately pelted, ancient in its knowledge of hyperesthesia.

I went down the corridor. It had an odd look of being out of true, as though the right angles had suffered a distortion through pressure. And when I went into the big room and saw them there, saw them glance at me, their faces were odd, like cinema faces seen from a seat too far to the side of the screen.

I saw a chair beside Judy Jonah and sat in it and asked, too loudly. "What's up, anyway?" My voice came back to my ears with that timbre of the voices of doctors and nurses as you are going under anesthesia. No one answered.

I leaned closer to Judy. "Did they find the body?" I asked her.

She gave me a surprised look. "Oh, yes. Almost an hour ago."

I looked over at Noel. Her eyes moved across me and away, a bit unsteadily. Something about her puzzled me. As though she were newly vulnerable. No longer cold and classic and remote. Needing something. As though she needed to be

137

reassured. She looked exhausted. And she sat awkwardly, with none of her customary grace. In some odd way she looked younger.

Steve was the last one. He had hurt his face somehow. He looked angry. Deputy Sheriff Fish stood and began to talk. I tried to follow what he was saying, but I could not. It was like one of those foreign movies without subtitles where you have to try to follow the plot from the actions and the facial expressions of the characters. They all had an odd look in the morning light. Peculiarly distorted. I was aware of a feeling of shock in the room and I leaned forward and I believe I probably frowned earnestly as I tried to translate. It seemed to be something about Wilma. And I saw Noel leave the room and I wanted to follow her and have her explain all this to me. It was as though, at a party, I had joined a group in the middle of a conversation and stood there, smiling and nodding, laughing when the others did, utterly unable to pick up the thread of meaning that would make everything clear. A group that I did not know, using its own private language, erecting little social walls, and waiting for me to go away. Voices heard under water. The voices of others on a train when you are more than half asleep.

It happened to me once, in college. I had gone into the wrong lecture. A lecture on symbolic logic. Each individual word was a perfectly good normal word, but try as I might, I could make no sense of what was being said. It made me wonder if I were going mad. As if communication were being blocked.

I wanted to go to Noel. There was my only safety. The only known place in the world.

But first . . .

Chapter Fifteen

(MAVIS DOCKERTY—BEFORE)

ON THE WAY UP he had to make one of his usual snotty
cracks about Wilma, on account of how he is crazy jealous.
What he ought to have is a dandy mechanical wife. Take her
out of the closet and plug her into a light socket. He doesn't
want me to be a *person*.

After I put him in his place we drove on without talking,
and I cried a little bit. He drove too damn fast, but I
certainly wasn't going to say a word about it, no matter what
he did.

I sat 'way over there in my corner of the seat and I
thought about the lovely new clothes I would wear. And
about being a house guest where there are important people.
Big people. The only flaw in the ointment was having to go
up there with Paul. Like a race where your feet are tied
together, like on picnics. I couldn't be myself, not with him
along. I couldn't be free. And I decided right then and there
that I'd let Wilma know that the next time there was a party,
I'd certainly appreciate it if I could come without that dead
stone weight hanging around my neck like the bird on that
sailor in the poem we had in seventh grade.

And she would know what I meant, all right. She had him
typed right down to the dotted i. "Mavis, dear," she said,
"he's just a very ordinary man. He's good in business, and
I'm glad he works for me. But I couldn't *bear* being married
to him. God! Pipe and slippers and a household budget. You
see, dear, he's no challenge to you. And you need challenge.
You need life and excitement. You didn't know how dull
your life really was, did you?"

She has him typed. He's Rotarian and stuffy and provincial. He's living in the Middle Ages. I just wished and wished
that somebody else was driving me up to Lake Vale. Because
I could see, from his snotty mood, that he was going to try

139

to spoil things for me. That's all he does. Spoil things. And someday he's going to make me so mad that I'm going to let him know about Gilman Hayes and that afternoon in Wilma's apartment. I can just imagine the look in his eyes.

Wilma had told me about the place, but gosh, words can't describe it. It was like in *House Beautiful*. Only more so, if possible. I got real excited when I saw it. I could hardly breathe. And there was cars there already, like you don't see just anyplace. One of those big sporty Buicks, and a little black English car with red wire wheels, and a gorgeous white Jaguar, with a cute little cartoon of Judy Jonah on the door of it. I wished I'd put my foot down harder and we had got a Jaguar. They're so smooth looking. But no, Paul has to have this thing because he says there isn't enough room in those.

I nearly made a terrible booboo when a man came hurrying out. He was kind of foreign-looking and I thought he was one of the guests and then I remembered Wilma talking about the Mexican servants and I realized, just when I was about to stick my hand out and smile, that it was José. I would have been mortified to death if I'd done anything as terrible as that, shaking hands with a servant. It would be nice to have a little Mexican maid, to live in.

The servant told us to take the path around the house. He was very polite, even if he was sort of fierce-looking. We went by a big croquet place and around to a big terrace overlooking the lake. It was like a picture, really. You could see right away that Wilma knows how to live. Like she says, gracious living is an art, and you have to work at it all the time. There were two fast-looking boats tied up at the twin docks. I saw Judy Jonah down there and Gilman Hayes was near her. They were sun-bathing. I met Judy a couple of times in the city at Wilma's apartment, but she's sort of strange. I mean she isn't like you would expect, being so famous. She even looks a little plain, somehow. The others were on the terrace. Wilma hurried right over to us. You could tell she was glad to see us. Glad to see me, anyway. She gave me a little hug, and explained that we were all friends here and it would be a sort of informal-type house party. I acted pleased, but honestly, I had been hoping there would be some other important people there I hadn't met before.

I told her her house was lovely, and she took us back to

our room. I bet that next to hers, it was the best room in the house. Like she says, it was gracious living. José was just putting the last of our suitcases on one of those rack things.

Then Wilma said José would bring us a drink and we could freshen up and then join the others. I ordered an extra-dry Martini, but Paul, he had to ask for that damn bourbon he likes. It doesn't even sound like a drink with any class. Now, if it was Scotch on the rocks or a Scotch mist or something. No. Bourbon and water, bourbon and water. He hasn't got any taste. He hasn't got any sense of gracious living. He's provincial.

Not only that, but after the drinks came he had to try to tell me not to get drunk and complain about the last party we went to. I know when I'm drunk and when I'm not drunk. He just doesn't like to see anybody having any fun. He's like a big schoolteacher. If he had his way, everybody would sit in a corner and he'd give lectures and mark papers.

I made the mistake of standing there drinking my drink and wearing just my bra and panties. And of course, he had to start leering at me in that way he has. I told him not to get messy. Honestly, he wants to get messy at the darnedest times. There's never any buildup. He just looks at you and boom. Right then and there. He's got about as much romance as a toad in the grass. I didn't even wait for him to come out of our private bath. I went out and joined the others, and believe me it was a relief to be away from him for just a few minutes after spending the whole darn day with him. Wilma helped Randy start the music and it was lovely. Honestly, I just lay back on that couch thing and José brought me a fresh drink and I looked at the blue lake and heard the music and it was like being on a cruise or something. It was perfectly lovely. Nice people and nice civilized conversation and somebody to wait on you. Judy and Gilman Hayes came up from the dock and after a while that nice Wallace Dorn arrived. I wish Paul would dress like that and act like that. Wallace is so obviously a gentleman. Paul could be just anybody. He looks like a hundred other men on the street.

There we were, all friends, just drinking and talking and enjoying ourselves. I guess Paul would have tried to be a damp blanket if somebody had given him half a chance. But maybe he was smart enough to keep his mouth shut and not try to spoil the party for the woman who, after all, is his boss, any way you want to look at it. Anybody could see that Wilma was having a good time. She positively sparkled. It made me feel warm and good just to look at her.

I was glad when finally it was time to eat. Everything had got sort of swarmy and when I stood up I didn't think my legs were going to work just right. But the food was so spicy hot it made my eyes cry, and it was what I needed to make all those Martinis behave. After dinner I felt just wonderful. Floaty and half excited. I kept wishing Paul wasn't around. I didn't feel the least bit provincial.

Gil Hayes had changed into pale slacks and a white shirt. He had knotted the shirttails in the front, just above the edge of the trousers, and he left it unbuttoned. The white shirt made him look real tan, and wearing it that way made his shoulders look broader and his hips look slimmer. After dinner and after some brandy Gil Hayes asked me to dance. He'd found some South American records.

It's funny about him. He's a wonderful dancer. It's maybe like it would be dancing with a big cat. He doesn't talk at all, and he leads very strong, so it's easy to follow him even when he's doing very fancy things you've never done before. The lights were kind of dim in the big room. I knew we probably looked special the way we were dancing together. I hoped Paul would look at us once in a while. His dancing! I suppose it was just fine 'way back when he was in college, but it certainly is old-fashioned. About the only thing he *doesn't* do is pump your arm up and down and count out loud.

It was real magic, dancing like that. The way he'd swoop and the little touches of him. It made me feel all prickly all over and like I couldn't get breath enough, or get close enough to him. At first it was just exciting, making me feel awful sexy, but when it went on and on and on, it turned into like a kind of torture. It was like pain or something. When he danced me out onto the terrace, I felt almost the way you do when you're about to faint. I wanted him to take me out of the light, out there in the darkness where there was grass. I wanted to scream at him. It would have been the quickest thing that ever happened. And then I knew that he was doing it on purpose. I knew he was torturing me. Because he kept doing things and then stopping. I didn't want him to know how hard I was breathing, but I couldn't stop it.

142

I sort of half saw when Paul and Judy went down onto the dock. And 'way in the back of my mind I was thinking how that was. He'd probably forced himself on her. And then he could go back to the city and go to one of those stupid lunches of his and say, real casual, that he had a nice chat with Judy Jonah that week end. I bet he would bore her ears right off her head. Because what could he talk about to her? When he tries to talk about something besides his job he gets into a lot of deep-sounding stuff about life and things and I don't think he knows half the time what he's trying to say. It's a kind of showing off, because he happens to know big words. What would a person like him know about life? He's in that office all day, and when he comes home he wants to sit like a stuffed dummy and read books. There isn't any life in him or any fun.

When the records ended Gilman Hayes backed away from me and gave a kind of funny jerky bow and said, "Good night. I'm tired. I'm going to bed." I could have killed him dead right there where he stood. Leaving me in that condition. I said good night and I went right by him and went to my room. I almost forgot to say good night to Wilma.

I got in the room and I wanted to pace up and down like a tigress or something, and chew my nails right down to the hilt. Then I realized that Paul would be coming back to the room soon. I got ready for bed and ready for him quickly. He came in and, thank God, he didn't want to chatter. When the light was out, I started pretending, even though Wilma has told me it's a childish game. I pretended I was alone on a cruise and this was my stateroom. And I'd met a man during the day. He looked just like Gil Hayes except he was dark, and he had manners like that nice Wallace Dorn. And now we were together, and there was nothing provincial about either one of us.

It was hard to make the game work because I'm so used to Paul and used to the way he goes about things. But I pretended hard and it made it a lot better and a sort of crazy thing happened. When, toward the end, I sort of lost my hold on the pretending, when everything goes kind of crazy anyway, I had the ridiculous idea that it was Wilma there with me. Nothing could be sillier than that, I guess.

Just as I was going to sleep I thought that Paul hadn't kissed me even once, but I was too darn tired to even wonder about it. He can do what he pleases. I needed him

143

and he was there and that was that. He had no kick coming. Not after the way he'd leered at me when we first got there. Wilma says he has a pedestrian mind. You'd know that just to look at him.

Paul was snoring when I woke up. I got out of bed quickly. It was a wonderful day and I felt just divine, just perfectly and wonderfully alive. It was warm and sunny, so after I showered, I got right into my new swimsuit. It's one piece, a funny olivy green with a texture like velvet and no shoulder straps. I wore my robe over it and went out to breakfast on the terrace. Everybody got whisky sours first. Or rum sours, if you wanted. I think that's a perfectly marvelous idea. I love that sour taste in the morning, and it's so gay to get a little edge before you even eat your eggs.

I wished Paul would sleep all day. I wished he'd sleep until it was time to go home. Gilman Hayes was in his swimsuit too. I looked at his hand and wrist in the sun. It surprised me to see his fingernails. Little bits of things, nibbled 'way down, so the pads of his fingers sort of curl up over them. His hand looked strong and square and brown in the sun, and there was a gold watch strap around his heavy wrist, and the sun-bleached hair curled over the gold of the strap.

I was just leaving when Paul came shuffling out. Steve and Noel Hess were sitting talking together. Wilma was down on the dock with Judy. I heard Wilma laugh. I went down and swam and then Gilman Hayes got on the water skis. Later he showed me how. He was very strong. I was clumsy at first, but I have natural good balance, and my legs are husky, so I was able to do it pretty well with him teaching me. I guess it was after the skiing that I noticed how Paul was drinking a lot. I looked at him and his eyes didn't seem to work together quite the way they usually do. And his voice was blurry. Noel was drinking a lot too, which sort of astonished me. I never saw her drink before.

Paul didn't really get messy drunk until the croquet game. Then he was awful. For a time I was sort of ashamed of him, and then I felt good about it. He'd certainly lost his chance to ever say anything to me again about drinking. I never made such a spectacle of myself as that. We were all drinking, but Paul was the worst. I certainly wasn't going to lower myself by helping him.

Later on it turned out it was Judy who helped him. If he could remember it, I thought he'd have a nice story for one

144

of those silly lunch things. Judy Jonah put me to bed, boys.

After I ate I suddenly felt terribly sleepy. I went into our room like a mouse. The last thing I wanted to do was wake him up. I was real pooped, but he made such gargling snoring noises, I couldn't drop off. I remembered seeing Steve and Noel go across the lake in a boat. It had sort of surprised me, but I guess if she was provincial, Wilma wouldn't have her around. And it didn't look like Steve would be back. I tried his door and it wasn't locked, so I stretched out in there on his bed. It had been made up. Alcohol does sort of let you down, and then the best thing to do is sleep for a while, and when you wake up you're as good as new, usually.

I slept about an hour and then I went down on the dock. I got some more sun. The party had turned sleepy, but I guessed it would pick up again when it got dark. When the sun got too low, I put my robe back on and went on up to the house. Randy was sitting on the dock staring at the lake. And one boat was still gone. I wondered if he was a little sore. But he certainly had no cause to get sore, not the way he acts with Wilma. I guess Noel doesn't do anything about that, because it is a pretty good job for Randy, and he doesn't have to work very hard for his money.

I did little dance steps as I went across the terrace so that the hem of my robe swirled. Gee, I felt wonderful. Life had kind of opened up. Like going down an alley for a long time and then coming out into a park. Sometimes a person gets a feeling of how things are going to be in the future. And I just *knew* that Paul wasn't going to be in my future. It was funny, I was almost feeling sorry for him, the way I was going to leave him behind. Like something you outgrow, or you decide the style isn't right for you or something, and you hang it in the back of the closet and then one day you give it away and feel just a little bit sad about giving it away.

Wilma always says you've got to be objective about yourself. Look at yourself kind of cold. I looked, but I couldn't find anything about me that I really didn't like. I know that's kind of awful to say. It sounds conceited. But Mary Gort had come one hell of a long way, brother, and she was going to go a long way further, too. And travel light while she was at it.

I had José make me a drink so I could celebrate. Celebrate the end of the alley. I couldn't even be mad at Paul any more, now that I knew how it was all going to come out. Any pretending I did from now on was going to be for real.

It got real gay again, like I knew it was going to. It was Saturday night, wasn't it? I like the feel of Saturday nights. There was a buffet thing, where you could fill your own plate, and Paul was still sleeping off his drunk. That was fine by me. Noel was wonderful. Gee, she'd always been so quiet. She got real gay and funny and wonderful, just laughing all the time and making cracks and staying as close to Steve as she could. Steve is nice enough, but golly, even in flat heels I can stare him right straight in the eye, and that does nothing for me, but nothing. Men like that make me feel like some kind of a horse, but she's little enough for him. We ate and drank and then did some swimming. I had to go to the room and put my suit back on. And when I turned out the bathroom light and went back through the dark bedroom, Paul had to say, "Mavis?" and know what time it was. I told him I hoped he felt dreadful. He certainly sounded as if he did.

My suit was still damp and unpleasant. We drank on the dock under the floodlights and swam some and it was hardly cold at all. Of course we had some antifreeze, but I mean there wasn't any of that wind that makes you feel cold.

I guess it was Wilma that said swimming felt better without suits on. That was a fine idea. Randy wasn't swimming anyway, but of those who were, Judy and Wallace Dorn were the only ones who said they'd keep their suits on. Steve went up to the switch box. Then he played a joke on us by turning the lights back on again. He's a riot sometimes. He kills me.

Wilma was certainly right about the swimming being better. It made you feel free and crazy and wonderful and naughty and bold. We horsed around, playing tag around the end of the docks and stuff like that. The water sort of slides by you, and it was just a little bit warmer than the air right on top. If you went down a little bit, though, it got real icy. It was all dark and mixed up. Gosh, you couldn't tell who was getting fresh with you, but I didn't care a bit. I kept thinking that it was just the sort of thing that stuffy old Paul would look down his long nose at. He doesn't want anybody having any fun, especially me. I wished he'd come out.

I got kind of tired and I floated for a long time. I was

146

close to the dock. I kept my eyes kind of squinty, blurring all the stars. Then I saw somebody on the dock right near me, and I could tell from how skinny he was it was Randy. He was looking down at me. That was the first time I felt even a little bit creepy about not having anything on, but he certainly couldn't see much. Not by starlight. Then I saw him lift something. One of those water skis, and it looked for a minute like he was going to hit me with it or something. I guess he was going to splash somebody.

"Hey!" I said, and he made a funny little grunting noise to himself.

"Mavis?" he said. And he put the ski down.

I realized I hadn't heard Wilma laughing or talking in quite a while. I called her. She didn't answer. I wondered if she'd gone up to the house without telling anybody she was leaving.

It's funny how alarms go off in your head. All of a sudden, as Gil started to call her too, I just *knew* something was wrong. I just *knew* it. And all of a sudden the water was cold. Awful cold. And all the stars didn't look friendly any more. They looked cold too.

"Wilma!" I yelled. "Wilma!"

"All at once," Steve said, and his voice was shaky. "Now!"

"Wilma!" we yelled. The night didn't care. The stars didn't give a damn. Our voices came back from the mountains. All faint and haunted and horrible.

"Wilma!"

Chapter Sixteen

(GILMAN HAYES—AFTERWARD)

SHE HAD those big books of reproductions. I had put on a shirt she had given me, and some comfortable ragged khaki shorts from the old days. I sat and turned the pages. Dufy, Rouault, Utrillo. What do they say? The honored dead. They leave patterns behind them. They couldn't even draw. I drew every leaf and it went up on the cork board. Sister Elizabeth said it was pretty. There was something the matter with one of Sister Elizabeth's eyes. It didn't look at you. The other kids made jokes. They said it was the eye that looked at God.

It was dawn and I turned meaningless pages.

One eye looked at God and you couldn't tell what she was thinking, but her arms were warm. Her clothes smelled musty and sweaty when she held me close. I was her favorite, so I didn't mind being held that way.

She was holding me and I was laughing silently against the mustiness that day. When she held me away so suddenly, I barely had a chance to make a crying face again.

He'd held me out in the air over the bricks 'way down there. Then he pulled me back and dropped me and hurt my head and slapped me and turned his back on me, leaning on the railing. I was crying. I reached down with both hands and I grabbed his ankles and snatched and lifted as hard as I could. I knew I had to do it fast and hard and strong, because if it didn't happen to him, he would slap me again.

"Aaaaaaaa!" he cried on the way down.

I was looking down when they came out. I was watching, 'way down there, the blood running in a little river down a place between two of the bricks, and he was like he was lying down to see it closer and better, his eyes right near the little river. Sometimes when it was after a rain, they would let us race toothpicks in the gutter. I never cared if I won or not. I like to watch it.

148

Sister Elizabeth said it was a dreadful shock to me. She held me close. She smelled funny. I said he was trying to show me how he could walk on the railing. What happened was I was off balance. I did not see him go down, because I was staggering back. That would have been a good part of it. I did not know how many times he went over in the air. And that would have been a good thing to know.

It's odd that I should sort of forget that I'm different and it was Wilma who made me remember it all over again. I guess I never did really forget. It's more that I didn't use it. If you're different, it's something to be used, or it's wasted. I only used it in little ways. Like that night in the park and hearing them, and creeping close through the bushes, creeping so close to them I could have reached out and touched them. They were like animals. I hit them both, and it was funny I only had to hit him once, but I had to hit her three times. I had been planning to do something humorous with them. Something to make you laugh. But I felt tired and I had forgotten what it was, so I left them there. It wasn't even in the paper. So what good was it?

Wilma saw the importance of me. She brought it out. So that people pointed at me, and tried to talk to me, and even said sir.

I could do the pictures very quickly, and they were four hundred dollars for each one at first and then six hundred and fifty. And now one thousand. But Evis gets one third of that. I don't see what he does that he should get one third. I ask him and he says things about the high rental area of the gallery and the cost of packing and shipping and things like that.

It's important. One of them, I did this: I took the tubes. I squirted the raw colors into my hands. Then I made a washing motion with my hands, then smeared the canvas. The first time I had done too much of the washing motion. It came out gray, for some reason. So the next time I did it not so much and the colors stayed bright and raw and smeared. Then I turned the canvas around and around until it looked like something. Then with black and a little brush I made it look more like what it looked like. That one took a long time to dry, I remember.

Now I wish I could ask Wilma why she did it. There are a lot of things in the world that make you do other things. And people are always watching and thinking, and you can

149

only guess what the real reasons are, because they all have their own.

She talked so long.

They were down there on the dock in the lights, swimming, and the lights were not on where we were. Our legs were over the bank and we sat on the clipped neat green grass, our hips touching, our thighs touching, like friends.

"I don't understand," I said.

"It was a bet, darling. I've been telling you and telling you. You're sweet sometimes, but really you are terribly dense. Why did we bet? Because there was an argument, that's why. A stuffy and self-important man. One of those cocktail-party arguments. He said that, in the mass, the people have taste and perception. He said you can't kid them. My answer, of course, is that the public consists of slobs who like what they are told to like. He was a tiny bit drunk. Drunk enough to bet me one thousand dollars that I couldn't pick somebody off the street and turn him into an artist. Or at least what the public would consider an artist. I looked around. I thought it would be more amusing if I could find somebody pretty. And there you were, dear, behind that counter, wearing your silly little hat and positively reeking of sex. With Steve Winsan's fees and the money I've spent on you, dear, it has cost me nearly seven thousand to win one. But it has been delightful, really. So I'm just telling you that the party is over. That's all."

"But the critics . . ."

Her voice got harder. "The critics worth a damn said you're a farce, and you are. The sheep went along with the big fad. They didn't understand those globs because nobody can, and because they couldn't understand them, they said they were good—pushed in the right direction by Steve, of course. And that created a stir and the stir meant more publicity and that meant more sales, and I got my thousand dollars over a month ago. My God, I couldn't let you try to draw *things*, objects, anything recognizable. Your work would be infantile."

"But you told me . . . Wilma, you said I'm different. You said I should be . . ."

"Arrogant. Of course. You had to take yourself very seriously. So others would. You had to believe in yourself. That was part of the stage setting, darling. Good Lord, if you keep telling a frump she's lovely, she'll start believing it

150

and even start improving in looks. You can pat people into shape like *tortillas*. Almost any shape you want."

"I'm a good artist," I told her.

She patted my knee. "Poor Gil. No, baby. You aren't any kind of an artist. Not any kind at all. You're just a big guy with muscles and you've had a good time, haven't you? The end of the line, baby. All out. Evis may be able to unload a few more, but a year from now nobody will even remember who the hell you were. Unless you can keep on paying Steve's fees, and I know damn well you can't, because you haven't saved a dime. And I'm not going to keep on with it, certainly."

"I need you," I said. "I need to come and talk to you. I get shaky and then I need to come and . . ."

She took her hand away. "Now listen! How can you be so goddamn dumb? This was a gag. Get it? Wilma had fun. So did you. Now Wilma is bored. With you and with the gag. You just aren't good company, Gil. You haven't any conversation and damn few manners and you go around preening yourself and flexing your muscles. I'm throwing you off my back. If you're smart, you'll find a nice clean counter and get behind it and put on a monkey hat and start making with the cheese on rye."

She left me there. I saw her down on the dock. She was laughing with Steve. They were laughing at me. I knew it. I was nothing and they had made me into something and now they were making me back into nothing again. I sat up there and I was empty. I was like a figure you could make out of twisting wire coat hangers so they were the outline of a man. You could see through me. See the stars and the lights and everything. And sounds went right through me, and the tiny breeze that there was, up high where I sat.

And right in the middle of all the wire a little round thing started to grow. Round and solid and shining. It grew and grew until it filled up all the wire and then I was me again and I wanted to laugh out loud. The best part of the joke was on her.

They put it up on the cork board. It was on thick white paper and they put it up with four yellow thumbtacks, one in each corner. I drew every leaf. It took me hours. Every single little leaf, and each leaf had five little points. One day it was gone and I asked, but nobody knew what had happened to it. I wanted to do it all over again, but there wasn't time.

151

Because by then we were planting the garden. I hated the garden. I worked all one day, squashing each seed between my fingers when I put it down in the hole I made with the stick. Nothing grew there.

She had thought she had made me. I had made myself. But I could see the danger, even in that. The danger of her mouth. The laughing of it. And others laughing. The way they were laughing down there. I could not permit that. I could not allow it.

I stood up and felt tall. I felt that my shoulders were against the sky. I looked around. The light reflection was dim on the croquet wickets, on the striped posts. I walked over, and my body felt as if it were made of leather and springs, tireless. I pulled the post from the ground. It was hard wood, striped in gay paint, and the end that went into the ground was capped with brass that ended in a sharp point.

The wood was hard. I held the post in both hands close to my chest. I increased the effort slowly. My shoulders made popping sounds. The muscles of my arms creaked. My throat closed and the world darkened and my hands were bright with pain. It had to happen, or nothing would happen. This had to be true or nothing would happen. This had to be true or nothing would be true.

And the hard maple made a faint crackling sound and then broke sharply and I fell to my knees in the sudden weakness, my ears ringing, the depths of my lungs burning. In my left hand I held the turned brass tip, with four or five inches of the glossy wood attached. I threw the rest of the post behind me as I stood up, heard it roll and clatter on the gravel. I tucked the small end in the waistband of my trunks. The brass was cool against my belly.

It had broken and I was strong and important and known to myself. Whole again and significant. I went down to them and laughter was something that ran gaily around in my chest, little running silver bits, like spilled mercury. I went down among them. It was significant that I went down from a high place where I had proved my strength in the lights. Sister Elizabeth had read the pagan myths to us, of the ones on Olympus who, for amusement, coldly and without compassion, would go down to play among the mortals, concealing the godhead, concealing the shining uniqueness the way the striped bit of wood capped with brass was hidden from them. It was hidden because it was proof of strength they could not know, and if I displayed it openly they would look

152

too knowingly at me and be ashamed. I was grateful to Wilma because she had made it necessary to undergo the trial of strength, the final proof.

I swam with them, careful not to lose the symbol. It was enough to know that it was there. And I found that I could talk with them cleverly, so that they knew nothing. That was enough. It pleased me.

When at last, after a long time, we swam in naked darkness, I swam with the symbol of strength in my hand. I played their childish games because it pleased me to do so.

And then there came a time when I was beside Wilma, stars pale on her body in the black water. And the meaning of many things was revealed to me. It was a new secret I had discovered, a new measure of my growth. It's something you must learn to do, and it's hard. You must open your mind to a blankness, and then what you must do will be told to you.

I felt a great tenderness toward her. A gratitude, because she was making this possible for me. She became a part of the design, and once it was unfolded, it was so evident that I wondered why I had not seen it before. It fitted together. It was an art form in which I had not worked before and the laws of the form were rigid. If it were not done to precise ritual, it would all be spoiled. Out of my strength and importance flowed the plan and I felt humble. It was an honor for her that she could share this uniqueness, share it as a mortal proving her mortality.

She swam slowly and, beside her, holding the symbol of strength in my right hand, I slid my left hand under her arm lightly across one breast to cup her right breast, the water-cooled surface and the living warmth underneath. I drove the sharp brass tip into the back of her head with one quick blow and pulled it free. I felt a tremor run through her body and then a stillness. She seemed to grow heavier. I released her.

She was motionless, face down. She sank slowly beneath the surface. For a moment I could see the gleam of paleness under the water and then that faded down and was gone. I had been true to the vision, and I had accomplished it to perfection. She had shared the perfection and it had honored her. I had been given a new reassurance of strength, and out of it I had become stronger. There would be other assurances until I would at last be so shining that they would not dare look directly at me. My shining would blind them.

When they began to call, I called too, and laughed inside.

She lay below us, honored and dedicated, and it was not yet time to explain it. I put the shorts back on in the darkness and hid the symbol again. I dived for her as they told me to. It amused me. Later, back in my room, when I changed to the khaki shorts and the striped shirt, I put the symbol of strength and art in the pocket of the shorts. They searched through the night. It surprised me that they found her. I thought at first that to bring her up would spoil the exact form of it, but then I realized that it was part of the ritual, a part I had not understood. It was fitting that she be brought up as dawn was coming, because then it would form a new symbol of birth into death, the dawn of her honor and of the importance I had given her by selecting her to complete the design.

They called us and I sat there on the floor and turned the pages of the big books. Utrillo, Rouault, Dufy. They had left patterns behind them. But they could not even draw. I had drawn every leaf. And then I had progressed beyond them to this new form. This new art form had a rhythm and a symmetry that could never be captured on two-dimensional canvas. It had a richness of color beyond anything that can be purchased in a tube. And a brush is an artificial thing. It comes between the artist and the art form. I wondered why they had not seen and understood that. The art form must be done with the body itself. The dance is artificial because it merely acts out a symbolic drama. It imitates the meaningful. The body must be used for a meaningful act, and each meaningful act must be accomplished with the rhythm and design inherent in the act. And the art form cannot be undertaken by anyone except those few who have the special insight and strength of the new shining race of man.

I wanted to tell them. I could hear them babbling about car keys and criminal investigation and newspaper reporters. It made me impatient. I wanted to stand up and roar for silence and then explain what I had discovered. If I could make them understand, then they could stop this babbling foolishness. They could not learn the methods and the plans, of course. But if they could follow my words, they could see how it had been given to me to open this new frontier. I put the books aside, those books that were merely exhaustive records of failure, of the lack of comprehension. I sat there filled with contempt for them. No, you could not tell them. It was too intricate for them. Their standards were too mortal.

I felt the excitement coming, and I did not know why. I looked carefully around the room, looking for the source, knowing that this was, as it would always be, the first warning of a new design, a new creative act. The form was still new to me, so that it took me a long time to find my way through to the inevitable.

As with Wilma, it was ridiculously easy. They were mortal. They could not be convinced with words. But they could be convinced with deeds. With demonstration. Then they could see, all at once, the beauty and the significance of it. And then there would be no awkwardness and no delay in interpretation. Then we could discuss it calmly and I could explain to them why the form had to be exact each time, balanced to meet the symmetry of the moment, precise in its beauty, brilliant and deathless.

Mavis Dockerty sat six feet from me, her back to me. I felt differently toward her than toward Wilma. I felt grateful to Wilma. But I owed this woman nothing. It was I who would honor her, who would make her this gift that would provide an eternal moment of meaningfulness to her shallow life, so that, in effect, she would live forever.

I stood tall behind her, my feet planted strongly, and I took the godhead symbol from my pocket and held it tightly. I learned another thing in that moment. That it is important to achieve a special expression for the need of the moment. The face must be utterly slack and expressionless. All expression is in the muscular rhythm, so the face must not detract. I waited until they began to notice me, to look at me rather oddly. Then, as with Wilma, I slipped my hand under her left arm, bringing it across to cup her right breast. She tensed in shock and in my mind I told her strongly to welcome this and not to resist it. I drove the symbol into her skull with one sharp blow, sensing that I must leave it there for a time. I stepped back and it was a gay wooden decoration, bedded perfectly. She bent forward from the waist in slow worship, and there was but one flaw to mar it. Her leg kept making a rather ridiculous kicking motion.

I looked up, waiting for their awe and their appreciation, hoping the flaw had not disturbed them, that the flaw had been overbalanced by the perfection of placement, and I saw her husband and the largest uniformed man running at me, while Steve Winsan bounded from the room.

The uniformed man yanked his gun from his holster and

155

struck me across the side of the face. I fell heavily. I could not move, but I was aware of what was going on. It puzzled me. It seemed such a ridiculous thing to do. Ridiculous to hear the scream of a woman. And then, suddenly, I realized my own error. I had expected too much of them. The act had been truly beyond their comprehension. They would make no effort to understand. They had completely missed the significance of it. And I smiled inside and knew how I would punish them. Later, when they realized, they would beg and plead for an explanation. They had acted hastily. They had hurt me. So it was my right and my privilege to deny them access to me.

They pulled my wrists together and put handcuffs on me. They had moved my body. And that gave me a problem that bothered me. True, I could refuse to speak to them, but even in the movements of my body there would be meaning for those who watched carefully. It was beyond my powers to do anything at all devoid of meaning.

After a time I resolved that difficulty. I would give them no clue, by word or movement. When they saw that I was conscious, they sat me in a chair. I gave them no help. Once they sat me there, I stayed there, far back inside myself, looking at nothing, and I was laughing at them. I would give them nothing. No matter how they pleaded, I would give them nothing. They kept at me, shouting at me, pulling me this way and that way. I assumed each position into which they pulled me, but I made no motion of my own. And soon I found a new talent that pleased me. I could make my thoughts loud, so that their voices came to me from far away, fuzzy and insignificant and without meaning. Once you are able to do that—and only very few, I am certain, can accomplish it—it destroys the meaning of the passage of time. A year is a minute, or an hour is a lifetime.

I was aware that others had come. New ones. Older ones with grave faces. I sat there. I stared at nothing. I let my mouth sag open. And I felt the rope of saliva from the corner of my mouth to my chest. I could shut them out entirely. They would get nothing from me. There were great depths in me, a thousand hiding places. Where no one could follow me and drive me out into the light.

And in one of the dark places I began to redo that picture of long ago. Every leaf. Each leaf had five points. It would take a very long time, and once it was done, I could do it over again. With the ultimate of care.

From a long way away somebody came to me and he took my chained hands and lifted them up so that they were over my head. Then he let go of them. I held my hands there. I would not betray myself. I would hold them up there until they withered and died, until my shoulders locked in place, rather than betray myself by any conscious movement.

And then somebody took my hands quite gently and lowered them back to my lap. I knew then that I had defeated all of them. It was the final test.

Now they would leave me alone. I would never let them know how. Then I would be the only one who had ever found out, in all the history of the world.

Chapter Seventeen

(Joseph Maleski—Afterward)

Roy Carren dropped me off at Shattocks' Pine Tree Restaurant. It's just down the road from the barracks. By then it was eleven o'clock in the morning. Sunday morning. I watched him drive down the road. Slow. I felt like somebody had peeled the skin off my face and stuck it back on again, using too much glue. When I rubbed my jaw I felt the whiskers. I felt real strange. It made me remember a time when I was a little kid. I had to go to a Halloween party all dressed up funny in the daylight. I had to go alone with everybody laughing at me. All the grown-up people.

I went on into the restaurant. On Sunday they serve a big breakfast and serve it up until noon. Usually I sit at the counter. But as soon as I got in the door and saw them all looking at me, I knew that if I sat at the counter they were going to start asking all those questions. Usually I don't mind all that. I guess maybe I sort of like knowing what has gone on. Like with a bad accident on the main route or something. I go in and they ask me about it and I tell them. But I could see they wanted to know all about the drowning and those people and all, and I just didn't want to talk about it. So I turned and went on over to one of the booths and slid in and hiked the holster around so the gun wasn't digging into me.

I guess I didn't look so friendly. Benny, from the garage, came over to the booth sort of uneasy and stood about four feet away and said, "Guess it was kind of a mess out there, that guy going crazy and everything, eh?"

I gave him a look and nodded and picked up the menu and opened it, even though I knew I was going to have what I always have on Sunday when I go in there. Sunnyside up with ham and a double order of toast with the wild strawberry jam Mrs. Shattock makes. Out of the corner of my eye I saw him stand there and then go away.

I looked at the menu but I didn't see the printing there. I kept seeing that crazy one, and me moving in slow motion while he stuck that thing in the woman's head. Roy told me a hundred times I couldn't have risked a shot, and even if I had, I couldn't have squeezed it off fast enough, but it's a thing you remember and wonder about.

Janey Shattock came over and stood by me. I looked up at her and tried to grin at her like always, but it didn't work right.

"The usual, Janey," I said, and my voice was too loud. It was as though the other people in the place weren't talking the way they always do. And there didn't seem to be the usual noise coming from the kitchen. They seemed to be looking at me as if I was some sort of a freak or something.

She brought my order after a while and I said, "Bring yourself some coffee and sit down, Janey."

She did. She sat across from me. I looked at her and I knew she wasn't going to ask any questions. I said in a low voice, "It was bad and I can't talk about it yet."

"I know by looking at you it was bad, Joe," she said.

It was only after I started eating I knew how hungry I was. She was quiet, the way I wanted her to be. She's a strong girl. She's big, and I thought when I glanced across at her that she really isn't plain. She isn't pretty and she isn't plain either. Maybe handsome, if you can call a girl that.

And I felt ashamed all of a sudden. Ashamed of me. Ashamed of Joseph Maleski. Because this is what I have been doing: dating Janey and not liking some things about her. Like how her hands are sort of rough and red-knuckled, and she all the time hides them in her lap when you're out with her. And how, unless she has just washed her hair, there's a little kitchen smell in it, because they serve a lot of fried stuff and she's in and out of the kitchen all day.

What did I want? My God, one of those females at the place where I'd spent the night? What the hell was I? I kept eating and looking at her in a new way. There I'd been dating her, and not liking the things that meant she was a good kid because the family had it tough getting the place going good, and she worked like a dog.

Being with her, it made me feel good and clean, like I had already taken the shower I was going to take before I hit the sack. I finished and pushed the plate away and she poured my coffee cup full again and put the pot down and started to pull her hand back into her lap, but I grabbed it. I held her hand tight. She got red and I knew they were looking at us and I knew it was Sunday morning.

I wanted to kid around. I wanted to give her some kind of a line like I always do. But I sat there like a big dummy and I held her hand hard and I said, "Janey." A great line that is! Lots of laughs.

My eyes began to sting like I was a little kid again. I let go of her hand and she put it in her lap. And I couldn't even look at her any more. I walked all the way to the barracks before I remembered I had walked out without even paying.

When I hit the sack I was hoping when I woke up all those people would be like people in a dream. Not real and alive and warm. Like Janey. Like Janey and me.